EVISCERATE

PRAISE FOR ERADICATE (THE CUSTODIAN BOOK ONE)

"With a brass-knuckled, blood-dusted prose style that picks up where brutal icon Mickey Spillane left off, author Jarrett Mazza pushes men's adventure fiction into darker territory. *Eradicate* pits mercenary Kyle Quinn against a sinister cult lodged in the bowels of the Louisiana bayou, and with no limits on his methods, bodies start hitting the floor at a rapid clip. Don a crash helmet and mouthguard, because Quinn's termination list is long and full of wrenching twists and turns. Highly recommended for fans of concrete-boiled, fast-paced novels. Mazza doesn't skimp on violence and thrills, and doesn't shy away from challenging the protagonist's—and the reader's—sense of right and wrong in a dangerous, grey world overrun by monsters."

—Jarret Keene, author of the *Kid Crimson* series

"Jarrett Mazza's novel, *Eradicate*, thunders ahead, gaining speed like a locomotive as protagonist and black ops assassin Kyle Quinn strikes a secret sect that harms children. Quinn also seeks to understand the demons driving him to kill. This intense tale entices readers to dive into scene after scene late into the night and even until dawn."

—John G. Bluck, author of the *Luke Ryder* series

"This book is a masterful, truly original work of suspense that has strong characterizations and clever twists. Eradicate is a quick, smart, engrossing read featuring a character in Kyle Quinn who readers will wish had their backs in any situation."

EVISCERATE

THE CUSTODIAN
BOOK 2

JARRETT MAZZA

ROUGH
EDGES
PRESS

Rough Edges Press
An Imprint of Wolfpack Publishing
1707 E. Diana Street
Tampa, FL 33610

roughedgespress.com

Paperback ISBN 978-1-68549-544-2
eBook ISBN 978-1-68549-543-5
LCCN 2025930621

For Mom.
Always there, always prepared.

EVISCERATE

PROLOGUE

THE TUNNEL WAS BLACK.

Almost.

All that appeared amid the darkness was an incandescent light that shined quaintly at the end of the subterranean lair—where the Custodian, Kyle Quinn, lurked in the dark. Like an apparition, he could see his targets, but they could not see him. Crackling in intermittent bursts, gunfire rained down on the elite assassin, yet Quinn enjoyed days like this. So often, he worked alone, but for this mission—*this task*—he was ordered to join a sweeper team assigned to eviscerate a drug operation overseen by the brutal and deadly Sinaloa Cartel.

There was one condition attached to his latest mission.

Everyone dies. Everything burns.

Armed with his TR-1 Ultralight gun, Quinn hunkered inside a dusty crevasse. In full tactical gear, Quinn opened up on several fleeing silhouettes. Unlike the strike team, who was dressed in fatigues and traditional camouflage, Quinn was sheathed in black.

He wore a mask with a white hand painted over its face. With a penchant for drama and some showmanship, Quinn also owned night vision goggles which allowed him to detect his targets with absolute clarity.

Quinn flicked the trigger of his TR and executed another Narcos.

Headshot. Shoulder. Chest. Heart.

Quinn crouched. Staying low, the strike team's purpose and Quinn's were aligned...for now. The cartels were, in Quinn's mind, deserving of a brutal demise due to their savage, uncivilized ways, and given his newest mission parameters, he had input on who he was to kill and how they were to die.

Quinn hated the cartels and had no problem sending them all to Hell.

Under direct orders from Priest, Quinn was also told to acquire an asset. If he succeeded in acquiring said asset, then Priest would continue to work with Quinn and support his pursuit of retribution and justice.

"Get this first," Priest confirmed. Quinn nodded. "Then we'll see what comes next."

The rest of the unit was there to neutralize and close down the tunnel.

Quinn, however, was just sent there to kill. Careful about how he selected his targets, Quinn preferred to execute those who were guarding passageways and other remote areas of access. Clusters of armed men scurried, but Quinn was keen on marking each one carefully.

"Ha!" Quinn heard a fool yelp from the dark. He lowered his TR-1 with the canted rail and Magpul PMAGs and dropped his hand to his thigh rig to pull his sidearm. While traditionally, Quinn's pistol of choice was a Glock, recently, he switched to a new model: a Colt M1911A1 with customized triggers and thread-on compensators. Loud and merciless when fired, as Quinn held one with an outstretched arm, he stared down its sights and nailed another square in the chest.

"Go! Go!" the Narcos leader ordered.

Into another tunnel, Quinn parted from the team. He shot another in the leg before another snuck up near Quinn's shoulder. Quinn headlocked the poorly masked attacker and launched him into the wall. He finished with a boot to the cocksucker's face and a shot to the temple.

Find the asset.

Now, Priest's orders were clear. Quinn was to seek and find, but mostly he was to recover. This was a compromise established with Priest.

In the next passage, Quinn stopped dead. Head up, he had a look around. Now in a room with paneled walls and tiled floors, it was not the kind one would discover in such a location.

Therefore, it must also have been a secret.

Now Quinn understood why Priest wanted him there. When he examined the space, which resembled a lab, Quinn scoped until he located what Priest wanted him to find. What Quinn saw first was a stark metal table that blended in well with the other plain furniture arranged nicely in the brightly lit space. Hit by strobe lights and walking on gleaming tiled floors, the stoic mercenary instantly saw the item that did not belong in the admittedly sparkly setting.

Stomping in, Quinn looked dead ahead.

Sure to his assumption, there it was. Quinn passed the table and gawked at the steel briefcase. Lifting it to his chest, Quinn didn't know the combination. This was all that was in the room. Despite Priest removing the sanctions, Quinn would honor his request. It was to find any secret worth protecting because that's who he was now.

In some ways, Quinn supposed, he was now a man of honor.

"Quinn." Hearing his name, he turned.

"Jesus Christ. Don't shoot." He stared at another operator who was dressed in woodland fatigues.

Stewart was a Green Beret in charge of the raid. As Quinn lowered his gun, he secured the case under his arm.

"You good?" Stewart asked.

Quinn nodded. Stewart glimpsed at the case and noticed what Quinn had but said nothing about it.

Everything was compartmentalized here, and Quinn was required to execute as well as obtain, and so he did his job while the other operatives did theirs.

"We're heading for extraction now," Stewart informed. "Area is secured."

"Right." Quinn followed Stewart but paused to examine the room again. *So peculiar.* Priest owed Quinn a solid explanation as to what was happening.

Everything seemed odd—out of place.

With no questions and no answers, all Quinn had were concerns and ideas. But first, he had to answer the most important question of all. It was simple:

What the hell is inside this case?

CHAPTER 1
A NEW ORDER

UNLOCKING SOMETHING AS FORTIFIED AS THIS CASE was like opening a bank vault with a machine gun. *It just ain't gonna happen.* Quinn fidgeted with the locks, though he was not the worst locksmith among Custodians. Nevertheless, he also wasn't one for damaging valuable products either.

"I have it. Come and get it."

"Outstanding," Priest said to Quinn. He was communicating using a traditional iPhone. Quinn called him as soon as the mission was complete.

When the strike team was finished with the tunnels, a Blackhawk escorted everyone, including Quinn, to a secured location. In this instance, the location was a base located ten miles from the tunnels. It was a timely exchange, and suddenly, Quinn was with Priest, who arrived at the base in his platinum BMW in just under ten minutes.

Priest's new vehicle was sleek, but Quinn's affinity for American muscle toppled his taste in prototypical luxury automobiles. He saw cars like this as a cheap export for flashy men who liked flashy things. Quinn himself owned a 1970 AMC/AMX 3, his pride and joy, and in his mind, better than what Priest was driving.

Once he landed, Quinn ventured off on his own. He was aware Priest worked for SAC but this operation was one ordered by the NSA. Nothing was said between Priest and Quinn besides good luck and you did well after.

When Priest pulled up, Quinn kept a close watch on his employer. He removed all his gear and stood in his military-issued pants.

"This it?" Priest asked Quinn.

"It is," Quinn confirmed.

"Nice." Priest pulled the case close and inspected it. "Betcha it wasn't easy to get, huh?"

"Is it ever?" Quinn replied.

"Hmm," Priest said. "*No, it never is.* And I take it you got your fair share of assholes this time around?"

"I left no one alive if that's what you mean," Quinn replied.

Priest grinned and winked. "*Nice.* Eradicate permanently, I like that."

Quinn reverted his attention back to this mysterious case and watched as Priest stepped closer to the table.

"Either way, I'm glad to see you're back."

"So am I," Quinn said, "because now, I can tell you what my next batch is going to be. The cartel is trafficking kids, Priest. You know this, and they need to be stopped... *now.*"

"Yes," Priest replied. He gripped the corners of the briefcase and pushed in the locks. Normally, this type of case was opened with a key, however the one Priest had was a digital key. It was shaped almost the same as its more traditional counterpart but was built with a smooth shaft and a circular bottom. Priest waved the digitized key in front of the locks and the case beeped and he was free to open it.

Priest continued. "And we will discuss all of that." When he heard the beeping, Quinn peered into the case to examine its formerly veiled contents. "But before we do," Priest paused, "there's more we need to talk about first."

"Hmm."

Quinn could see from Priest's brightened complexion that what he had was something precious, something interesting.

What is it? Why did he want Quinn to kill for it?

What Priest recovered from the case was a metal canister, thinly shaped and glistening under the little light cast in such a small space. For Quinn, this case resembled containers used to house toxic, often unstable materials. The first detail observed by Quinn was the canister's biohazard symbol. Along with its cylindrical shape, the container was galvanized and needed to be opened using another method Quinn didn't know.

"What the hell is that?" Quinn asked.

Priest's flushed demeanor highlighted his giddiness. Quinn paid little attention to his boss's infatuated expression of glee or his awful dry wit. No, Quinn stayed on the canister. A reveal like this was unexpected.

"This..." Priest said, "this is what the Sinaloa Cartel has been up to, something they're trying to manufacture and perfect."

"What is it?" Quinn asked. He squinted to focus.

"We don't know yet, but what we do know is it's a combination of some highly powerful narcotics blended together to form one single, highly *unstable* formula with tremendous human potential. It doesn't have a name yet, so we've been calling it...NX-17."

Quinn didn't hear Priest say the rest.

Quinn's head slanted curiously. He questioned if he heard Priest even at all. Quinn shook his head. The very notion of combining substances sounded like a terribly dangerous endeavor, even for a dangerous man like Quinn.

"What is it?" Quinn said.

"Well, based on our research," Priest said, "the cartels, and a whole lotta other assholes, want to move this shit into the US. And the only way to do that is to rely on previously successful forms of transportation, the same kind they use to move people and drugs. What you saw in those tunnels is just a taste of what's to come."

Quinn examined the case. "How unstable is it?" Quinn asked. "Can it kill anyone who takes it?"

"Depends," Priest said.

"On what?" Quinn asked.

"On the test subjects, which, in this case, is exactly who you think..." Priest inserted the canister into his black Samsonite briefcase. Who Quinn was thinking of, however, put a bad taste in the custodian's mouth.

"*Kids.*"

"Correct."

"Why is it always kids?"

"Do you really need to ask that?" Priest said. "Hey, you wanted to hunt bad guys and blast them into oblivion and distribute your own form of brutal justice while operating under your own rules, well, there ain't nothin' worse than what's goin' on here, I can tell you that. I sent you to the tunnels to wipe out these damn pricks, and if you want more, I can and will give you more."

Quinn stood in silence. He was considering the best way to go forward.

"Where?"

"There's a freighter we've been tracking through the South Pacific," Priest said. "It's a shell company linked to Sinaloa. Last I heard, they were sending a SEAL team to bury the op and rescue a few hostages, but I think I can arrange for you to join if you want. No doubt, they'll have more of this stuff onboard, as well as some of the Sinaloa fucks you want so bad. Can't think of anyone more worthy of your criteria than these guys."

The stuff Priest had referred to was called NX but Quinn chose to call it *Hyper-X* on account of its hyperactive results. Cutting-edge, a new drug was what Priest had discovered here, and a new drug meant new problems, new conflicts, and above all else: new enemies.

"And I want it all," Priest said. "And you can be the one who gets it for me."

"Another *tag along*?" Quinn asked, concerned.

While he worked alone most of the time, Priest insisted Quinn go with another team, which was now becoming a more common change under the Custodian's new criteria. The US government was exacting their own form of brutal justice and was eradicating their own enemies too.

"If you want to make bad people pay, you gotta go with another team sadly." Priest added, "At least for right now. Otherwise, people will start asking questions about the one-man army who's offing all sorts of scumbags without any oversight. At least here, you can pretend like you have one, and you know as well as I do, *custodians clean*. So, for now, this is all I can do for you."

Quinn nodded. He didn't disagree.

He was in the *bad guy killing business*, and so, Quinn was now seeking out those who tormented and tortured and were considered to be "evil". There were few criminal organizations who patented their own unique brand of pain and there were few who did pain like Sinaloa. And so, if they were moving a new product into the US to use on children, Quinn had no choice but to go.

He had to stop it before it escalated into something far more horrifying.

The term custodian, for Quinn, meant something more. It meant protecting and guarding true justice and real values—a code and a creed—and so far as the safety of kids was concerned...Quinn couldn't think of a more noble cause.

"I take it all of this meets your standards?" Now soft-spoken, Priest seemed to express a relative degree of sympathy. The criteria Priest referenced was Quinn's new, *modified mission morality*, as he liked to call it. He no longer eviscerated enemies based only on Priest's assessment. His opinion regarding his own targets mattered to him now too. Going forward, Quinn decided what was to be destroyed and who was to be kept alive.

For now, *he* was to be his own master.

Should anyone pose a threat to Quinn's newest principles, then removing them was both justified and necessary. Therefore, he was willing to do what he did best in these cases. However, Priest also gave him his word that this was the new direction of his duties as a Custodian. He could kill bad guys, and in this case, the bad guys were exactly who Priest wanted dead too. It was, essentially, a *win-win*. And so far, Priest honored his agreement. He stayed true to his oath and to his own creed too.

"I take it...we have an agreement then?"

It was at this point Quinn heard only what he wanted to. He wanted a contract, a plan, and a directive. And now, Quinn had all of those things. His mission was to locate the cartel and eviscerate all its members. He was to prevent them from testing their new product on children and kill anyone who stood in his way.

This was the mission. It was *Quinn's* mission.

"Where's the ship?" Quinn asked. "And the team? How long before I can get out there and play?"

With an intrigued smile, Priest knew it was on as soon as Quinn asked this question. "On their way. You ready?"

The Custodian turned to the door and left the case as well as the synthetic in his rearview.

"Always."

———

Quinn was told to convene with the SEAL team before commencing his op.

He was informed how he was to board a Blackhawk after arriving at a military base in an Air Force base just north of Austin, Texas. There, Quinn would be briefed about the freighter's cargo. The fact that he was in the room among other military personnel coerced stares from some of the other operators. Quinn cared for none of the men's thoughts or feelings. He was here on his own accord.

"Straight op. Extract and eliminate. Rescue hostages and neutralize all Tangos, is that understood?"

"Yes, sir." The team responded to their leader in unison.

Quinn had met this team leader once before. His name was Luke. Luke Kift. A heavy-hitter, Kift was also a West Point Naval Academy graduate and somewhat of a hothead. He was also known to be an excellent tactician, a quality Quinn respected. Quinn didn't care to know too much about anyone these days. Although Quinn was joining this team, he was focused on his own objective. He was to locate any traces of the new synthetic known as Hyper-X, which he recovered for Priest just yesterday.

The entire time, Quinn stood near a table in the stark briefing room. Beneath the dark lighting and black walls, Quinn remained separate from the rest of the SEALs. Knowing his role, the team gawked at Quinn. Custodians were a classification that coursed through the entire United States military. Some Custodians were former SEALs, but those that weren't, were aware of who Quinn was and where he came from.

A Custodian at level five meant something to everyone.

"Any questions?" Kift looked at the team once again.

Quinn watched him push off the table and step back. No new questions surfaced.

"All right," Kift yelled. "Let's move!"

It was the last order given and the team marched toward the hangar door. On their way to the Blackhawk, Quinn secured his Kevlar vest by fastening the straps. As Kift passed Quinn, the SEAL leader gave an inquisitive, watchful stare. It was clear Kift didn't want Quinn along for the ride, but he had no choice.

The man was here and he was staying.

Quinn didn't care how he was perceived. He returned Kift's scowl with one of his own.

Cleaning was Quinn's game and extraction was theirs, and that's how it should stay. Either way, it was best if both men stayed out of the other's way. Quinn held no qualms or grudges against anyone. In the end, it simply was what it was. Quinn strapped on his vest and his utility belt and joined the SEALs on the chopper. He said nothing to anyone as they prepared to board the rogue freighter.

The Blackhawk flew and the team inside was fitted

with the traditional military-issued gear, including L3 Ground Panoramic goggles, the standard M4 Carbines, and Beretta 92FS.

Quinn possessed none of these weapons.

Instead, he was armed with his new Sig-Sauer MPX assault rifle, semi-auto. The gun was equipped with a hybrid cartridge case and was very light. It included a carbon fiber handguard with a Grandmaster silicon carbide treatment and also acquired a fourteen-inch barrel. Having all the bells and whistles, the guns performed well with minimal kick. Quinn reflected on the challenges ahead, his role, and the permission granted by Priest.

Quinn could kill whoever he wanted so long as he uncovered Priest's asset—so long as he recovered this secret.

"Hang tight!" Kift yelled. Every SEAL raised their hands and gave the thumbs up.

Quinn didn't.

Head down, Quinn was a ghost. As the chopper eased down toward the freighter, fat clouds hung above the roiling sea. Seabirds shrieked to provide a bleated warning to the strike team as torrential winds forced the men to move fore and aft in the hold of elite transport.

They looked down.

"Dropping in *five...*" Kift counted down while everyone prepared to deploy. They dropped their ropes and exited in tight groups of four. "Go! Go!"

While Kift was next, Quinn went on ahead.

Mask on, Quinn's MPX was slung over his shoulder. He clenched the tethered rope with black gloves and dropped down in one fell swoop. He slid with ease and landed successfully on the deck along with the rest.

Motioning inward, Quinn would not rely on his Colt

for the close encounters. This time, Quinn chose to see what he could do without the assistance of a semi-auto. For now, he went for his KA-BAR 1211. Quinn's OTF blade was generally how he liked to play. In this case, Quinn made an exception.

Knife out, Quinn stayed low as he stepped across the dock. The ship, Quinn was told, was supposedly a shell company designed for the secret transportation of narcotics.

It was commandeered by the Sinaloa Cartel.

Anywhere was a potential target.

Always in Eradicate mode now, Quinn was his own judge. For him, it was less about orders and more about *morality* and *retribution*. Eyes down, the SEALs scoured the boat for hostages while Quinn's parameters were to recover and remove, and that was all. Quinn memorized everything he passed. Always on guard, Quinn neared the railing, stared through the thin bars, and spotted his first target.

Wielding an Uzi, the man was tattooed and standing guard.

Quinn pressed the KA-BAR to his side and slipped along the ramp.

When the Narcos turned, Quinn pounced. Swinging the blade, Quinn knocked away the man's weapon and sliced his arm in a complete and perfect circle. Quinn cut the man's neck and chest. After completing a nasty gash, Quinn opened the fool's jugular and opened arteries with zero hesitation or resistance. Later, Quinn finished the man with a spinning back kick. The henchman's neck bubbled with blood.

Quinn sheathed his knife and retrieved his MPX.

Smoking a few more, Quinn depended on his rifle's Hiperfire trigger. Always, Quinn was amazed at how well a gun performed whenever it was modified. The SEALs had their own modifications, yes, but Quinn's was more than its modifications. It was elevated to become the perfect sculpt of what a gun *could* be if it was used in the right way.

Quinn marched and clipped another tango in the leg and then once more in the chest. Quinn then finished with a clean shot to the man's face. Doing so, Quinn was completely exposed. The remaining Narcos posing as seamen emerged from various intersections like zombies.

Quinn carefully mapped his targets and visualized them all before opening fire. Quinn executed two more near the railing. They all fell one at a time. Quickly, Quinn shot one bullet in a thug's sternum and fired another one in the heart. The last fool got blasted through his jugular. It was dirty yet clean at the same time.

On route to the ship's control center, the SEALs were ordered to go to the cargo bay and extract the hostages. Quinn moved south. From out of nowhere, a crazed sicario armed with a Beretta stomped. Quinn dropped and hammered his gun's stock into the fool's knee.

"Gah!" The sicario buckled as he grabbed his throbbing joint.

Once down, Quinn heaved the henchman with a solid knee. This was not enough. Another sicario reached for another weapon. "Fuck..." the killer gargled.

With a firm right cross, Quinn went on to end the fight with a quick bullet to the hitman's face. Head turned, Quinn glimpsed and saw more armed men. Like mice drawn into a trap, Quinn *was* the trap. His enemies were starting to swarm the doorway—the very passage Quinn needed to enter.

They shot in Quinn's direction, and the Custodian ducked and fired.

Getting as many as he could, Quinn's clip emptied as he reached for his Colt. Chalking up two more headshots, Quinn shot two more dead center. Approaching the door, Quinn was curious about what the SEALs were doing while he was busy with this.

Why were there so many surrounding this passage?

Were more men working for Sinaloa or were these people expendable mercenaries, almost like Quinn?

These were Quinn's questions, but no doubt this was where the custodian needed to be.

Priest said he wanted the synthetic—Hyper-X—and this was where it had to be located.

The room was as quiet as it was ominous. It was bright, but upon entering, Quinn felt a shadow beginning to close in. Though he thought the space was vacant, when Quinn moved, he felt like he was being lured, like he too was being baited.

Reaching back, Quinn slid his hand past his shoulder. He brought his fingers up and across to grab a tool he hadn't used in a while but one he was very much looking forward to wielding.

Quinn squeezed his tonfa and fastened the weapons against his forearm. While a gun would have sufficed, Quinn's instincts assured him this was the right call.

He was now on the lookout for a trail. He was searching for a path capable of showing him the way. In truth, so far, it had only brought Quinn here, which was nowhere.

Tonfa still secured and rifle still loaded, a subtle breeze fluttered Quinn's hair. He detected a noticeable change in the atmosphere. The shadows expanded and Quinn's fingers tingled. This still could be a trap. If it was, Quinn had fallen right into it.

Shit. That's exactly what happened.

A firm uppercut popped Quinn's chin and rang his face like a bell. A solid and accurate strike, Quinn hadn't felt a wallop like this since his last pro fight back in Wyoming. Shaking his head, the hit forced Quinn to stagger, but it was instantly followed by a just as ferocious roundhouse kick.

"Gah!" Quinn had no time to fall into his defense.

Honestly, he was impressed. *Damn impressed.*

Quinn slammed into a bank of computers, gripped his tonfa because he was aching to use them. But, before Quinn could, he needed to see exactly who he was fighting. Quinn fought through the pain and attacked this new assassin head-on.

Swinging his tonfa, Quinn stepped with his left and tried to connect with the masked man's skull. Between each swing, Quinn was attempting to get a better look at who he was fighting.

Appearing only as a figure in black, the assassin's armor was angular and matrixed. Layer upon layer, it outfitted with folded navy plates somewhat similar to Quinn's own armor. This new assassin's visor was divided into two sections. There were two slits along the mouth for breathing, like a hockey goalie from a time long ago. The assassin looked heavier yet somehow maintained his mobility. His reaction time made Quinn think he was lighter than he appeared.

Whoever he—they—were, Quinn noticed an emblem carved into their chest. The symbol was an inverted diamond and shined despite the darkened exterior. Looking more like a stone than a jewel, it was a piece of something Quinn didn't recognize. Quinn had no idea what it was like or what it should be, so he gave the killer a name that was easy to remember.

Blackstone.

Distributing a few solid hits, whatever Quinn managed to land, did not have the desired effect. One hit, and the assassin was back up seconds after. Unloading several kicks onto Quinn, each one was different and delivered perfectly on target.

Front kick. Roundhouse. *Double. Double.*

So solid, this new assassin was superior in ways Quinn didn't want to admit.

After the fourth kick, Quinn charged. He grabbed the leg and tucked it under his arm. Thrusting his elbow down onto the joint, Quinn hammered Blackstone in the knee. If not for the padding secured around the leg, Quinn would have definitely broken it.

This should have happened, but it didn't.

"*Grrr.*" Quinn spun.

With a sweeping kick, he knocked the assassin off the imaginary line created between them. No time to retreat, Quinn spun his tonfa. Quinn's hits were fierce but his opponent always found a way to counter. Therefore, when the one called Blackstone tried to deliver a punch, Quinn blocked using his Shotokan. Then, trying to hit back again, Blackstone deflected using the same hard movements as before. Endowed with a certain feral rawness and fortitude, Quinn felt like he could be fighting his own reflection.

Every block and blow exacted by Blackstone was textbook—astoundingly on point.

Executing a solid delivery, Quinn's attacker possessed an innate resilience he hadn't seen in another fighter. To overcome this, Quinn needed to resort to dirtier, more surprising moves.

He heel-kicked Blackstone's knee and then jumped in with a sharp elbow. Clobbering as if trying to take off the man's head, Quinn pounded Blackstone's helmet.

While fashioned from pure metal—or some other durable alloy—even at full force, Quinn couldn't make a dent.

During Quinn's fourth shot, Blackstone retaliated.

He kicked Quinn's legs, opened his stance, and disrupted the Custodian's stability.

Blackstone drove in with the elbow, Quinn was knocked back. Freeing himself, the assassin dashed. He leaped over the control panel, stormed at Quinn, and retrieved the canister.

"Fuck."

Seeing his man taking what belonged to Quinn, the Custodian drew his Colt. Triangulating Blackstone's rapid cuts and curves, Quinn did land a few shots. None stopped his new rival. Blackstone was protected by elite body armor that left him unscathed.

By the time Quinn returned to his set position, Blackstone was gone.

"No." Quinn followed Blackstone through the control center, hot on this package.

The assassin was only mere steps from the door.

Quinn reloaded and raised his weapon. Now aiming for the spaced-out sections on Blackstone's armor, before Quinn could shoot, a beeping noise sounded seconds before a black ball was tossed in his direction.

"Son of a—"

On the verge of detonation, Quinn pushed off his back leg and flew.

What Blackstone had wasn't your standard grenade. A device designed to supersede the power of any ordinary explosive, when it ignited, waves of crackling fire swarmed the control room. Avoiding debris, Quinn hunkered down. Armed with his M1, the Custodian emerged from the cloud of smoke but hoped his enemy was not out of sight.

Soon as Quinn exited the putrid dust, he looked at the doorway.

The entrance was scorched. Now bent in the middle, Quinn looked up. There was no sign of Blackstone.

"Smoke in the control room!" a miscellaneous voice yelled from an unknown location.

A thick plume of fire had formed in a near-perfect circle. As the flames dispersed, the tendrils burned anything it touched. Once the fire settled, the cloud broadened while Quinn lowered his gun.

"Quinn?" Behind Quinn was Kift as well as the rest of the SEALs, having completed their own mission.

Quinn had yet to finish his.

"Jesus, what the shit happened here?"

"Bomb," Quinn said. He didn't want to explain anything else to Kift, not at this moment.

Someone slipped through Quinn's fingers. This was all the Custodian was thinking about now. Quinn shook his head as he regained his faculties. With Kift asking too many questions, he was broaching into Quinn's territory.

Both men had their missions. As long as that synthetic was missing, then it would be tested on kids certain to die a painful death. It was critical and deadly, according to Priest, and now it was in the domain of a rising, nefarious power.

"But he's got something he shouldn't have." Quinn stomped alongside Kift. "Something that belongs to me."

As far as Quinn knew, Blackstone was still on the ship somewhere. And, if there was even the slightest chance he had not vacated the freighter, then Quinn would pursue. He had given his word to Priest and that was an untradeable asset never to be compromised or taken away.

"Wait." Kift snatched Quinn by the wrist and squeezed.

Quinn scowled at the SEAL commander. Until now, Quinn had not laid a single finger on Kift. Yet, Kift decided to perform this gesture from out of nowhere. And that was not okay.   `

"We need to go. Extraction team is ready. We have to get these hostages to safety."

Quinn's head dipped. He was perplexed by Kift's statement. He didn't work for him.

"Then go. I need to stay," Quinn said. "I'm not finished yet."

Quinn's stare deepened until it became a scowl. Before Quinn was only informing Kift of what needed to be done. Now, he was insisting.

"Orders are to bring everyone who arrived back with us."

"Who's orders?"

"No time to explain," said Kift. "We just have to go, now."

Kift spoke to Quinn like he was his subordinate. But Quinn wasn't on Kift's team, nor was he on his side. Still, Quinn continued to feel Kift's firm grip around his wrist.

"Let go of me," Quinn demanded.

Putting a hand on another soldier was a clear act of aggression. It was one made so clear that even the remaining SEALs eased back due to the tension.

"*We* can't stay. *You* can't stay," said Kift. "We gotta move now, understand?"

"I said let go of me," Quinn spoke as clearly as his sore throat would allow. "Now."

"You really wanna do this?" Kift asked, hand still on Quinn's. "Because if you wanna, we definitely can."

"I'm only gonna ask you one more time," warned Quinn. The intensity between him and the SEAL had escalated. Holding true, Quinn stayed where he was. "*Let me go.*"

Quinn felt Kift's fingers starting to strain. This was the SEAL's answer.

With Kift's hand still on Quinn's body, the Custodian's response was immediate and hostile. Quinn's hand whipped out for a quick distraction and then clocked Kift square in the face. Then, curling his hand, Quinn torqued Kift's joint and pinned the SEAL.

In aikido, this move is known as *nikajo* or *the second control wrist lock*.

From here, Quinn could break Kift's wrist. Yet, Quinn's only intention was to express disdain for what the man had done. Bending the joint, Quinn applied only a slight amount of pressure. It was just enough to send the Navy commander a clear warning.

Do not touch me again.

"*Fah!*" snapped Kift, a rictus formed on his formerly shocked face. The other SEALs stepped in as soon as one of their own was attacked.

Quinn released Kift as three other SEALs stomped.

Spinning to avoid them, Quinn was skilled but not skilled enough to take on an entire SEAL team. No one was that skilled. Seeing Kift's head shaking, Quinn rose to stand tall. Moving back, Quinn kept his distance.

"You really are a motherfucker, ain't ya, Quinn?" Kift barked at the Custodian.

Kift spat, and more SEALs approached.

"There's two ways this can go, you know that, *right?*"

This was a nice way of saying Quinn had no chance. He knew this already.

But, according to what Priest had said, he was only *piggybacking* with the team. He was by no means obligated to engage or interact with any one of them.

So then, what the hell were they doing to Quinn now? Why were they so insistent on ensuring his departure?

"Yeah," Quinn said, displaying a look of sheer disdain.

"So..." said Kift, hand on his sidearm. "What's it going to be?"

Quinn had no intention of facing off against the SEALs. He was brave, not stupid. Quinn lowered his hand and gave Kift an askance. The deed done by the team leader was uncalled for and out of line. It irked Quinn to his core. After he nodded to show he had no intention of resisting, he proceeded toward the door. On his way out, Quinn stopped after two SEALs stepped in his path.

"What?" Like two walls, Quinn had already made it clear he was done.

Still, these men stood like they weren't going to let him go. They were going to beat Quinn senseless despite the fact he had already surrendered himself over to these men.

"Well, since you attempted to resist," Kift said, "you're now a hostile prisoner, Quinn."

"Hostile prisoner?" Quinn wasn't surprised by this classification. He *was* acting hostile, but he was no prisoner. What Quinn didn't like was how Kift tried to be intimidating. If he wasn't scared, then why were more SEALs protecting him?

"You attacked a SEAL captain, brother. You broke the rules, and now, I gotta take you back and explain what happened."

Quinn watched the SEALs with crinkled lips and rolled his fingers up into his clammy palms. He imagined hitting Kift again. Maybe Quinn would get an opportunity to pop this asshole, but being unable to now, Quinn grunted his reply. "Fine. Take me in."

CHAPTER 2
GHOSTS INSIDE THE WALLS

IN THE CHOPPER RIDE BACK TO THE SHIP, THE Custodian sat alone.

Like a prisoner being escorted through a cell block, Quinn was a passenger before, but now he was just cargo. After deboarding the chopper, Quinn was back at a base.

There, wearing his usual suit with no tie, stood Priest. With his shirt unbuttoned below his neck, he sported his classic Aviators sunglasses despite there being a clear absence of sunlight.

Quinn stepped off with his hands in zip ties and Kift marched with his hand on the Custodian's forearm. Together, they walked toward Priest. Quinn watched his boss's lips coil. And, struck by the sight, Priest fervently stepped in.

"What the hell is going on here?! What the fuck is this?!" Priest shouted over the propeller blades.

Quinn observed his lord's demeanor. Pulling his glasses off his face, venom boiled in the contractor's bright eyes. Priest was a man you definitely didn't want to piss off, and anyone who did suffered incredible consequences, no matter who they were.

"The hell is my operative doing with his hands tied?"

"Nothing personal," said Kift. "But your boy here got a little too amped on our mission. He tried breaking away."

"Your mission?!" Voice raised, the veins in Priest's neck bulged as his yells overcame the chopper's booming engine. Quinn chose to remain silent. Right now, he was awaiting further instruction.

"It ain't your mission!" Priest was now shouting at the top of his lungs. "It's mine! *Ours!* You rescue your hostages, and we take care of our asset! If my man said he was going after it, then that's because it was his fucking job to go after it! You had no damn right to interfere!"

Witnessing Priest's tirade, the entire SEAL team huddled around the spook. With his head still down, Quinn had no dog in this fight. Now he was cooperating and so he wanted to avoid creating other problems. The shame he felt—if it was shame—existed because he *hadn't* succeeded in his mission.

Quinn hadn't grabbed the mysterious item Priest was hellbent on retrieving.

An assassin Quinn called Blackstone was now on the loose. This made Quinn's administering of retribution null and void. He didn't keep his word like he said he would. Quinn didn't fulfill his duties. So far as Quinn knew, he did fail. He lost.

"Now take these goddamn zip ties off my man," demanded Priest. He was nearing the end of his diatribe. "And step the fuck back."

Only a ghost in the shadows or a snake in the fucking grass would talk to a SEAL with such derision. Head up, Quinn looked at Kift.

The SEAL commander, who had survived Priest's tirade, pulled out a Ka-Bar and cut the bands secured around Quinn's wrists. The plastic strips fell to the ground and Quinn rubbed his skin and moved away from the SEALs. Nothing to say. Quinn didn't want to wait for Priest to say more.

For now, he spoke only to Quinn.

"Let's go," Priest said. Quinn followed.

He could feel Kift's stare warming the back of his neck. Now that they were off the airstrip, Quinn and Priest headed into a bunker, which was a more secured location far from the tents. Quinn approached a set of steel stairs at the end of a narrow hallway and then to a galvanized door ten steps ahead of them.

Here, Quinn was surrounded by intertwining pipes while cold air tickled the back of his solid neck. He didn't like being here. It smelled, and Quinn was already smelly enough.

"Sorry about that. Fucking SEALs," Priest said. "It's like every one of them thinks they're bloody DEVGRU these days. Besides, they were only there to do complete by-the-book, bring 'em out-without-getting-shot civilian horseshit job. I had a deal with their fucking COS the entire time, made sure no one asked any questions or interfered. Either way, sorry to have put you in with them," Priest continued. "I couldn't send one in without garnering the attention of the fucking brass, and you wanted your retribution, so..."

Quinn sat on a metal chair in the middle of the stark room while Priest moved to the other side of this table.

"I didn't get it," Quinn disclosed while riddled with shame.

Priest scratched his earlobe. "What didn't you get?"

Holding his gaze, Quinn mentally prepared for Priest's reaction.

"*The compound,*" Quinn expressed. "The asset. I didn't get it. Someone else was there. They got to it before I could."

"Shit. Another operative?" Priest asked.

Quinn nodded. "Yes."

"Who?"

"Don't know," Quinn said, "but he was well trained, not so much in the Custodial arts, but still...still very good."

Custodial Arts was a term Quinn coined himself. He liked it a lot. It reminded Quinn of the Jedi arts from *Star Wars*. He was a fan of such films, had been since he was a kid.

"I see. Damn it," Priest said. His hand slid along his cheeks and his tongue pushed against the inside of his mouth. It was rare for Quinn to let Priest down. However, there was more to the story, more to the mission than Quinn previously knew. This changed things.

"I take it you're disappointed?" Quinn was careful about how he phrased his response. He did, after all, *fail*.

"Disappointed?" said Priest, seated at the end of the table across from Quinn. "No, I'm just...surprised."

"Unless you know who he is, it's no secret then," added Quinn. "There are people out there who know about this thing, know about us too. Maybe it's more than we think."

Priest's nails clicked against the surface of the table.

"Maybe he was Sinaloa," Priest replied. "This assassin you encountered."

"Doubt that very much," Quinn said, head shaking.

"What makes you say *that*?"

"Too skilled to be a *sicario*," added Quinn. He used

the appropriate term. Sicario is Spanish for *hitman*. "And he was well geared too, stood out and he fought as if he knew me. He knew how I fought, how I moved too. Also, he was nowhere near the others I killed. It was almost like...he was *protecting* the asset. It was his job to make sure no one got anywhere near it."

"Hmm," Priest said, hand on his chin. "Is it someone you think you've seen before, maybe?"

"I don't know," Quinn said. "Possibly, but I'm not sure."

Quinn skimmed through all the former adversaries he encountered throughout his intricate and complicated past. Some of these people were formidable. Others were perfectly forgettable.

There were only a few who could stand toe to toe with someone like Quinn, though. And, recalling the Eradicate order back in Louisiana, Quinn had faced off against a fixer named Kardinal. He also fought his greatest enemy ever: his father. However, none compared to who Quinn fought on the freighter. None of them were as good as this Blackstone.

"I see." Priest's fingertips were pressed together and he was posed like a maniacal supervillain. "Well, either way, cartel's still got their hands on that shit now," Priest said, "which means they'll be using it and breeding a new kind of addict, potentially creating a very serious threat. You know this."

"I do," Quinn said. He was despondent after hearing Priest's comment.

Priest referenced a new kind of addict. This substance, apparently, was a potent mix of certain narcotics that manufactured zombies rather than junkies. Quinn felt the comparison was suitable. Essentially, that's what drug addicts were, they were zombies.

"We have to stop them now, while we still can. Now I've got a few leads that I think might be able to assist us," Priest said. "I'll reconvene with CIA and FBI. I'll get in touch with some narcotics agents and find out where else Sinaloa is operating, and then you can hit 'em there. Sound good?"

"Assuming they'll even let us do that," Quinn said as he nodded. "Hitting hard means nothing if there's people standing in the way." Quinn was referencing the situation he had with the SEALs. As a result of what happened there, both Quinn and Priest thought *others* might interfere with their concerted attack.

Sinaloa was theirs and no one else's.

"You let me worry about who's in the way," Priest said. "I'll clear the playing field for you, but if I do that, then you gotta promise me something there too, Quinn."

Quinn thought about the promises Priest might request of him now. Yet, Quinn had already arrived at a response of his own. "*I won't fail again.*"

"That I know," Priest replied, "but if I do getcha to take these cartel fuckers out, I want you to do what you did for me back in Louisiana."

Quinn remembered.

"*Eradicate.*"

A smug smirk formed on Priest's face, and Quinn was struck with déjà vu. He recalled the same expression from two months ago. Set to exterminate every psychotic supervillain that plagued this Earth, Quinn's mission had now expanded. He was now chasing a new assassin as well as a valuable substance capable of changing the entire war on drugs.

It wasn't just about killing bad men. No, all of this presented a significant challenge Quinn had never observed before and yet, there was no going back on his new cause or his new creed.

"No," Priest said to Quinn. "This time, I want more," Priest continued. "This time...I want you to...*eviscerate. I want you to tear them apart...from the inside.*"

"I see," Quinn said. When given this new kill-order, Quinn contemplated his new level of brutality. Kill them from the inside? Take out the leader, go for the head of the organization, the head of the serpent, so to speak, Quinn understood the difference. He knew what he was supposed to.

"But before you do any of that," continued Priest, "there's something else you need to know."

Priest motioned closer to where Quinn was sitting.

Quinn's hands folded and he made not a sound. In Priest's hand was a mini tablet Quinn barely noticed. He was so focused on Priest, but their time together had not yet come to a close.

"There's something else besides the cartel that's now starting to emerge from behind the scenes, something we haven't seen until now," explained Priest, tablet still in hand. "And I think your assassin might be involved."

Quinn glimpsed at the tablet. Priest hadn't handed it to Quinn, who was tired of waiting.

"Who are they?" Quinn asked, looking at the iPad.

"To be honest," Priest said, "at this point, we don't exactly know. When we got word of the new compound that the Sinaloa Cartel was in possession of, we found out that it was synthesized by a defunct program the NSA had running a long time ago. It was them and the Canadian government."

"*Canadian?*" Quinn asked.

Priest nodded. "Apparently some scientists out of UBC had the initial formula for the synthetic before it became what it is today." Priest finally handed Quinn the tablet. The photos on screen were taken at a lab. They showed men and women in white coats, all standing there in a row. Quinn skimmed the next few—which featured the same men and women in the same lab—provided an entirely different shot. In these new images, the lab was ransacked and destroyed. All the scientists were dead, their throats were cut and their bodies were left slain at the scene.

"Jesus." The sight even caused Quinn to shudder.

Every corpse displayed multiple wounds, a clear sign of overkill in Quinn's opinion, and he was all about overkill. But, whoever did the job was making a statement: these men and women needed to be more than dead...but *terminated*.

"Once it was perfected," Priest said, "it was absorbed by a new initiative known as KEYS."

"KEYS?" Quinn asked.

"KEYS," Priest confirmed.

"That stand for something?"

"Maybe," Priest said. "But right now, all we know about this terrorist network is after they were shutdown, their work was supposed to be confiscated, destroyed. Now, I found out recently that it wasn't, and that the cartels have somehow managed to get a hold of it, and now they're using it to experiment on people, specifically on children."

"And you think maybe they're not working alone, that maybe this KEYS, or whatever it is," Quinn said, "might be helping them?"

"That is what I think, yes," Priest said.

Quinn handed the tablet back to Priest and his eyes narrowed into a squint. Quinn was now concentrating on all the details supposedly hidden inside each kill. Doing this, the Custodian was also weighing his options. Quinn saw one scientist slashed across their neck, which indicated a strong knife hand, similar to Blackstone's.

Quinn perused a new photo. The gunshot wounds there were next for Quinn's inspection.

Taking a closer look, he spotted two in the chest and one in the head. This method of marksmanship was identical to his own. And, if it *was*, then it was likely the *same* assassin Quinn encountered back on the ship.

He moved the same, acted the same, fought the same, even killed the same.

Always known to trust his instincts, Quinn was a hunter, and every hunter was supposed to know their prey. These drug cartels and a top-secret government project were not what irked Quinn. What did, was this new elite assassin, a killer who might possibly be just as good a killer as Quinn.

And what was at stake—what was unfolding—Quinn couldn't imagine.

"First order of business will be to get to the cartel," Priest said. "Get to them before they start trading, go for them, confiscate what you can, and bring it all back to me. You get the bad guys but I get the compound. Deal?" Priest said this as he pressed the button at the base of the pad and eliminated all the corresponding images. Priest then set the device back on the table. "Seek and destroy, clean and mop, and do what you do best. Find what you can, take what you can, and ensure justice is served and that no one stands in your way."

"Not justice," corrected Quinn. He remembered his new creed and what he wanted now. None of this was for Priest. It was only for Quinn and no one else. "Retribution."

"Aye," Priest said with a wry smile. "*Retribution.*"

CHAPTER 3
THE SHADOWS TALK

QUINN AND PRIEST LEFT THE BASE IN A EUROCOPTER EC155 and not a Blackhawk. But when they did vacate the premises, neither one of them said a single thing to Kift or to the rest of the SEAL team.

According to Priest, there were a few hotspots in Texas that were operating under the guise of the Sinaloa Cartel. For Quinn, every one of them was primed for evisceration. Priest claimed to have reached out to a few of his so-called pals in the DEA, one of them named Paul Heinreich. According to Priest, Heinreich was a narcotics agent. He was also someone who worked with Priest in the past, or so Priest had said.

Quinn brought his gear and was set to touch down in just twenty-four hours.

With the intel provided, the scope and scale of the upcoming mission were fully outlined and established. What Quinn was primarily concerned with now was Blackstone.

Who the hell was he? Where did he come from? Who did he work for?

When Quinn arrived at his desired location, Priest told him to meet another contact. Quinn was told more than one person would be assisting him during his Eviscerate mission. This next contact, however, was someone Quinn was actually familiar with.

Quinn's heart thumped when he saw who they were, aroused as he recalled the face of a woman he definitely wanted to see again.

"*Ally?*"

Playing it cool, Priest knew how Quinn felt when working with Ally Shepherd. Therefore, there was nothing else to add to their exchange. All Quinn wanted now was to talk to her. Unfortunately, he didn't have a clue what to say.

The last time Quinn saw Ally was when he was busted up and in dire need of repair.

It was here where Ally helped Quinn. It was here whereby Quinn began to see her as something more than just a friend. Quinn was always careful who he let into his life. In this game, anything could happen at any time. Quinn thought of Ally more often than he cared to admit. He was always quick to deny such feelings but these feelings had grown into something not even a man like himself could resist.

In the end, they were real. Quinn simply could not stop thinking about Ally.

He thought about her because he needed her. He adored her.

"Hello, Quinn," Ally said as she grinned. It seemed she was as happy to see the Custodian as much as he was happy to see her.

"Hey ya, Ally," Quinn replied, still playing it cool.

A moment surged between them and the chemistry was so present Priest couldn't help but chortle in its wake.

Quinn was crushing hard, like a boy in high school and yet he knew he needed to stay stoic, professional. He stared at Ally for a few more seconds and then stepped back and away.

He was still working.

————

In the middle of July, a scorching summer heat had assaulted good old Texas. The air was thick and sticky but nicer and prettier compared to Louisiana. A state comprised of fields and long roads, here, Quinn encountered some very friendly people, even friendlier if he respected their valued and upheld traditions.

While there, Quinn wasn't relegated to a new safehouse.

Thanks to Priest, Quinn was checked in at a hotel, at least for the first day.

In a Hilton not far from Austin's airport, Quinn was damn impressed and was quite comfortable with the current accommodations. Quinn slept after he landed and was brought to this room by helicopter, and not in his own Cirrus Vision jet.

For now, Quinn's jet stayed where it was.

Well rested, when Quinn woke, he headed to the gym for a quick workout. Slinging dumbbells, Quinn completed a set of heavy thrusters and a hard cardio circuit. When he returned to his room, he packed everything he needed for the assault.

Quinn received a text earlier that day.

There was more information he and Priest needed to share before commencing the slaughter. As Quinn headed to another room to meet with Priest, he saw his boss wearing a crisp polo and teal pants. Seeing Priest dressed this way was unexpected, then again, Priest was also with a new man who appeared around the same age. He was a bald fellow, in a fleece jacket as well as a pair of Nike sneakers.

Still a visitor, Quinn prepared for the worst.

Hand on his Glock 26, Quinn didn't intend to use it, not unless things went in a direction he'd prefer they did not. Walking through the door, Quinn's hand shot down. Soon as it did, Priest's hand shot up. "Easy there, Quinn. *He* comes in peace."

"Whoa," this other man said to Quinn. "I was going to say don't get too excited, but I guess that's why you're with this guy over here, huh?" The man pointed at Priest. "You're always prepared, aren't you?"

The man's head tilted to the side. By referring to Priest as *this guy* suggested to Quinn this man was familiar. Still, Quinn refused to take his hand off his gun, not until he was told who the fuck this guy was.

"Jesus," the man said. He spoke with a voice sweet enough to be gentle but not quite so gentle enough to be kind. "You're everything he says you are...*ain't ya?*"

"Well, you know me, Heinreich, I'm not just good at finding good killers, and the one you're looking at now is grade A, Level 5."

Priest gave Quinn a friendly tap on the shoulder. He was next to Quinn, smiling at the man called Heinreich. And so, Quinn had a name.

"Kyle Quinn, this is Paul Heinreich. DEA. He's the special agent in charge of narcotics as well as monitoring any and all cartel operations. No one knows more about Sinaloa than he does, I can goddamn guarantee that."

Quinn took his hand off his gun but maintained his stoic, unfeeling demeanor. With introductions made,

Heinreich made the conscious decision to offer his hand. "Nice to meet you there, Quinn."

Quinn was hesitant to shake. He never cared much for cordialness. He was here to discuss a job and nothing else.

"I understand you're going to be...well, assisting us on the little problem we have," Heinreich said.

Quinn glanced at Priest. He didn't work for the FBI or anyone. He barely worked for Priest.

"In a matter of speaking, of course," Heinreich specified.

"Yeah," Priest replied. "In a matter of speaking."

Quinn said nothing. Again, he assisted no one.

"Before you go and start, well, taking care of things because, well, I hate the cartels more than anyone, it's important to note that the cartel has changed its leadership. See Sinaloa, I'm afraid, is now under the reign of Mr. Ramos Mandilo."

Quinn watched Heinreich look at Priest, who came forth with more clipped papers. Quinn scoffed. He had no time for minor details and felt he knew enough about his enemies already. He wanted to get on and get going. Nonetheless, Quinn had a look at an eight-by-eleven-sized photograph of the man referenced.

Ramos Mandilo had dark hair, wore heavy jewelry, and, in this one picture, was surrounded by an entourage of tattooed bodyguards. In this photo, Ramos was holding a phone and was also wearing a cool pair of sunglasses. To Quinn, he looked like the prototypical poster boy for cartel leadership.

Nevertheless, Quinn didn't care about any of this.

He stood back and waited for this boring exchange to come to an end. He wanted to start, like right fucking *now*.

"Ever heard of him?" Heinreich asked.

Quinn was stone-faced. He responded with a look so cold you could almost see the frost coming off his mug.

"Well, he's a real nasty one," Heinreich said after Quinn refused to answer. "Brutal and with a wife who's equally deranged. Together, they're more than you think they are. They have a taste for that good old ultra-violence, if you know what I mean? Ramos is surrounded by some pretty sadistic fucks."

Quinn wanted to scoff like he did before.

In the past, Quinn had tangled with some pretty bad fuckers, all of them fit this profile. When Quinn heard the same thing about Ramos, it didn't change his plans for evisceration. It definitely did not coerce someone like Quinn into backing down or declining to accept.

Always, the less he knew about his enemy's reputations, the better.

Where, when, and how were the only questions Quinn cared about.

"When he took control," Heinreich continued, "he waged war against Los Zetas and began a full-fledged takeover of every single cartel spread across the vast Mexican landscape. It's been a bloodbath ever since. And now that he's moved everyone off the board, Ramos has been trying his hand at experimentation. To do that, he's dispensed with a few choice villains to safeguard his investment."

"Like the assassin you encountered back on the freighter perhaps," Priest said.

Quinn saw how others were present in this photo. Some people looked younger, leaner, and wore heavier chains. This new man Quinn was looking at was tatted up, yes. He looked the part, the same as Ramos Mandilo.

Yet, Quinn's concern for neither still remained.

"No," Quinn said as he expressed his disapproval. His boredom had now reached astounding levels.

He turned to face Priest and hoped to see him standing there hunched. Instead, Priest was nibbling on his thumb like an anxious teenager. He continued to look at the photographs. It seemed that Priest cared about all this information, even in spite of the fact that Quinn was bored out of his freaking skull.

"The assassin I encountered was *not* a member of the Sinaloa Cartel," Quinn noted.

"Clearly you haven't seen some of the people under Ramos's command. Like this one," Heinreich said. He switched to a new picture.

This new one showed an image of a shirtless man with his torso covered in frightening imagery like dragons, demons, and other Gothic creatures. All clearly showed the man's preference for scary things, but Quinn was not scared.

This man's pose was also not so candid, like those Quinn had seen before.

This one was more of a portrait rather than a photograph.

"This is Javier Ramirez, chief enforcer to the Sinaloa Cartel," Heinreich informed.

"Wow," Quinn said, pretending to be impressed.

"Called the Cataclysmer, whatever the hell that means," Heinreich said, "but he's a man who has a particular fondness for skinning his enemies alive."

"Uh-huh." To Quinn, this was all just fearsome acts. Men who liked to torture weren't warriors, they were butchers and utter disgraces. And the victims of torture were those weak enough to get kidnapped or captured. Quinn had strategies in place should any of this happen to him, so did Priest.

"Needless to say, he might be at one of cartel's safe-houses," Heinreich continued. "If he is, we want you to—"

"Execute 'em?" Quinn interrupted. "You really need to tell me to do that?"

Heinreich humbly took a step back and raised both his hands to modestly surrender. "No, just want you to know what you're heading into is all," he said. "You make a move against these guys and they're going to do everything they can to take you out. And now, with whatever it is they're doing, this synthetic and this apparently deadly organiza-tion, I can only imagine the resources they have at their disposal. I know you got skills there, Mr. Quinn, but this isn't going to be a cake walk. Just want you to know this before you start."

Heinreich sounded surprisingly caring for an agent.

Quinn appreciated the show of humanity.

In the end, he was not just a killing machine. As well, Quinn understood what Agent Paul Heinreich was here to do. Quinn was about to travel into the eye of the storm. To Quinn's new DEA agent pal, that meant something.

"He can handle it," Priest assured.

Quinn preferred he speak for himself. If he did, he would not have said what Priest did.

"We need to hit these potential spots and find the location of possible facilities and other underground lairs. I can guarantee one of them will be testing this new drug on kids. We just have to get to them and shut it down. We do this, the cartels will scatter, but at least their primary asset will be taken away. It's that easy."

"So out in the open," Heinreich said to Quinn. "Not sure it's the best idea."

"Well, I am," Priest insisted, "which is why Quinn needs to go to one of those damn hotspots as soon as is humanly possible. We only have so much time to make our move, and we need to use that momentum now, while we still have it."

"Right." Quinn agreed. He was still struggling with Priest doing the talking for him. The matter was urgent, no doubt, and Quinn understood this very well.

"Time to go," Priest said.

Quinn nodded as Heinreich turned to look at Priest. "Right," Heinreich said. "Yeah, we should go."

"Thank you, Agent Heinreich," Quinn said, offering his hand. "I'm grateful for your time and your consideration." Quinn was kind but was rarely sweet. Here, he decided to be a bit of both.

"Okay," Heinreich replied. He gave Quinn a firm handshake. "One of the cartel's houses is in Austin, we think. You'll get your intel soon. Good luck."

"Quinn don't *need* luck," added Priest. He walked ahead of Heinreich and moved past Quinn's left shoulder. "All he needs is ammunition, ain't that right?"

While Priest wasn't wrong, Quinn did have a time and a location. All that was left was for Quinn to acquire his much-desired firepower. Other than that, he was ready.

Set.

———

Locked and loaded, Quinn shuffled up to this cartel house one hour after the briefing held in the hotel. Now armed with his Stealth Recon and his TR-1 Ultralight AR-15, the carbine was slung over Quinn's shoulder. Quinn's M1 pistols were holstered, and his tonfa was secured behind his back. On his mask, Quinn had spraypainted a grim reaper.

It was ugly and badass. Quinn counted four guards outside the doorway, all armed with the usual AKs. They loitered awhile. Unbeknownst to them, they were being watched by a man hidden behind a tree. With his Stealth Recon, the Custodian's plan was to execute the two guards at the front and then knock out the remaining two.

Soon as the four were down, it was only a matter of time before everyone was made aware of the impending assault. Quinn needed to be quick when outside and even quicker once he was in. Staring through the scope of his rifle, Quinn looked at the first guy smoking a cigarette and chatting to the cartel member next to him.

He would be the first to go.

Shooting this man dead center, Quinn popped him through the chest, and the shot alerted the man next to him. So the Custodian put a bullet through another Narcos's brittle chest and knocked a new target off his damn feet.

Quinn pulled the stock in tighter to his shoulder and then shot again.

Now executing a third man and then the fourth seconds later, Quinn hit them both square in their heads.

After splitting their skulls, the two Narcos collapsed like two inflatables stripped of their air. Now left strewn like bags of trash, Quinn discarded his recon. He marched to the decrepit home with his next weapon prepped to draw. The house had blacked-out windows, and its porch was lined with flimsy wooden planks. It was three stories high and looked like a manor wrecked by a violent storm. Quinn hopped onto the porch with his TR-1 ready. He tickled the trigger and held his breath.

No mercy. Quinn booted down the door.

Whatever was on the other side, Quinn had only seconds to interpret. Anyone armed was going down. Quinn didn't care who it was. With the door now off its hinges, Quinn found himself standing in a narrow clearing along with four other Narcos.

"Hey!" One pointed as he stood up to shout.

Quinn heard the first scream and was ignited. He shot the shouting man and fired at the remaining three. Quinn sent shots through the abdominal cavities.

It was now a completely ransacked house, a hellhole.

Having killed six Narcos total, with not even two minutes passed, there was already plenty of blood on the Custodian's hands. To Quinn's right stood a man in a tank top and flip-flops. While armed with a gold-plated pistol, Quinn smoked the fool through the forehead and watched as he descended to the ground. Suddenly, there were three more in the man's place, all jumping into the room and all wielding Uzis. Setting the room ablaze, Quinn's gunshots shredded walls and cratered floors. He rolled.

"Aye-yeah! Eat shit, pendejo!"

Quinn's Spanish was not quite as good as his knowledge of other languages. When he heard this comment, he stopped to reload. Slapping in a fresh new clip, Quinn peeked out from behind a table. While he was not going to eat shit, Quinn did possess a certain method for returning the gesture.

He shot straight and he shot low. He picked off all the men individually, and meticulously distributed each round and left holes in the men's chests, abdominals, and in their faces. Everything, which so rapid and accurate, was due to the TR's ability to shoot fast but also straight. The weapon provided all the advantages one would want when owning such a heavily modified, highly reliable firearm. Something like that was perfect for this kind of job.

Quinn entered a new room with round tables. So far, he hadn't seen any narcotics or any sign of the valuable substance known as Hyper-X. All of this was so strange, considering that narcotics was what this location was supposedly known for.

Soon, the space fell deathly quiet.

Quinn cooled his nerves as he inhaled. With his gaze set on a new door, Quinn stepped to the side and made sure all points of access remained in his purview. TR up, Quinn heard a scuttle. He pivoted so fast his heel rubbed into the wood. Foot planted, Quinn rotated and soon...he came face-to-face with yet another madman.

"Ah!" This new man jumped out of the closet, chopping away with a rusty machete.

Charging at Quinn, the Narcos screamed wildly, and ferally swung his weak, pathetic arms. This man was either high, insane, or both. As he attempted to stab Quinn with broad, sloppy strokes, the Custodian cross-stepped and made big circular movements. Using aikido, Quinn twisted and kept his AR-15 low. Then, Quinn snatched his attacker's wrist and bent the bone. Using his attacker's momentum, Quinn whipped him back around and unleashed the full power of his *kotegaeshi*. He flipped the man over and delivered a snapping kick into his ribcage. Then, Quinn knelt over the top of this stupid man.

At point blank, Quinn shot the feral cartel henchman with his M1 and left him to bleed out on the floor. Quinn then instantly returned to his former position. Feeling a surge of adrenaline, Quinn stomped into the next room and there, he hit another fool in the chest.

Bang bang.

The room was now all cleared. Quinn checked the tables.

"We know you're in here, you motherfucker..." This

new voice, Quinn knew, belonged to Javier Ramirez, the so-called Cataclsymer.

After Quinn heard the grumbles from a man-eating maniac, the Custodian peeped over his shoulder but remained steady. There was no point in showing himself if Quinn didn't have a clear shot. And, if Quinn was going to shoot this Javier asshole, goddamn it, he was going to shoot him dead.

Quinn came closer to the cartel's main Narcos, he thought about his next move.

Judging by how close his enemy was, Quinn lifted his leg and delivered a sidekick that pounded Javier in the chest.

"Ah!" Javier raged. Quinn reached for his tonfa. Removing his signature weapons, Quinn spun the batons into his forearms.

No more guns.

No more bullets.

Time to go old school.

Quinn pummeled Ramirez with the first two knuckles in a tight fist. Quinn was sure to keep the tip of the tonfa out, and, therefore, the punch delivered was enhanced. It was heavier and sure to leave a mark. After Quinn hit Javier with his tonfa, he rotated and drove his arm up and then down.

Quinn hammered the enforcer in the chin.

For this fight, Quinn packed one hell of a wallop.

Javier shrieked like a stepped-on mouse. From here, Quinn went into full attack mode. He struck repeatedly and connected three times. Then, Quinn flipped the tonfa back to its traditional position. With the weapons now against his forearms, Quinn finished Ramirez with a push kick that forced the madman into the next room.

Watching Javier go down, Quinn could kill a man with the tonfa; had before and was prepared to do it again now.

In the midst of setting himself up for the final blow, Quinn stopped.

He was not alone.

In the company of a new opponent, Quinn was in black, while this visitor was also covered in dark gear. The only difference between him and Quinn was the mask. This visitor's mask was painted with three red lines drawn across the center, also quite badass.

"Fuck," Quinn said after being kicked. "Well, hello there."

Quinn was relaxed and unaffected by the arrival of this assassin. With no expression or face, this assassin's movements were mechanical and efficient, like a machine.

"See you found me. Good job," Quinn commended. "Nice moves back at the boat. Didn't expect any of them. Who are you?"

Refusing to answer, Blackstone looked Quinn up and down.

"Not much of a talker, are you?"

It was a stupid question. Blackstone was here to kill, not talk.

"Okay then. Nothing to add," Quinn continued. "Let's get started. It's getting late, and I'm already tired."

The one who came to save Javier was the same assassin Quinn encountered on the freighter.

Blackstone had arrived.

Blackstone's weapon of choice was an HK UMP45. Coming out of his hiding place, Blackstone looked like a cloaked villain from a children's play. He unleashed a relentless stream of bullets while Quinn dove with the tonfa still in his hand.

Quinn took cover but got clipped just under his right arm.

Thankfully, Quinn was protected by his body armor. Still, it stung like a bitch.

"Ah," Quinn squirmed, and he slipped his tonfa back behind him.

He reached for his Glock 26, but the gun was holstered around his left ankle. Still, the Custodian snagged the gun and shot three times. He was unsure as to where he was aiming. His goal was to provide cover fire so he could run. Nevertheless, with Quinn's hand up and free, he fired his Glock. But Blackstone was firing too, at the same time and in the same direction.

Quinn's boots smacked the floor as he sprinted. Running away, Quinn heard the straining yells from the wounded cartel guardian, Javier Ramirez.

"No! Don't let him get away!" Javier's voice was gut-wrenching. His mouth was full of spit or what Quinn hoped was blood.

Although Quinn wouldn't say, he was *far away*. He barreled through the doorway and landed on his shoulder. He tumbled and smashed the wood and went straight down into the floor below. The fall, though short, still hurt. Quinn didn't process this or any of his injuries. Whenever Quinn felt any pain in any part of his body, he paused and waited for it to sink in. Soon as it did, Quinn would welcome it, where he stored it for future use. This strategy, which had served Quinn well so far, was a good way of combating the pain always growing inside.

He didn't think about it, he just fought through it and then moved on.

And that's the way it was for as long as Quinn could remember. He was thinking differently. Since his encounter with his father, he was thinking about everything differently, more than he liked to admit.

He touched his spine, stopped, and peered up. Quinn heard Ramirez from the floor above.

The man was impassioned when speaking with Blackstone.

"We have to get back to him!" Quinn heard Ramirez shouting from above. "We have to find this asshole before he gets away!"

Javier was speaking Spanish as Quinn reached for his belt. He unclipped a flashlight and clicked its end to light it up. Quinn cast its beam onto the shadows and lifted as much of the darkness as he could. Quinn's breath was again taken away, but it was not due to fatigue or pain. The sight Quinn was previewed to, even for an often unfazed man like himself, was too much.

"No." In the humid basement, Quinn encountered rows of cages.

He counted five, six, and then seven, going on and on.

Inside of these prisons were several groupings of raggedy, unkempt, discarded people—prisoners. Quinn stared at the grotesque assembly of battered women and sobbing children. Each one emaciated, they were malnourished, and trembling in the muggy setting. With scars drawn along the women's cheeks and necks, they were broken by whatever horrors they'd been subjected to. It was a terror even Quinn couldn't imagine.

He didn't find narcotics but found this instead.

How long the Sinaloa Cartel had these people? Again, Quinn dared not guess.

Quinn preferred not to think about it. He stared into a child's frail eyes. The woman standing the closest to him stepped back when she saw Quinn. Raising her hands to show she meant no harm, she bowed.

"Please," the woman pleaded. "Please, don't hurt us."

Quinn shuffled.

Shame had now become his only emotion as he gazed at all these prisoners. Although Quinn was not responsible in any way, it hurt. If he wanted retribution, and Quinn did, then he knew this was the cost of getting it.

"Help us," a woman no older than twenty said to Quinn through steel bars.

Clutching the cold steel, she stared at the elite mercenary. Next to her was a boy around the age of four. He cuddled himself into the woman's skinny arms. The boy's face covered in dirt, he gazed at Quinn. He looked closer at this little boy. He observed a hollowness that was all too familiar to the Custodian. A prick instantly punctured Quinn's heart and he recalled the dark days of his past.

Quinn removed his M1, smoked the padlock, and blasted the steel. The cage creaked and the women and children all looked at Quinn magnanimously. Proceeding out of this cage, Quinn lowered his sidearm. He did not acknowledge any of the people passing by. If they only knew the kind of man he was, the act of releasing them would matter far less.

This was how Quinn chose to see his good deed. He was just someone who was in the right place at the right time. After everything that happened, it felt like Quinn couldn't be in a worse place.

"Thank you." The woman spoke to Quinn in Spanish and nodded. Quinn said nothing as he stepped back and let everyone pass. He glimpsed at the woman, and what Quinn saw first was the scar across her stomach.

This was a weird detail for Quinn. He asked himself why he was there.

Was it to release hostages?

Make sure innocent people were protected?

So far as Quinn could see? Yes, unquestionably.

He wanted retribution and nothing else.

But after this escape, Quinn grabbed his phone and dialed Priest. He waited and removed his mask. Quinn's black makeup appeared smeared around his eyes. His mission was to clear the room, and that's what he did. As for Javier Ramirez, well, Quinn should have killed that bastard, and he would try to do this now, but would fail if he did.

"Yeah?"

"Room is all clear. It's done." Quinn cut to the chase and informed Priest soon as he heard him speak.

"All dead?"

Quinn refused to lie. "Most."

Priest's breathing went from moderate to heavy. "Not all?"

"No," Quinn said. He admitted how he had not slain every member of the cartel. He could have provided more detail regarding but he refused. "Not all."

Quinn ended the call. He slipped his phone into his back pocket. Though the cages were cleared, the house containing the broken women and children was also empty. The last child to leave the cage suddenly stopped to tug on Quinn's shirt.

"Thank you," the boy said. "Thank you for saving us."

What Quinn wanted to say was *don't mention it* or *no problem*. He wanted to utter these words or some other overstated phrase people said whenever they are thanked. He wanted to tell the boy that everything was going to be all right, that Quinn was here to help.

Why would Quinn say these things? Why would he speak the words he never had?

Quinn thought he should say it because that's what people were *expected* to say in these unforgiving circumstances. They were the words and phrases of good people, of Samaritans and of heroes. It was what people said who believed in good things. It was the same people who believed that good things happen to good people. It's the heroes who win and the villains who lose.

But Quinn was neither.

He wasn't heroic. Even his newfound *ideology* didn't elevate him to such a level.

No, right now, he was just a man standing in the way, a man with a gun and nothing else.

It was for these reasons Quinn couldn't say to this one kid that *it was all good* or that *it was going to be just fine.* Quinn was growing a soul but it wasn't done taking shape. It also wasn't about saying the right thing at the right time. The reason Quinn set the kid free was because he knew what it was like to be in a cage. Quinn would have given anything to have someone break him out at a time when it counted most.

Unfortunately, no one did. No one heard his cries, knew of his pain, or could see his scars.

And so, when Quinn watched the boy race off with his mother, he saw how the two were holding hands. Together, they vanished into the night, but Quinn stayed behind. He stayed because he wanted to be sure everybody disappeared the same as the boy and his mother.

Soon, everyone was gone, never to be seen or heard of again.

CHAPTER 4
A TALE OF TWO WOLVES

BACK IN MEXICO, A WEARY AND FATIGUED Blackstone said nothing as he waited in the fortified mansion belonging to one Mr. Ramos Mandilo. Still shelled in his gear, Blackstone's hands were all bloody from the fight he shared with his new and deadly enemy. Holding tight to his HK, the assassin stood outside the Sinaloa's great lair and there, continuously shot a single target in a practice range set up for the killers to use.

Upon his return, Cane said nothing to Ramos until he was confronted later.

"So...what the hell happened?" Ramos barked at his main hitman, Cane.

Cane Quinn, a.k.a. Blackstone, provided Ramos with only the minimum detail. Despite working for the cartel as their primary tool for murder and destruction, in Cane's opinion, Cane worked for no one. In his mind, he only collaborated, and that was an entirely different process.

"Attacked. We were fucking attacked."

When Ramos asked who and what attacked one of his other houses, Javier was the one to answer.

"An assassin. A fucking ringer." Ramos stood with his wife, Alessandra. She and Ramos were now poised by the balustrade, a stunning railing crafted out of pure alabaster. The property it overlooked was just one of many. After Javier informed his master about what attacked them, Blackstone responded while making his way back.

"Not an assassin. A *Custodian*." Blackstone skulked through the foyer.

His arms swayed, and he transitioned from the back of the house to the front. Without acknowledging the head of the cartel or his wife, Blackstone carried on like the two were barely there.

"Would you then explain to me *exactly* how you were made aware of this man who attacked you twice in one day?"

Blackstone slapped another clip into his SIG. He cocked the weapon and lowered his hand. He looked at the head of the cartel. Mask removed, Cane's identity was now fully revealed.

"Because," Blackstone said, spit shelling his every word, "I know him because it's my job to know him."

Ramos's head shook. The explanation Blackstone gave was too standard. It was too by-the-book for someone in his position.

"No, I don't think so," Ramos said. "I think there's something else going on here, so I'm going to ask you one last time..." Ramos bit his tongue and flexed his chest. "How much do you know about him, this Custodian you mentioned?"

There was a pause and Blackstone's head gradually began to turn. He was looking at the man in charge. Blackstone's eyes burned as the hatred within continued to build. It was obvious he could no longer refuse Ramos's question. No, now was not the time to hold back the truth.

Certainly, it was not to deny it either.

"*He's my brother.*" Cane Quinn raised his SIG and glowered at Mandilo.

Unfazed by the interrogation, Cane was loyal to his unwillingness to be intimidated or threatened. The servant and the lord were locked into a heated moment that neither one of them could break free of.

"Your brother?" Ramos asked as he stood next to Cane.

"My *older* brother," Cane said.

"I see. And he's been trained, same as you?"

Cane ignored Ramos and reached into his belt for another magazine. Then, Cane tilted his head and replied. "You could say that."

"*Interesting,*" Ramos Mandilo said.

"So, our attacker...he's your brother?" This next question was phrased by Alessandra.

She stepped along in her silk nightgown and glared at Cane. She was barefooted, and her luscious brown hair flowed elegantly behind her as she moved.

"Yes," Cane said. He phrased the answer as simply as he could. Yet, he refused to make eye contact.

"How did he manage to cross paths with you, I wonder?" said Alessandra.

"Got wind of the product from a spook working for the DEA or NSA probably," Cane said, "or some other black ops division."

"Black ops?" Ramos asked. "So, that's who your brother's working for?"

"Most likely," Cane said.

"So," Alessandra said, her arms crossed. "We find a path that leads to your brother. We find anyone who knows him, and then we fucking kill him."

Cane laughed hearing Ramos's wife's ridiculous strategy. "Finding my brother," he said, "would be like hunting a crocodile in the fucking Amazon. You wanna go pokin' around for one, be my guest. But chasing a man like him... not a wise decision."

"In case you've forgotten, we're Sinaloa. We are the fucking crocs in the Amazon," Ramos said.

"Not in this case," Cane said, gun in hand. "You're not even close."

"So...that's it?" Ramos switched back to Spanish. "We brought you onboard so you could help us," he said, "and now you're saying your brother *can't* be stopped? I thought you were someone who was willing to live up to his stunning reputation. Perhaps I was wrong."

Cane shot another round into the same spot as before. His SIG emptied. He lowered the weapon down to his waist.

"*My* reputation is not what's at stake here," Cane affirmed. "I'm afraid it's *yours*."

Cane stepped up to the brutal kingpin and received a gawk from the one known as Alessandra. Although Cane was facing Ramos, at this moment, he was speaking to him *and* to his wife.

"You want to stop someone like him, you have to know how the game is played."

"Is that so?" Ramos asked.

"It is," Cane confirmed. "The one who's hunting you, my brother and his employer...*his kind*..." Cane stressed the word *kind* because he wanted to emphasize the sheer rarity of those labeled as *Custodians*. "They come from a world that doesn't play by your rules. There is no cause and there is no effect, see? They don't negotiate, hesitate, or question. They see, they target, and they eliminate," Cane explained. "My brother could come in here right now and wipe out your whole fucking house if he wanted.

He's not afraid of torture or death, because he comes from the same place that I do, *the dark place?* I know what he wants, and I know what he's looking for. And, because I do, I'm the best chance you have at stopping him."

"And how *exactly* do you plan on doing that?" Alessandra, so pretentious and embittered, curled her tongue as she spoke. "How do you plan to stop him?"

"He found me, didn't he?" said Cane. "So, that means he's after what we are, and he won't stop until he gets it."

"Then we double our efforts," Ramos said. "We use more men."

"No," Cane said. He glared at Ramos and Alessandra. "We do *not* engage."

"Excuse me?" Alessandra barked back at her chief assassin.

"He will return," Cane said. "And when he does, I'll handle what comes next."

"And how many of my men do you expect to sacrifice as you do?" Ramos asked.

Cane's impulse was to grin but then he chose not to. He knew exactly how many men would be sacrificed at the hands of his dangerous brother.

"As many as are needed. This is a war, is it not? And the one who wins the war is the one who chooses to treat his enemy like almost a better version of themselves. You want to stop my brother, this is how you do it." Without saying another word, Cane pivoted and faced the target in an open field.

"Okay," Ramos said. "We will allow you to lure your brother as you see fit, but you will *not* be doing any of this alone, do you understand? Javier and the others will accompany you. We stop this brother of yours while we still can. You give the orders and they...they will follow them."

"And I have your word they will?" asked Cane as he agreed to Ramos's plan.

"Yes," said Alessandra. She didn't break eye contact. "You have our word."

Just as fearless as her husband, both Ramos and Alessandra respected Cane Quinn. However, this didn't change his status. Still, he belonged to Sinaloa.

Cane cocked his gun again and lifted the pistol to his cold face. "Good," he said. "Very good."

CHAPTER 5
RED SKY IN THE MORNING

Quinn used a laptop to check in with Priest just like he did back in Louisiana, but now he had a MacBook Pro, which was better. Quinn sent a message using a special messenger interface specified by Priest.

With the platform opened, Quinn was greeted by a new order.

You're going to take out a truck.

As Priest reported this to Quinn, it was Heinreich who said the truck was another way the cartels transport their products across their country. Apparently, it was one of their chief methods.

A Kenworth, eighteen-wheeler semi. According to Border Patrol, one was seen moving at 09:00 yesterday. It's on track to head through Austin in the next two hours, which means you'll be the one intercepting. Quinn, you gotta get on that truck. Get on and take out anyone and grab what you can, if there's anything to grab. You have to stop it from reaching its destination. Remember your

new rules. Take out the whole gang. All of them deserve to die.

Priest sent his messages via his own laptop using this Messenger. No calls.

Quinn wrote to Priest.

I know how it's supposed to go.

Priest replied back. **Right. Of course, you do.**

Quinn was unsure how many shipments of this Hyper-X were in the possession of the Sinaloa Cartel currently. But, at the very least, there was one, and the cartel decided to transport it using a hulking vehicle like this truck. It was built with an angular front section. It included tinted windows and a flat-nose hull seven feet in diameter.

In addition to Quinn's weapons, the Custodian also had a Ducati EVO 848 motorcycle, the black model. Liquid-cooled and with fuel injection, the bike included a twin-cylinder engine, and the puppy was capable of reaching 140 HP. It could even hit a full mile in under twelve seconds!

Not bad at all.

Onboard the sleek and explosive puppy of a ride, Quinn wasn't much of a cool rider. His affinity for bikes didn't rival his passion for guns, jets, or cars. But his plan was to use the Ducati to get close to the truck. Speeding along the almost empty highway, Quinn swerved in and out of the intermittent traffic and the bike's dexterity allowed him to bend around the neighboring vehicles with little resistance.

Quinn accelerated the Ducati to the base of the eighteen-wheeler. Then, he veered in, and then...he jumped. Leaping off the bike, Quinn nimbly landed on the front of this truck and the driver stopped and turned to look at his rearview.

Quinn pulled himself onboard and also pulled his M1.

The transport lacked stability. Still, Quinn stayed balanced. With his legs wide, Quinn's stance was strong. He clutched his gun with two hands but heard footsteps shuffling along the side of the vehicle.

Damn ready, once he had a glimpse of the target, it was over.

One shot, Quinn pushed the first slain cartel crony onto the street. Quinn kneeled and shot two clean holes in the next fool's jugular.

From there, Quinn hastened.

With two down, the door to the hold was guarded by two other cartel operators. Quinn cleared the path and tried to get to the cargo hold. After, he distributed a heavy, exploding kick that knocked the door right off its hinges and into a new storage facility. Inside, Quinn saw that most of the vehicle's interior was occupied only with rows of packaged cocaine.

Quinn shook a prism loaded with white powder. He sought to weigh the package and tried to gauge whether there was more. Quinn wouldn't know until he cut it open. Quinn holstered his sidearm and went for his switchblade. He ejected the blade and was about to jam it into the package when he stopped after seeing someone else standing in the doorway.

"Drop it. Let it go." Exposed, Quinn was a turkey shoot from where he was standing.

Javier Ramirez was Sinaloa's right-hand man, next to Cane. Right now, he looked at Quinn while holding a gold-plated AK47. The gun's barrel was dipped too far as Quinn raised his hands anyway.

"Step back now, *jefe*." Quinn did as he was told. He

faced a cluster of cocaine packages but so far...found no sign of the synthetic known as Hyper-X.

"You boarded the wrong ride here, motherfucker, and you messed with the wrong—" Quinn ignored Javier's bogus threat. Although Quinn was close to Javier, he inched himself even closer.

This man's words, so pointless in Quinn's mind, as the Custodian slid in, he lifted his hand to latch Javier's wrist. Pulling the Narcos closer, Quinn twisted Javier's wrist and locked him in a solid *kotegaeshi* and slammed Javier into the floor. Soon after, the brutal sicario was stripped of his main weapon.

Bobbing back and forth, Quinn delivered two kicks into Javier's chest, someone who was now in a partial fighting position. It wasn't much of a stance, but then Quinn struck with a sidekick and knocked Javier back down. Seeing him slam into the floor, Quinn was out of patience and out of time.

Quinn lifted his blade and sliced Javier's chest with a clean aikido *giri* cut. Quinn drew more blood after severing Javier's aorta. Once this was done, Quinn pushed with his shoulder to thrust Javier down again. Quinn squatted and pushed his knees hard into Javier's ribcage. Quinn cut and delivered another clean gash along this man's jugular. He then jammed the weapon straight into Javier's trachea.

Quinn pushed the blade in nice and deep.

A thin stream of arterial red sprayed Quinn's stoic face. It was as brutal as it was wet, and Quinn was drenched as he looked at all the cargo. He turned and motioned to one of the holds. Busting it wide open, Quinn scavenged for any signs of the material called Hyper-X. He kicked another door aside and found a new compartment hidden there.

Quinn's face was brightened from the discovery.

He reached in and grasped a smooth cylinder.

Bingo.

Quinn gripped the sleek container. He slipped it into his pocket. Then, Quinn moved back to the door and exited the cargo hold. Ditching the bike, Quinn raced to the front of the truck. He looked at the driver. Quinn wielded his Glock and hurried to the window. The driver popped open the window and pointed his Beretta.

Quinn had a clean shot well before he did. He nailed him.

Quinn shot the driver's face. Quinn opened the door and slipped the dead man from his seat. Quinn watched as a corpse tumbled onto the road. With the truck accelerating, Quinn was on a crash course, certain to destroy all cargo. Before any of this could happen, Quinn looked back and saw a silver Audi racing to the truck. Quinn squinted. He could see who was driving. As it turned out, Quinn knew them well.

"Ally?" Quinn whispered her name.

He couldn't believe Ally had come all this way to find him.

The tires shrieked and Quinn could smell the foul scent of burned rubber. He watched as the car peeled off. In that second, Quinn was airborne. He leaped off the truck and clashed with the roof of the Audi. Quinn was connected but bounced for a second before he latched his hands along the car. Jamming his fingers in, Quinn held the indents of the roof while the truck exploded. The car fled in a twisted cloud of smoke and exhaust.

"You good?" a voice screamed from below.

Turning, Quinn saw the voice was Ally's. He squeezed the roof and was relatively secured. Quinn's body was stretched as he pressed his chin into the metal.

"Good!" yelled Quinn.

The eighteen-wheeler exploded toward a bend in the road. Its nose plowed straight through a row of guardrails. Splitting into a cluster of big yellow tubs, the truck tilted—wheels blitzing while heading straight for a gathering of trees. The truck rolled over like a massive, oversized mule. It descended before being swallowed up by debris. Escaping the cacophony, if Quinn hadn't jumped, he'd have ended up the same as the truck.

And, had Ally not been there, the destruction would have only been so much worse.

Quinn rested his head against the roof of Ally's Audi. The car slowed onto a new highway. What Quinn needed now was a cold drink and another few seconds to fall into Ally's arms.

Maybe, Quinn thought, he'd do that first.

CHAPTER 6
KEYS

AFTER ATTACKING THE EIGHTEEN-WHEELER, ALLY stopped so Quinn entered the car. The Custodian couldn't hold on to the roof for long.

Once he was inside, Quinn said nothing to her or to Heinreich.

Quinn was escorted to an office six miles north of the freeway.

He was there, but Priest was not. Quinn looked at Ally and she stared back at him.

So far as Quinn was aware, everything that happened fell under Heinreich's jurisdiction.

He was the special agent monitoring all cartel activity. In essence, Heinreich was tracking Sinaloa, except he wasn't executing them. Instead, he was working with Ally, or Ally was working with Heinreich. Either way, Quinn didn't care. Whatever the reason, everyone was working to discover how a Mexican drug cartel had managed to discover this new and powerful asset.

Or did *they* discover it or someone else?

Quinn was now beginning to suspect that maybe it

wasn't manufactured by the Sinaloa Cartel at all. No, maybe it was never about the cartels at all.

Maybe this was about something else.

"Look, Quinn, this...Hyper-X...it's not what you think." Quinn's eyes twitched as he looked at Heinreich.

When Heinreich told Quinn that the synthetic wasn't as it appeared, Quinn hissed. "I know," Quinn said.

"Well, what you might *not* know," added Heinreich. He was in a room filled only with tables and chairs. "Is *how* it was manufactured."

"See," Ally interceded. "We know the cartel couldn't have made it on their own," she said, "but where they got it from and why...well, Heinreich has been telling me all about that."

"And she," Heinreich said. He was referring to Ally. "She's been telling me a whole lot about you."

"How do you know each other?" Quinn looked at Ally and Heinreich. He didn't like that Ally had just fallen out of nowhere. She did, but Quinn wanted to know why.

"We used to work together," Ally said. "Old friends, see?"

Quinn nodded. He did see.

"And Priest?" Quinn asked instead, changing the subject. He trusted Ally and trusted whoever she interacted with, so if she trusted Heinreich, maybe Quinn did too.

"We still think he's trying to get to the bottom of this as well," Heinreich said. "Working shit out on his end, you know? I mean, he's logistics and you're field. Besides..." Heinreich grumbled his next response. "This was all *his* idea," Heinreich continued, "to have you start this war in the first place."

Quinn didn't respond. It was Priest's idea about how

to properly incentivize Kyle Quinn. Still, Quinn was doing this mission because he wanted to.

"So what *exactly* does this Hyper-X do?" Quinn asked. Whenever he didn't like where the conversation was going, he switched to something else.

Now, it was not a question meant for anyone specifically. Quinn asked it because he was frustrated by all the claims being made so far. But, no one was providing anything precise, not until Heinreich elaborated on his previous statement.

"It's an enhanced pain suppressor," Heinreich explained, "able to subjugate not only physical pain, but emotional pain as well. The way beta blockers drown out noise, Hyper-X drowns out trauma, causes adrenaline levels to spike, and allows the subject to channel all their energy to a solid level but only for a very short amount of time. See, it reharnesses all this pain and then siphons it into various parts of the body capable of speed and strength."

"A *lot* of speed and a *lot* of strength," Heinreich specified.

Heinreich mentioned this and Quinn's stare shifted to Ally.

"You mean, like...*a super soldier serum?*"

"Well, we would hardly call it that," Heinreich said, "but it does allow for optimal performance, at least that's what we've observed. However, it's tough to beat someone who can't feel any pain, wouldn't you agree?"

Quinn's head turned so it was straight. "And how exactly do the cartels fit into all of this?" Quinn asked.

"During my time with the agency," Ally said, "I did take a look into our biological engineering division, specifically engineering linked to PTSD and other forms of trauma, but Sinaloa was labeled as a terrorist organization by the CIA. There were rumors that some were on the lookout for a new asset to replace some of our old products."

"No more cocaine," Quinn said. "Basically?"

Ally nodded. "Basically."

Quinn looked around the room. Everyone was on the same page.

"The cartels have been searching for something new to bring to the US for years. I mean, first, it was drugs, and then it was people, human trafficking," Ally said. "But now, now it seems as though they might actually have a more valuable commodity than all that, if they combine both of those things together."

"But I thought you said," Quinn replied, "*they* didn't make the drug."

"No," Ally confirmed.

"No," Heinreich confirmed as well.

"Well," Quinn said, "then who the hell did?"

A brief period of uncomfortable silence surfaced and Ally did as she always did whenever she was previewed to something too difficult to grasp. "KEYS." Ally said this.

Quinn's fists clenched.

It was not the first time he heard the word.

"KEYS?" Quinn queried.

"Yes," Heinreich replied. "Heard of 'em?"

"I have," Quinn answered, "but I was told they were working with the cartels, a private op of some kind, maybe even cooperating, but not much after that."

"Well, KEYS...is...well," Heinreich said, "let's just say...that's where the story gets *complicated.*"

At this point, Quinn had more questions as he continued to survey the room. Searching for familiar faces, the only one he wanted to see was not here.

"Where's Priest?" Quinn asked.

"Well, Priest is trying to stop the spread as much as we are," Heinreich said.

Quinn looked at Heinreich. Fat droplets of sweat lingered on his forehead and chin. Quinn was uncertain if this was because of the heat or if it was the topic itself. Was this causing Heinreich to feel a whirlwind of doubt?

The last time Priest spoke to Quinn, the custodian thought he had all the information.

Sinaloa Cartel. New Drug. Government Program. KEYS.

Take out, neutralize, or, as Priest had phrased it: *eviscerate*. And yet, with no sign of Priest at the engagement, he was not providing Quinn with orders.

"All we know is that KEYS, this organization, is closer than we thought," explained Ally. "They might be the ones responsible for creating this synthetic and they might also be the ones who are trying to cover it up."

"And you've been selected to mop it all up, Quinn," Heinreich added. "That's been the goal since day one."

"I was selected to do nothing," Quinn said. He was speaking to Heinreich but was keeping his eyes on Ally. "I accepted this mission on my own accord. I don't want the cartels moving bad shit into my country, and I don't want to see any more kids getting hurt because of it. That's the only reason I'm here now."

"Kids?" Heinreich questioned.

"*Trafficked* kids," Quinn specified. He recalled what he saw back at the house owned by Sinaloa. "I know Sinaloa controls most of the flesh trade here," Quinn said. "I know they've been testing this Hyper-X shit on children. I saw it. I know."

"What do you mean?" asked Ally. "Know what?"

"Yeah, how do you know?" Heinreich asked. He seemed to believe all of Quinn's claims except for one.

"The house I hit," Quinn said, "*it was filled with women and children.*"

"Shit," Ally said.

"No sign of the synthetic though," Quinn said. "None."

"Son of a bitch," Heinreich said.

"Actually," added Ally, "I think it's here where things get complicated, like you said, right?"

Quinn felt a deep singe in the base of his spine. He gawked at Ally because even Quinn didn't expect her to use the same justification that Heinreich did.

"Based on the intel from some of our own DEA agents," Ally said, "traces of this synthetic weren't actually found in any kids."

"What?" Quinn barked. The phrase made him so sick he had to spit.

According to Priest, that's exactly who was being tested!

"Well, not *exclusively*," Heinreich corrected.

It was as though Heinreich's only reason for being here was to defend Priest. Quinn remembered how it was both Heinreich and the Lock Smith himself, who was Priest, who had explained this mission. It might be their thoughts and idea, but it was Quinn's reasoning. It was his motive.

"Mostly, it's been given...*to women.*"

"What?" Quinn asked Heinreich. "What do you mean...women?"

"Well, *expectant mothers.*" Now Ally was the one making corrections.

For some reason, she knew more about what was happening than Quinn did. Maybe she knew more than Priest too. Maybe Heinreich told her everything.

But why?

"Right," Quinn said.

If he was going to be honest, Quinn couldn't figure out whether Heinreich could be trusted or if his interests lay only in killing the cartel. Being more honest, Quinn was tired of waiting to find out. He stayed with the mission. He stayed true to the plan.

"Well, when the two of you are done talking," Quinn said, "I do have a plan for getting rid of Mandilo, if you're up for it."

Quinn cared less about the victims and more about the perpetrators.

And that was the point. It was these bad people who were Quinn's mission. He had come to kill, not to question or uncover. So, he switched from talking about the situation to taking severe steps to end it. He was back to cleaning, back to removing stains.

"Then, tell us," Heinreich said. "We're open to hearing anything now."

"All right," Quinn said, "well, it's real simple."

"Simple?" Ally asked.

"Very," Quinn added. "I'm going to walk through the front door and shoot Ramos Mandilo right in the fucking head."

CHAPTER 7
DO NOT GO GENTLY...

QUINN WAS IN MEXICO.

He crossed the border in a RAV4 hybrid model, which was Heinreich's former vehicle. It was red with thick-ass tires and plenty of trunk space. Before leaving America for this new country, Quinn asked Heinreich if he could *keep the roads clear.*

Absolutely, Heinreich confirmed.

Mexico's heat was worse than Texas's. Quinn was scorching and it was almost nightfall. Still, the inescapable warmness engulfed him. Although he had yet to suit up, when Quinn told Priest what he was about to do, he received no response.

Why?

Later, Quinn popped open the trunk loaded with bags and unzipped each one.

His pants were loose and his shirt was tight. Quinn geared up for the approaching slaughter. He started with the basics. Quinn happily returned to using his Glocks. There were three with him now.

A 34, 26, and 17.

All were included with sound suppressors and each one was loaded along with five spare mags. Once Quinn had his pistols gathered, he inserted them all into his thigh rigs. He declined to bring an assault rifle to this party. Too noisy and too unnecessary, Quinn wanted a more intimate experience, and pistols were enough for the road ahead.

"Okay," Quinn said. He cocked one of his Glocks. "Let's get it."

————

At Ramos's mansion, it was well past eight at night and, therefore, almost the cartel leader's dinner time.

When Quinn infiltrated the Mandilo property decked out in full gear, he pattered along like a wolf strolling through the dark woods. He scaled the wall guarding the property in a series of gallant leaps and impressive high-pulls. Like an Olympic gymnast, afterward, Quinn spotted all the cameras. Coming to the first, Quinn nudged it with his tonfa but didn't alter its position too much.

He just needed to turn it so it didn't see him. Then, Quinn crawled through a palm tree and escaped along one of its narrow branches. Once he was in, Quinn flipped up to pass the perimeter. In order to avoid the motion sensors, Quinn jumped onto a pillar located beneath the second-level balcony. He concealed himself beneath a stone balustrade, for Quinn was a python slithering on a tall tree.

Waiting for one guard to pass, Quinn swung and appeared from under the pillar. But, by the time the guard spotted the railing, the cut was already delivered.

A stream of blood ejaculated from the guard's neck and Quinn motioned to the second level, still holding his knife. Wrapping his arm around the guard's severed neck, Quinn held his mouth shut and jabbed the man once more in the pancreas and the first sight that emerged after was another guard.

He wielded the standard HK. Quinn found him and flicked the trigger of his silenced Glock. The shots were so quiet that Quinn felt like he was playing a first-person shooter game. He fired one in the asshole's chest and the next in through his right temple. Being a clean cut, both dropped.

Quinn stepped over the bleeding bodies and approached the bedroom.

There, the Custodian heard another footstep tapping the space around the corner. Another cartel man dressed in a suit stood by, wielding an Uzi. He jumped soon as he saw Quinn. The man's hand shifted, but Quinn shot him through the head.

The man was knocked into the alabaster wall before sliding down to the floor. The wall was painted with his own blood. In the room, Quinn heard the voice of someone singing a soft melody.

He peeped inside.

Alessandra stood in her silk bathrobe, but there was no sign of her husband, Ramos, anywhere. Poised in front of a circular mirror, Alessandra rubbed lotion in her hands. A person is never more vulnerable than when they're in the bedroom or bathroom. Though she was a strikingly beautiful woman, Quinn thought Alessandra looked quite fine in her robe. Then, Quinn was reckoned when he considered the person she was.

Anyone who knew Sinaloa also knew of Alessandra and her reputation.

Most would shake when hearing tales of Ms. Demerez.

She castrated, boiled, even ate some of her enemies alive. According to one story, Alessandra watched as one man had his balls chewed by a wolf. She was said to have poured whiskey on the wound just so it would sting.

Now, these stories were ugly. Quinn had heard far worse.

But the stories about the Custodians were far more terrifying than the parables told about a drug cartel. Priest made MS-13 look like a boy-band when he unleashed hell in the name of America. At this moment, Kyle Quinn was gripping his Glock while peering out from behind the door.

He could see Alessandra blending moisturizer into her cherubic face. Quinn watched her walk across the glowing marble tiles. With a direct line to Alessandra, Quinn had her exactly where he wanted her to be.

Although Quinn had the headshot, he pressed his finger lightly to the trigger and delivered a clean shot straight through Alessandra's left calf.

Quinn listened to her scream.

It was louder than he thought, and he didn't like it, not one bit.

CHAPTER 8
AN INTRUDER

HEARING ALESSANDRA'S TERRIBLE SQUEALS, THE WIFE of the cartel leader fell to the floor and held her bleeding leg. Yelling loudly for all to hear, all of this was part of Quinn's plan. He wanted only to wound her so he could draw out the other men. As Alessandra screamed expletives, the Custodian spotted another man creeping up behind him.

"Drop it." When this man warned Quinn, the Custodian lowered his weapon and stared at the one who threatened him.

Quinn wasn't fearful of any other shooter but he did recognize this speaker's voice. While familiar, the man was armed with an FN F2000. It was a bullish Belgian assault rifle outfitted with a scope. A red dot shined in the center of Quinn's forehead.

"Nice piece." Quinn leaned into his humor to keep things interesting, maybe even easier.

Although he recognized the person standing before him, Quinn also knew the presence and the smell. Black-

stone was unmasked and so he possessed a certain famil-
iarity that impaired all of Quinn's senses.

"I said put it down."

"*Cane?*" Quinn said, shocked by the sight.

Head bent, Quinn's posture was crooked, almost to the
point of being unbalanced. His arms felt weak. Quinn was
never off-guard, unwilling, or distracted. No, the man was a
fucking hawk. There was absolutely nothing that could level
Quinn to such a degree he couldn't complete his mission.

But this was different.

No, this was something not even Quinn expected or
wanted to see.

"Kyle." Hearing his name, Quinn tingled.

Hand on his Glock, he had Cane aligned. But being
Quinn's brother—his younger brother—he had his target
aligned too. Each Quinn acquired the kill shot both
desired, and both were unable to deliver. Right now,
neither could do precisely what they were born or bred to
do. They were weakened by the shock. All Quinn had to
do was let go, and it was the same for Cane.

But they didn't. They didn't, because they were
compelled to hold onto whatever the two were still shar-
ing. The Quinns could kill almost anything, except family.
Quinn refused to move even an inch.

"You're..." Cane sounded frail and weak.

With more footsteps heard, reinforcements trampled
through the Mandilo home. If Ramos was present, it also
meant he was aware. It also meant he was approaching
and would be here soon.

"Alive," Quinn said.

"Here," Cane said. "Just like we knew you would be."

"Knew?" Quinn asked. How did Cane know? *Who
told him?*

Cane's answer was delivered in the same broken voice as before. When it was done, however, Quinn embraced the fact that his brother was still alive. Quinn glimpsed past him. Alessandra Demerez was near the door. With more armed men, Quinn's strength had suddenly dwindled.

He was now in the most vulnerable position he'd ever been in.

If he stayed where he was, then he was a sure as hell... a fucking dead man.

"You're going to run, aren't you?" Cane asked.

"For now," Quinn answered.

"You know we'll find you," Cane said. He smiled to show his confidence, but Quinn didn't care. Now that his brother was here, Quinn could not finish the mission as he had planned.

In truth, what he was thinking now was better.

"I will see you again...*very soon.*" Head shaking, Quinn wasn't here to kill his brother. His fight was not with Cane. No, it was with the other men who deserved to die.

Did Quinn's brother deserve to die too?

Perhaps.

While struggling with this idea, Quinn heard more footsteps.

There was only one way out, and it was the same way he'd used to get in. Quinn could not go back that way. Now, he had to find a new exit or make one.

"Where is she! Where is my wife?" Quinn heard Ramos's vehement shouts echoing throughout the massive house. The Custodian stayed on Cane. He would stay longer but burdened by the possibility of ending his brother's life, Quinn chose the more difficult decision. He leaped over the balcony and bolted from the Mandilo estate.

"Where is the one who killed my men?" Ramos said in Spanish.

Quinn heard him after he landed on the terracotta roof and as he began to flee from the property. Quinn turned. He knew Cane wasn't going to shoot him. Even if Cane did try and do this, it would be a pointless endeavor.

Quinn was already gone.

The sicarios pounced from behind the door and marched away from Cane. Staunch, Cane was lost from the combination of incomputable sights. The bullets blazed and Quinn vanished. The distance obscured the Custodian's field of view. And yet, his brother was still there.

Still, he was breathing.

He was the cartel's chief assassin, and he was known to Quinn as Blackstone. He was the main killer working against Quinn and, being an enemy, followed a similar path. Both Quinn and his brother were trained by the same man. Both were raised to become living weapons capable of death, destruction, and endless pain. And this somehow brought Cane to the attention of the Sinaloa Cartel.

Quinn turned to the balcony and watched Cane step up to the balustrade.

By now, Quinn was gone. Despite this, Quinn observed his brother longer. He couldn't put into words what he experienced. It was best to say nothing at all.

———

"Who the hell was that?" Ramos asked Cane. "How did he get in here?"

The sicarios all stood in their suits while holding their automatic weapons. Each one glared at the back of Cane's head as he held his FN. Cane had yet to speak. However, the sicarios' thoughts were all so obvious, Cane didn't have to face them.

"Doesn't matter," Cane said. "He's gone now."

"Well, he won't get very far," said one sicario in Spanish.

"Aye," said another. "We're going after him."

Cane scoffed. He knew his brother. This was exactly what he wanted the men to do.

"Yes," Ramos said. He stepped out of the bedroom. "We're going after him. We're leaving now. Now, are you with us or not?"

Now addressing Cane, Ramos's hand rested on the door handle. Cane stared at the night sky and ignored Ramos altogether. No, he was thinking of something else, of *someone* else.

Cane's silence was his answer. He *would* go, but not with them.

Cane's brother had just raided a mansion belonging to one of the world's most dangerous criminals. During his escape, the younger Quinn understood what would happen next. Ramos and Alessandra and their battalion of loyal fools would pursue. They would charge. They would fight. But, as they approached a man who was truly anticipating their arrival, *all were sure to die.*

And this gifted Cane with a glorious opportunity.

He would wait for them all to go down. He would wait for his brother to tire, and then...then he would make his move. Cane would do this because, well, he wasn't working for Ramos, *not really.*

No, his calling was linked to a higher authority that was not this man.

Instead, it was to someone above him—a man in a suit so pristine it was almost a cassock. No, Cane answered to a different man. Cane's true master was actually...*a priest.*

————

"Kyle," Ally said to Quinn through the phone. "Please, tell me...are you—"

"I'm fine," Quinn said. Now that he had come to his car, Quinn was back across the border. He was secured and home-free, at least for now.

Cane Quinn was Blackstone and Blackstone was Kyle Quinn's brother.

Quinn could see Cane's face not as the man he was but as the boy he used to be. Quinn had a code, and his code was now retribution. Quinn wanted to make sure bad people suffered and those who were innocent were spared.

In the end, pain was inevitable but killing family was not. Suddenly, Quinn was back to where it all began. He returned to altering a plan he thought would never change. Quinn couldn't kill his brother, but his brother could kill him.

And yet, he didn't.

Why?

Cane let Quinn go and Quinn was alive *because* of Cane. A Quinn saving another Quinn was a fair trade, if not also completely unexpected.

It needed to happen this way, or so Quinn insisted.

It was all Quinn wanted to believe.

He wanted to believe his brother could be like him!

Maybe, Quinn thought...maybe, Cane could be saved.

CHAPTER 9
THE RATTLED CAGES

CANE DID NOT FEAR THE WRATH OF RAMOS MANDILO.

When he accepted the chance to work for *him*, something was offered by the man who actually employed Cane in this endeavor, and so, the second Quinn was told he was to be a watcher—a sleeper agent while working within the cartel's secret enclave. This didn't change how Cane was fully aware of Ramos's reputation as well as the cost of betraying him. Many stories surrounded the infamous Mexican drug trade. All these tales combined into a lore that was animalistic, savage, and utterly terrifying to anyone who heard it. Certainly, all criminals had their own tales of horror and brutality. There were many parables about how all of them chose to instill fear into their enemies. Nevertheless, when it came to embracing the nature of the cartels, Sinaloa was a group known for taking punishment in appalling, devastating directions.

Cane knew all about this lore.

He knew that should he betray the Mandilos and not fulfill his duties to them, then he would be sure to suffer terribly. They'd cut off his dick, burn him alive, or make Cane eat his own dick *before* burning him alive.

Still, Cane knew what Ramos was about to do was a mistake.

He was about to walk into a fucking trap, and Cane was not going to warn him.

Cane didn't want to kill his brother. As he was told by *the man behind the scenes*, Cane needed his brother because Kyle had something Cane wanted. It was about more than just revenge for Cane. It was worth more than this and worth a lot more than money. In fact, Quinn didn't know that Cane was being tested. As this *man in charge* had said to Cane from the beginning. *"This is all part of the plan."*

"Sir, I need to speak with you."

In the foyer, Cane stood beneath a gleaming chandelier. His FN F2000 was down by his side. The setting was grim. The atmosphere felt gloomy and hostile. Immediately after walking into this one room, Cane assumed Ramos knew why he was here.

But Cane was wrong.

"I don't want to hear it! I don't care how dangerous you think this man is! He came into my home and he almost killed my wife! He's a fucking dead man!"

Ramos, now assimilating all his resources, Cane had come to accept his employer's outrage. He saw someone react similarly. Cane's father was a relentlessly conniving, unfeeling man. He would beat his own children should they fail to act or succeed. Yet, while Ramos continued to load his weapons, he moved to his oak desk and poured himself a drink. It was at this point Cane sought to inform Ramos why his action was not justifiable, even if it was also understandable.

"I know your brother is your blood," Ramos said to

Cane, "and we are not exactly innocent men and against your assassin...the man's been hitting us from all sides! And now, he has come to my house and made a direct attack against me, and you didn't stop him!"

"He cheated," Cane said. "That's all. He cheated and he got away, but I assure you, I will find him and I will get him, but then that's something you have to let me do... alone."

"Ah!" Ramos vehemently waved his hand and sprang out of his chair.

Running his hands through his slick hair, he yelled until his face reddened from the burning aggression. Cane stood silent as he fell victim to Ramos's epic tantrum.

"It happened once!" Ramos screamed in Spanish. "And once is too fucking many! Do you have any idea what he could have done to her?!"

Ramos's hands flapped. He was now using them to graphically illustrate his inner turmoil. Seeing all of this, Cane felt none of it was necessary. He was aware. Still, he listened.

"Do you have any idea what I will do to him once I find him?"

"*If*," added Cane. "*If* you find him." He stopped Ramos from thinking he would be able to find Kyle Quinn or take him alive. "But he's waiting for you now," Cane said to Ramos. "I know him. I know what he wants you to do. He wants you go. He would have finished Alessandra off if he wanted to, but he didn't, and he didn't because I was there. He trusts me. And that's why I need you to stay. I will find him and I will bring him back exactly as you want him, but first—"

"Good!" Ramos interrupted.

"But see, he wants you to react. He wants you to retaliate."

"Good," Ramos replied, "because that is *exactly* what we are going to do."

"I know." Cane stepped forward. He sought to speak to Ramos with the utmost grace. This tepid situation required patience and timing. And yet, these were virtues the notorious head of the cartel did not possess, especially now.

"He wants you to do something *without* considering the consequences," Cane said.

"And you expect me to do what, stand by and *not* react?" Ramos snapped back.

"No," Cane said, "but if you want to truly stop him, then you must develop a new plan, a *real* plan, and not the one you have now."

"A *real* plan?" Ramos asked, his cheeks still red from rage. Ramos sucked back his drink and glowered. "What are you trying to tell me?"

Cane's eyes narrowed and he replied with the same stoicism as before. He spoke the truth and nothing more.

"What I said already. Let me go. Let me finish this. *Me*."

"You think I'm going to give you another opportunity to fail?" Ramos said. "You think I would allow you to let the man who's bested you at every turn make a fool of you, of *me*, of us?"

"I am the only one who can bring him down," Cane insisted. "Now, you hired me for a reason because I'm someone who can ensure your safety as well as your success."

With malice, Ramos stepped toward his astute soldier and pointed his finger. "If you weren't still an asset to me," Ramos said, "you'd be dead, do you understand? I would have you flayed, neutered, and then fed to my fucking dogs!"

Ramos spat on his own floor while Cane said nothing.

"Please." Cane addressed Ramos with the respect he deserved.

Cane could see Ramos Mandilo was breaking or was almost broken. And, when a man's sanity started to slip, it became clear that's what Cane's brother wanted to happen. Cane stepped aside. He had done all he could to convince Mandilo to back down. Despite assuring Ramos that this was not the way to kill his brother, bringing Alessandra along was beyond foolish. She was attacked too, and her wrath was equal to her husband's, but still.

She had no tactical experience or training.

She was a loose cannon, far more so than her husband.

"Sir," said another sicario who entered the room. "One of the patrolmen on our payroll has a lead on our infiltrator's location. We're ready to go after him."

The man spoke in Spanish. While so out in the open, Cane's head shook. If Quinn was so easy to find, then it was by design. And so, the true nature of Cane's plan had become impedingly clear.

Ramos gazed at the guards and nodded. *"Muchas gracias."*

"Do not go," Cane advised Ramos. "Don't."

"You are many things," Ramos said to Cane. "You are a gifted killer, and in this business, I needed gifted killers, as many as I can get my hands on, but..." Ramos stopped talking and Cane was uncertain as to who he was *really* protecting. "Right now, I need loyalty. I need results."

Cane was hired by Ramos because he wanted an outside professional capable of protecting him and his own cartel. And, while Cane was communicating with someone else, everything about Ramos's decision suggested there was an agenda.

Someone was rattling the family's cages and it wasn't Cane.

"This is suicide," Cane said. "If you want to survive it, you have to bring me with you."

Whether Cane would go or not didn't matter. Cane was aware of his brother's skills. He also understood how he worked alone. A freelancer, like Cane himself, there were rumors regarding the Custodian's employer.

This was something shared among the mercenary underworld.

Some said they worked for CIA doing wet work and taking down half-ass governments. Others said they were NSA operators who secured the borders and leveled scumbags or other disruptors. All were likely true, but whoever they were working for, their orders had come from the very top. Therefore, if Cane's brother *was* working, then he was working for a top branch of the United States government. And so, if Ramos and Alessandra were going after Cane's brother, then the resources protecting Kyle exceeded any held by any drug cartel.

But none of this was registering with Ramos.

With every warning given to the drug lord, his rubicund face showed how his rage had not ceased. And yet, as Cane proceeded to follow Ramos and Alessandra, one of the sicarios reached up and pushed his hand into the assassin's chest.

Being stopped, Cane gawked. "Take your hand off of me."

"This is not your op anymore, *ese*," replied the sicario.

"Excuse me." Cane glowered at the low-tier hitman.

Cane wanted to grab this idiot's hand and scrunch his fingers together and lock up this man's fucking wrist. With this move only, Cane could bring this asshole to his fucking knees. Instead, Cane stared past the fool's brooding face. Ramos and Alessandra then made their way to the black SUVs parked in the driveway and Cane managed to sneak in one last phrase. "You know you *need* me."

Ramos then looked back at Cane. Ramos Mandilo had now shunned every warning and cared less about anything Cane had to say now. And, what came after from Ramos was Cane's final order. It was the last time the other Quinn would ever hear from his so-called lord again and that...that was exactly what Cane's true master said would happen.

"If we fail, which we won't, then you are free to track and find your brother," Ramos said. "And if you do, and you kill him for what he has done to this family, you can consider your duty to my family fulfilled."

"*My* duty?" asked Cane.

"Yes," Ramos said. "It will be the last job you do for me," Ramos assured. "And, should you succeed, it will mark the end our time together."

"I'm not here because of something I owe," Cane insisted. "The reason I accepted this job was—"

"Whatever your reasons were," Ramos interceded. Still dismissive, Cane could see he was no longer allowed to speak in Ramos's presence. "I didn't care for any of them, so long as you delivered for me...it's all I cared about. Just know that our time together will be concluded just as soon as this is over."

"So that's it then?" said Cane. "This is where we go from here."

"Yeah."

Ramos's voice beckoned like the lead singer in an old-timey band. "That's it."

Ramos skulked across his long driveway while Cane stood there glaring. When Ramos hired Cane to secure his shipments and monitor the cartel's activity, he did so because he *knew him*. Cane Quinn was not just another skilled assassin. No, he had done things—bad things. Although Cane escaped the law many times, he also found a way to rise above it. Before any of this, there was a time when Cane Quinn was a sadistic, brutal menace to society.

He was a torturer and a rapist—an absolute monster if there ever was one.

He had come a long way since then, no doubt. But, still in the murdering business, Cane once did all of this purely for sport. And it was Ramos who knew this. It was also Ramos who questioned whether Cane's brother did too.

Ramos could see Cane was ashamed and remorseful.

However, this happened *before* Cane molded himself into the professional he was today. And yet, Cane tried to forget about his past. It was Ramos who made sure he never could. Ramos knew what Cane had done. He knew the animal he was and used this against him. Ramos lured Cane in with the promise of shelter and truth and this was how he was convinced to work for Sinaloa. This was the duty Ramos was referring to. Of course, Cane didn't care for the words of a nefarious man who only saw the world in one way.

Nevertheless, Ramos Mandilo insisted he could erase Cane's history of violence. This was another reason why Cane agreed to him. If he could be given a new life, then he was going to trust the person he believed could offer it. And now, his call sign, which actually was Blackstone, was called to deliver one last result.

Cane would not join the *find-'em-kill-'em* mission Ramos was now conducting. Cane was going to find his brother before Ramos and his wife did. Cane knew Ramos had a plan for locating Quinn. It was one Cane already knew.

He would be in the exact place the entire cartel was going, *or would he?*

Cane's plan was to wait for Ramos to find Quinn. He was going to follow him and wait for the cartel to fall flat and then stand toe-to-toe with his brother one last time. Although Cane was unsure how this encounter would play out, he had already fought his brother once before. And Cane believed his brother was just as willing and determined to see who was better.

In just twenty-four hours, both would know who was.

Kyle and Cane would know...and so would everyone else.

CHAPTER 10
ANOTHER ONE BURNED

WHEN QUINN CROSSED THE BORDER INTO THE GOOD old US of A, Ally told him to meet at an empty house in Austin. Quinn informed Ally about what he did and what his plan would be going forward. He also confirmed to Ally one last time his choice for completing his mission of evisceration.

"I'm going to lure the snake with the mouse and then scoop up all the remains."

Now in a dilapidated house, Quinn and Ally had selected a busted-up house in Austin to hold up. The entire time, Quinn's eyes stayed on the door.

"You really think he's going to come?"

"Unquestionably," Quinn said to Ally. "He's hot and fueled with something nasty," he said to her. "Plus, I made Heinreich leak intel to Sinaloa's cronies. Ramos knows where we are, no doubt."

"You're welcome for that, by the way," Heinreich added. He stepped to Quinn and Ally, both by the window. So far as Quinn was concerned, Heinreich was a player in this game now too, the same as they were.

Whether Quinn trusted him or not? Quinn didn't know. But, what Quinn did know, was some very bad shit was about to go down, and Quinn had already labeled it: The Massacre At Winslow. This was the address of the house they were in. Quinn actually liked the name. Quinn's plan to get rid of an entire drug cartel was hardly conventional. Still, the Custodian was also chasing a clandestine terrorist unit manufacturing a drug capable of enhancing human performance.

Who knows who else might be involved?

———

"Kill on sight."

These were the final words given by Ramos Mandilo.

He said them seconds before he left Cane to find his fellow killer brother, Kyle Quinn. And Cane, once the family's sole enforcer, responded with cool ease. He watched Ramos and his band of poorly trained, unskilled loyalists leave the mansion. All were off to try and face an enemy worse than anything they'd ever faced before; he was *not* breaking.

Where these men were headed was a one-way ticket. Cane had repressed most of the memories of his childhood. Since Cane saw his brother, he'd been thinking more about the past that shaped both into the men they are today.

Cane shuddered. He remembered these days too well. *Face your fears.*

This mentality, when grooming a breed of warriors, was a mystery to most.

There was to be a complete adherence to the concept of endurance above all other things. Cane had no loyalty to his brother or to the cartels, and yet he was thinking about both of them now. Cane loaded his SIG but was still in Mexico. He had no idea where Ramos was going, only that his brother would be waiting for him wherever that was. Cane's anticipation about what lay ahead was absolutely clear: *It was going to be a trap.*

And the best way to set a trap? This was a lesson taught by the Quinns' father.

"How do you defeat an enemy with more resources and more weapons than you?"

At the time, Cane and Kyle were sitting on their cold basement floor. Their legs were folded and tucked back. When training, the boys were required to sit in *seiza*; their legs folded and tucked back under the hips. The walls were stained with broken streaks of blood and there was a gun rack and a table stacked with melee-attack weapons. There was an ice bath there too. It was often used for healing after severe injuries. Kyle was ten and Cane was eight when the instruction was given.

Though it was years ago, Cane remembered it like it were yesterday.

"Fight dirty," Cane contributed.

"No," Kyle said. He acquired the same numb and rigid expression as his father. He also mimicked his dad's mannerisms too often. Kyle Quinn looked the most like his dad too.

"You fight smart. Fight smart, so your enemy will fight dirty."

"In some ways, yes," Quinn's father said. His hair was combed across his scalp.

Broder Quinn was wearing a pair of thin black pants, which were part of his *gi*. He motioned with his fist pressed beneath his right jaw and considered the suggestions made by his two sons.

"You force your enemy to react. You make them fight

dirty at exactly the wrong time. And, when they're thinking only about their fears and their anger, that's...that's when you trap 'em."

"*Trap 'em?*" asked Cane. "*How?*"

"*Same way you trap any predator,*" Papa Quinn explained. "*You make them think they have the advantage. You toy with their egos, see? You mess with their heads, but before you can do any of this, you first have to be willing to put it all on the line. In the end, you have to be willing to face the fire and do what needs to be done.*"

"*And what does?*" Cane asked. "*What needs to be done?*"

Broder Quinn grinned to show off his maddening visage. It was then that the boys' lesson had reached its conclusion. Broder stepped into another room and dragged out a fat cage. Inside were two squealing, frightened little bear cubs so small Kyle and Cane could carry them both in their little hands.

To this day, Cane remembers them exactly. They were perfect. Perfect and beautiful.

"*Today's lesson is about drawing out the big fish as it struggles to defend its own.*"

"*Then...shouldn't we be using fish or something else that's small?*"

This was Kyle's question, but Cane felt the same way.

"*Not today. Besides, it's much more difficult to do it this way. Anyone can kill something ugly, but it takes real courage, sheer fucking will, to kill something beautiful. You need to do what everyone else is unwilling or unable to do.*"

Cane didn't know if they were going to kill the cubs and then wait for the mom to come along. He chose not to remember. What he really did remember was his father opening the cage.

"*Do something that takes real guts and then wait to see what happens next, which one of you wants to go first?*"

No one answered. Cane was only eight and was unprepared to do something this ugly.

Then, he saw his brother reaching for a fat knife. He picked it up and brought it to his chest.

Kyle was willing.

"*Not you, Cane.*" Broder Quinn always knew how to taunt the smaller ones. And, being smaller, Cane was never the quickest to react. Broder glared at his second son.

"*You don't want to?*"

Cane's eyes were glassy. His lips quivered while sitting shakily in the dark. The very thought of killing these cubs caused him to tremble. And yet, their father's expectations were clear. The code during their training had not yet changed.

Face your fears.

After responding, Broder Quinn ordered. "*Stand up.*"

Cane knew what was coming whenever his dad glowered. The punishment for denying a request from him was always met with swift and brutal action. Broder smacked Cane in the face. He knocked him down to the cold floor. It wasn't corporal punishment but a precursor to eventual torture.

"*Ah!*" Cane exclaimed as he hit the cold floor. He landed sideways while his father spat.

"*Glad your brother is here, because at least he has what you don't. He's got guts.*"

Cane watched Kyle rising. The end result unfolded exactly as his dad said it would.

Quinn stabbed one cub in the neck but let the other one go. He did this while waiting for the mother to come and find them. Kyle and Cane waited for the mama bear to come looking. When she did, both Kyle and Cane shot her and then followed their father's orders.

Kill or be killed, or did you not learn that already?

Although it was a traumatic event for both boys after witnessing the horror, Cane never hesitated again. The lesson's purpose was to illustrate the best tactic for drawing out one's enemy. The experience with the bear cub and its mama was an unforgettable one.

Alessandra was the cub and Ramos was the mother.

But then, isn't that why Quinn did what he did?

He had attacked Alessandra. He left her wounded and then provoked what was to come after.

Why did Quinn do this?

Because it was Kyle Quinn's plan to engage with the head of this drug cartel, and although not pretty, it was the same lesson taught by the boys' old man and one the Custodian adhered to despite the trauma attached to it.

Always do what is necessary. Always do what needs to be done.

There was no arguing with their father. If Quinn was doing what needed to be done, then so was Cane. He was going to follow his brother, but he was not going to protect Ramos, his willing servants, or his wife...*no.*

No, Cane had other plans.

It was to draw out his brother. He was going to do this after he was done drawing out everyone else. And then Cane would be there waiting. He had the guts, not like when he was a child. This was who Cane was and who he always would be.

He had faced his fears and survived. Actually, he had done more than survived.

No, he beat them. He conquered them.

———

Quinn stood in the barren house selected by Ally and Heinreich. It was the location set for their final battle against the Sinaloa Cartel.

In a way, it was the same place it all began: on cheap soil and somewhere too dark to see. In Quinn's possession were his Glock 34, his 26, and his MPX assault rifle. Quinn had additional ammo stashed in his belt where his pistols were secured in thigh rigs. Tonight, he chose to go unmasked.

What was there to hide?

Completely exposed, Quinn's rifle hung over his back and he clutched his 34. As his new favorite weapon, Quinn had recently switched to the M1911s but Quinn never tired of using a simple, straight-shooter, and Glocks were the way to go for him.

Near the entrance, Quinn heard the footsteps of several marching men. He turned to Ally.

"Remember to stay in the outpost. You're the getaway if we need one."

Ally didn't like being told she wasn't allowed to join a fight. She gawked at her friend and checked her sidearm. "You know I can do more than that."

"I do," Quinn said. He motioned up to the doorway and slipped into full-on, unapologetic, *I'm here to kill your ass* mode. "But this is better," Quinn said again.

"Here they come," Heinreich said. He took his position.

Quinn didn't care whether Heinreich's skills were sound or not. He was too focused on refining and perfecting his own.

"Yes," Quinn replied. "Here they come."

The men stormed the property as gunfire rained down on Quinn like sharp hail before the coming of an aggressive blizzard. Quinn ducked and shot the first Narcos in the chest. Hitting one, Quinn pegged another, and shot this one in the neck. All were executed in just under three seconds and yet, there was no sign of Ramos or his wounded wife, but Quinn imagined they weren't far. In fact, they were likely waiting for the others to clear a path for them to both run. What they didn't know was there was no path, not now and not ever.

"Eyes up!" Quinn shouted. He pulled out a grenade from his belt, yanked the pin, and tossed the explosive into a cluster of five. He could hear their screams seconds before the bomb exploded and incinerated everything in sight. The heat from the grenade seared the back of Quinn's neck.

Keeping his gun against his chest, Quinn was up but found himself in front of yet another one of Ramos's men.

"*Puta!*"

Quinn clubbed the thug with the handle of his gun and broke his nose. Quinn then crunched the fabric of the Narcos's shirt and pulled him close. Then, he pivoted with his gun up and blew out the man's skull with a clean shot.

Blood splattered and juicy bits of brains wet Quinn's face.

There were more on the way. Pushing the stock of his rifle hard into his shoulder, Quinn lined up the others. He was always patient when choosing his targets. Quinn's chief principle when shooting was to aim small and miss small. It was so prototypical and cliché. However, his instructor in JTF 2 provided him with this guiding advice.

Quinn veered and spotted another target.

He saw a lanky fool who could barely hold his AK. Quinn shot this fool through the femur and then once more through the chest. After this other man fell onto a table, it collapsed under him. Once the first round from the MPX was off, the massacre accelerated.

"Ah!"

Among more screams and more footsteps, Quinn peered over his shoulder. He knelt and looked through the Trijicon scope to acquire more targets. Quinn spat the first two shots into more fools' heads. Both were tight yet both were clean.

The slaughter escalated. The second more of Quinn's targets were down, he moved onto the next. Shooting left, right, and center, the Custodian fired away. Quinn counted the sections: headshot, kidney-shot, heart, throat, and a few he smoked in the groin. And, when Quinn couldn't acquire a kill, he improvised. After shooting with his MPX, Quinn let one hand go free.

With it, Quinn removed his Ka-Bar.

It was not his OTF, though this new knife was more solid and longer.

Quinn wielded it like a sword. He used the blade the way he learned in aikido. Each move was done in big, circular cuts. Quinn performed a series of clean swipes, all methodical and graceful.

He cut the henchmen of Sinaloa around their necks and mid-sections. Unrelenting, Quinn stabbed and sliced. One by one, all the men fell. Either by bullets or blades, eventually, all were left to be mopped up.

Room cleared, Quinn reached for his belt. He loaded a new clip into his AR and retrieved a circular explosive. In Quinn's hand was a high-powered, portable explosive that could be detonated from a remote pinned to Quinn's belt, pretty high-tech for a mercenary. It was something provided to Quinn by Ally, for emergencies only.

Quinn wanted the entire house to crumble in no less than five seconds. Into the next room, Quinn smoked another henchman. Spitting rounds like he was dealing cards, Quinn lined them up in every corner and waited. With the trap going as planned, Quinn hit another target and stepped over a cluster of dead bodies. He counted twenty so far and heard chatter in the other room. Quinn slid and encountered a new idiot peeking out from behind the wall. The fool's lips bled and he looked ahead while yelling at Quinn. "Drop it!"

Now, Quinn had the man clear in his sights. All the Custodian had to do was squeeze and let go.

"Drop it now!"

Quinn jeered at the Narcos holding the gun. It was almost too enticing. Then, as Quinn lowered his barrel, he glimpsed at the Narcos's left thigh. From there, Quinn shot the muscle as the man yelped. The fool landed flat on his back while clutching his now bleeding wound.

"Ah!" The man knelt while Quinn lifted his Ka-Bar. "You fucker!" The Narcos's voice was a gargle of blood and spit. "You—"

The man cursed at Quinn seconds before the Custodian jabbed him square in his jaw and shook. Off-guarded by the stab, the man's nose gushed the same as his mouth. With his head likely spinning, Quinn inverted the blade and pushed it deeper into the man's trembling gullet.

"You know your boss, Ramos Mandilo, yes?" Quinn's question was rhetorical. He didn't expect the beaten henchman to answer. "Where is he?"

"Fuck you," the Narcos snarled at the Custodian's question.

"He's got two minutes to get his ass down here," Quinn said. "Tell him I'm fucking waiting."

"Fuck you!" the man snapped back. He spat on Quinn. "I'm not saying shit for you!"

This was exactly what Quinn wanted to hear now. No

one could get anyone in Sinaloa to cooperate. None talked in fear of the pain they would receive at the hands of their lord. However, what Quinn intended did not require words. All he needed to do was send a message, and that's what he planned on doing.

"Okay." Quinn slid the blade from the man's throat to his cheek and the tip grazed the fool's blemished skin. Quinn was ready to carve the message into the face. The entire time, Quinn knew Ramos Mandilo was either near or already there.

But, as Quinn wielded the knife, he squeezed the Narcos by the neck and was ready to start carving. When Quinn placed the tip over the man's forehead, he was only seconds from sticking him. Quinn pushed the knife in, but before the slicing could begin, the man was hit with a clean shot to the forehead.

Bang!

Spurting blood, the fool's face was left as a mushy heap of gooey mincemeat. Clumps of pinkish globules stuck to Quinn's hand as he let go of the knife. Reaching for his Glock, another gunman suddenly arrived at the scene.

"Ramos?"

And suddenly, there he was.

Standing in Kevlar and padding, Ramos Mandilo stood before Quinn armed with his HK UMP-45. It was equipped with a modified scope and a nice grip handle. A red dot shined on Quinn. El Patron was prepared for war.

Ramos was with Alessandra and she was armed too.

"Not alone, I see." Ramos was referring to Heinreich.

Quinn hadn't seen Heinreich since he entered the house. Where Heinreich was now, Quinn couldn't exactly say. And he didn't care to try. No, Quinn cared only about his kills and nothing else. Quinn held on tight to his 34.

He had yet to lift the gun or aim it. So far as gauging the situation, Ramos's presence was expected. Although Quinn was targeted, his intent was to keep Mr. Mandilo talking. In essence, Quinn sought to hold his attention for as long as he could and would do whatever he could before Ramos pulled the trigger.

"No," Quinn said, "and neither are you."

Quinn was speaking to Alessandra. She smirked as Quinn mentioned her.

"You," Ramos said to Quinn, "have no idea what she's capable of."

Ramos was referring to his wife. Quinn sighed and delivered an unapologetic look of hatred to the head of the most dangerous cartel in the world.

"Yeah," Quinn said. He showed a wry smile as he motioned in. "I do."

"You can't stop what's coming," Ramos said to Quinn. "This fight you're in...it's *beyond you.*" Smug and unfazed, Ramos grinned. "You think this is just about me?" Ramos asked. "You're just a mercenary! Clearly, you don't know what's happening! How deep this shit goes? Who's in charge? What they're planning to do?" Ramos asked again. Now, he was switching between English and Spanish. "You think something that can make people immune to pain was manufactured by me, by us? I knew you were a good killer, but I didn't know you were thick as that."

"I'm not," Quinn replied, hand on gun.

"So, you think you have it all figured out, do ya? You know what this is all about then?"

In an act of utter condescension, Ramos was dimwitted and misplaced. As well, Quinn detected the sarcasm and he didn't care what a disease like Ramos thought of him or who he was working for.

Quinn was going to kill Ramos and his wife, and that was it.

"Can we just kill him already?" Alessandra snapped at her husband. She was clutching her weapon so tight her hand was shaking.

Ramos's head jerked as he held his HK. With a peculiar squint, Ramos inspected Quinn as if he was totally lost. Quinn rubbed his gun handle and held Ramos in the center of his eye. Quinn memorized all the potential targets.

Then Ramos withdrew his weapon.

Once his enemy's gun was out, bursts of ear-numbing gunfire echoed throughout the narrow space. Furious rounds from Ramos's HK spattered the floor, and Quinn thought he was actually competent with the weapon. The debris sprayed Quinn's vest. The Custodian felt additional shots sprinkle his body.

Quinn understood Ramos did not have the ideal shot, not from his current position.

But Quinn didn't care.

He targeted Ramos's calves but his legs were protected with shin guards and knee pads. Still, Quinn's priority was the tendon. Once that was compromised, so was Ramos's ability to stand.

Alessandra scattered and fled from Quinn's sight.

Quinn didn't care where she was. He wanted Ramos dead and that was all. If anyone's stability is taken from them, then so was their balance. And once balance is taken, then it's not long before everything else goes too. This was another lesson learned from Quinn's father. And just like that, Quinn's trigger finger flicked and he felt the sharp bursts spit from his Glock. Quinn shot three until he got Ramos's leg. It was exactly where he wanted.

"Fah!" Though not a direct hit, it was a good one.

Quinn skimmed the calf and forced Ramos to stagger. He covered behind his men and was doing what is known as *creative cover*.

Every Narcos under his command was instructed about how to find unique yet effective means of hiding.

In this case, Ramos was using his own rifle to protect himself.

Here, Quinn's options were limited. The kill shot he once desired was now gone. So, Quinn improvised. He shot up and then down but kept everything simple. He only grazed Ramos. With each shot distributed, the head of Sinaloa emitted his share just the same. The cartel leader perforated the weak flooring and forced Quinn to turn and to keep turning. Over his shoulder, Quinn hopped into the next room. Inside, Quinn counted three shots left in his Glock.

Not enough.

Quinn dropped into the next room. Then, from out of nowhere, six shots popped the hardwood. Afterward, the wall looked like a napkin pierced several times by a toothpick. Still down, Quinn still tried to connect with Ramos in some capacity. The shots were mostly done to prevent him from retaliating faster than intended.

"Ah!" Quinn could hear Ramos shouting while wielding his HK.

"Gotchu, you dumb bastard!"

Quinn didn't have time to reload. So, he whipped his gun across the room. His aim wasn't great, but the amount of force generated to throw his gun was solid still. The pistol collided with Ramos's chin, ricocheted and disrupted his rifle's trajectory.

The Custodian took cover behind a table.

"God damn it! God fucking..." In a fit of rage, Ramos sprayed bullets and emptied his HK.

Then, Quinn slipped his MPX behind his shoulder and spared no time.

He shot back from behind the wall. Quinn gazed through the scope and found traces of the leader's silhouette. The fight between Quinn and Ramos was a measly back and forth exchange of blows. In fact, Quinn hadn't been pinned like this in a long time. He usually only needed to take one or two shots. But, in this case, Quinn hadn't hit Ramos once.

He skimmed Ramos, yes, but such a measly result didn't count as big success in Quinn's book. Consequently, Ramos Mandilo was not making the best use of his rifle. He dished out a few decent shots, and what he did hit was good, just not good enough. Ramos sprang from his hiding place and shot, but it was all quick-handed and rushed.

Quinn ducked.

He had a few rounds left. Then, Quinn acquired the shot he'd been searching for.

Straight into Ramos's left thigh, Quinn fired once, but his rifle skipped and the final round ejected from the barrel like gum from a chomping mouth. Solid hit.

"Ah!" The bullet pierced Ramos's thigh. The exit wound splattered against the nearest wall.

From there, Ramos dropped his gun, and his hand moved down to his leg. Wobbling, Ramos tipsily eased. Quinn thought he was about to fall, but he hadn't, not yet.

"Ramos!" Alessandra, now screaming, the Custodian watched as this mad woman lingered near the doorway. Having yet to get her own hands dirty, maybe she never would. Once Quinn managed to wound Ramos, he escalated into a full-on striking attack.

Quinn flew across the room.

Without fear, pain, or apologies, Quinn pushed off a

chair and completed a flying knee delivered hard into Ramos's forearm. Using all his momentum, Quinn successfully landed the kick. While his aim was far from perfect, the blow was delivered *precisely* as intended. Ramos pounded the wall and his shoulder penetrated the frail plaster. Ramos's body made a small dent and Quinn wrestled with the cartel leader.

Quinn wanted that fucking HK! He latched his fingers around its barrel and pushed.

"Fuck you!" Ramos yelled through gritting teeth, and Quinn could feel Ramos fighting against his hold. Quinn pushed Ramos's weapon back. It was down but not out. And so, it was not where Quinn needed it to be. Why Alessandra hadn't fired, Quinn couldn't understand.

He had no time to consider.

He held the barrel with his left hand and Quinn's hand snapped forward. He used his palm to clobber Ramos's fist. Quinn would make him let go of his gun. With the HK now loose, Quinn's hand snapped and he tossed it aside.

Stripped of his primary weapon, Ramos writhed.

Quinn ground his teeth and locked his jaw. He was not the kind to go down or give up so easily. However, with Ramos's rifle now lost, he hit back at Quinn. The El Patron, "The Boss", slammed the Custodian with a furious headbutt.

An effective counter, Ramos drove Quinn back and pushed him into the wall.

Where was Alessandra in all of this mess?

Quinn squeezed the straps of his vest. He found himself feeling pinned down once again. Body flush against the wall, Quinn stopped and looked up. He stared into Ramos's bloodshot eyes and exerted his rage to better demonstrate his overall assertion.

Quinn then went on to counter. He learned from years of experience that a well-placed chop is a more effective method of attack.

"Let him go!" Alessandra continued to unleash her rage on to Quinn.

After, Quinn opened fire. He believed that Alessandra saw her husband losing the fight and decided to intervene. A lousy shot, most of what Alessandra produced was haphazard. It was nothing more than panic fire. Quinn deployed his tonfa and whipped one straight into Alessandra, clunking her face. Though the attack was risky, it did give Quinn the time he needed to finish Ramos while he still could.

Alessandra's gun clanked against the floor.

Peripherally, Quinn could see Alessandra touching her bleeding nose.

Quinn sighed.

Now it was two against one. Quinn stepped in to close the gap. Turning, Quinn forced his back into Ramos's chest. Quinn grabbed Ramos's right hand. He pulled and flipped him forward. Up and then down, Ramos landed on his back.

Still holding Quinn, Ramos was down. He was not tired or unconscious.

Ramos jabbed Quinn from the floor. The Custodian blocked with a firm X blocking configuration. Ramos's hand slipped through the intersection. It was a subtle but highly creative technique. Afterward, Quinn uncrossed and moved his fist up to Ramos's forearm. He used the other to snake around and grab Ramos's fingers.

Once Quinn had Ramos's busted digits, Quinn bent his forearm. He contorted the El Patron's bones. And, with his enemy's joints now bent, Quinn used a *sankajo*—a third control manipulation as it is known in aikido.

Sliding his hand to the elbow, by doing this, Quinn forced Ramos into the wall.

"Ah!" Ramos's body thrashed and Quinn punched him in the kidney.

"Ah!"

The fight was now on.

Ramos turned and in came Alessandra—furious and ready. Quinn spread his fingers and guided Alessandra's strike. Snatching her wrist, Quinn flipped her forward and, with the full force of his fist, clobbered Alessandra's slanted head.

A fierce, hard-knuckled pound to the face, Quinn knocked Alessandra straight down to her knees. The angry woman spat up blood and Quinn responded with two succinct kicks—one for the knee and another for the shoulder. Quinn fended Alessandra off with a cross block, but she charged. She actually tried to tackle the Custodian. Quinn pushed back. Roaring like a linebacker, Alessandra's boots chopped the floor. Quinn jumped up to the wall and planted his feet. Now horizontal, Quinn straightened his body and used both the wall and Alessandra as leverage.

"Get the..." When Quinn heard Ramos belt again, he believed now was the time to end the pitiful brawl.

It was going nowhere. Quinn wrapped his arms around Alessandra's neck and, like a python, tightened into a choke. He was behind Alessandra and pushing his heels into her legs, an aggressive choke throttled the female kingpin from behind. Flat on the ground, Alessandra jerked as if being electrocuted. With each attempt, the lock became all the more secure.

Quinn held Alessandra by the throat. He could feel the air constricting as she squirmed. The more her legs pounded, the harder Quinn pressed. The Rear Naked

Choke was the death blow in hand-to-hand. Once initiated, there's only so many ways to break it. While Alessandra was trying her best to break it, she had absolutely no chance of succeeding.

Quinn had the upper hand. All he did now was wait for Alessandra to stop moving.

Ramos held his now broken arm and didn't stop to assist his wife.

He hurried to the door and escaped in a pathetic attempt to save himself.

Alessandra's pulse dwindled. The light in her eyes soon began to disappear. And then, just as he was about to let her go, Quinn gazed. He was many things, but a killer of women—even one as grotesque as the one under his arm—*he was not.*

At least, he wasn't anymore. Quinn let go.

He let go and kicked Alessandra aside. About to chase Ramos down, Alessandra coughed and held her neck. "You..."

The Custodian backed away and kept his hands up. If Alessandra wanted more, then Quinn would give her more. He just didn't want to. Before he decided what to do, Alessandra Demerez's head exploded right in front of Quinn.

Ducking down, Quinn turned to see where the shot came from. He checked the door.

Armed with an FN Five-SeveN pistol, Cane stood and glared. He executed the wife of Ramos Mandilo in cold blood, and so two facts were evident to the Custodian now. First, Cane had followed Ramos and second, Cane hated his employers as much as Quinn did.

Nonetheless, without a weapon, Quinn's heart raced.

He stood before Cane, hands up, and surrendered.

"Where is *he?*" Cane asked.

"Who?" Quinn said.

Cane sucked his cheeks back into his face. "Ramos. I know he was here," Cane said. "*Where is he now?*"

Quinn's feelings of aggression and animus soon stopped. Cane was not here to kill him.

"I don't have him."

"Where is he, Kyle?"

"Is that why you're here," Quinn said, "because you wanted to kill him?"

Quinn slid his hands along his elbows.

"I'm here to finish the mission, and my mission...it isn't all about you," Cane said.

"Isn't it?" Quinn said.

More tension arose and Quinn lowered his hands. Cane was here for blood, but not his brother's, not *only* his brother's. So, *why is Cane here at all?*

"You sure about that?"

Cane didn't answer. If he hadn't fired his gun by now, Quinn knew he never would. Still failing to act, Quinn responded with a flying propeller kick that knocked his brother's pistol. Then Quinn sprinted toward the door and drove his shoulder hard into his brother's gut. While Quinn thought he was out of the room, he assumed he was away from the gun. About to make a daring escape, Quinn slipped seconds before a new bullet skimmed his shoulder.

Quinn tripped but landed flat on his palms. He performed a somersault kip-up to get back up. Then, from behind, Quinn heard trampling footsteps and felt the rush of another person stampeding after him. Quinn turned and saw Cane racing after him.

Shit.

In a bold but faithful act, Quinn lowered his guard. He was willing to give his brother the benefit of the doubt —something Quinn didn't do back when the two were kids. Never would Quinn give anyone the upper hand. It pained him to know what his brother had been turned into. If he was willing to do all he had, then he was worse than Quinn thought.

Way worse.

Cane pushed off the wall and enwrapped Quinn by the head. Cane pulled Quinn down into a forward roll and accepted the attack like he was fighting in a demo. As he landed softly, Quinn's arm was a knot of tendons aches and possible muscle tears, but head up, Quinn looked at his brother.

Cane stood over Quinn and aimed his gun. Here, Quinn wondered how the fight was going to end. He kneed Cane and halted the shot. Cane wanted to fight and clearly, he wanted to kill too.

Quinn had other plans.

In this case, his plans were simple. *He was just going to walk away.*

His brother drove in with a hard swing and Quinn blocked in a perfect Shotokan show of action. He then swung with his elbow, clobbered Cane's chin, and pushed him to the floor. And, with Cane down, Quinn leaped. Cane's nose bled and his lip appeared cut. He fired two rounds into the wall, but by then, it was too late.

Quinn was gone.

Escaping like he wanted to, Quinn thought only of his brother. He knew him well. Quinn was outside the house but stopped to look back. His brother was not the assassin he once was. No, he was better. Maybe he was better than Quinn.

Quinn's father's voice returned. Broder had come back to taunt Quinn as he heard his father's screams. *"Finish! Finish him!"*

Right now, Quinn was ignoring his dad like he couldn't do back then.

This still didn't stop him from hearing his pop's voice. The sounds and the pain simply followed Quinn because they *were* him. They were him and he was them. Quinn didn't know any of the contacts in his brother's phone.

A useful tool.

Quinn held his breath, glanced at his watch. It was close to two in the morning and Quinn could feel Cane's firm, wide-eyed gaze stinging the back of his neck. He half-expected a shot, but none came. Though Cane might not be a solid fighter, killer, and shooter, maybe he was also a better man. *Maybe.*

CHAPTER 11
DOUBTING DEVIL

WITH SO MANY AT THEIR DISPOSAL, THE SINALOA Cartel was the most powerful cartel in existence.

The third-largest criminal organization in the world, to challenge its leadership was worse than suicide. It was downright dumb on levels undreamt of.

Quinn imagined Ramos was aware of all this by now.

But the cartel *was* trying something new.

And so, the other parties involved weren't necessarily criminals. They were not at the same level as the cartels, yes, but they were on someone's level. Ramos ran because he refused to help his wife. Now, Quinn assumed this was less because of cowardice and more a result of betrayal. Quinn could see how Ramos's arm was broken. Quinn saw this when the notorious drug lord was fleeing from the abandoned house.

He had come to a stop in the middle of the road.

Ramos turned to look at Quinn. Quinn crept with a rigid gait—*he was a ghost.*

The last encounter had escalated into a fight to the

death, but it was only after Ramos left his wife for dead that he obtained whatever courage he had left. And there wasn't much to begin with. Armed with his Beretta, Ramos sprayed the various cars. When doing this, Quinn let the measly bullets peg him in all the protected regions of his body. No, Quinn was aware that Ramos was in no state to land anything critical. None of this, however, was an attempt to kill but only to defend the madman's honor. And there was little of that left too. Quinn's plan was to kidnap Alessandra and provoke Ramos to act. Quinn would do this and then eviscerate whatever was left of the Sinaloa Cartel. And yet, it was not at all what was happening, not now.

"Get back! Get away from me!"

Ramos kneeled and reloaded and stared at Quinn as he marched. With Heinreich gone from the broken ware-house, he shouted at the walking Custodian. "Quinn!"

With so many bodies still left to take, Quinn wondered where the hell was Priest?

How did he fit into all this?

Quinn knew it was strange he hadn't heard from his boss. This was, after all, still his op. When Quinn touched down and was sent to complete the mission, suddenly, Priest was vanished. Gone. Then again, Quinn was supposed to be a man in control, or so he was told.

Ramos continued to rain fire.

He had decent aim as he capped another section of Quinn's chest. But Quinn's armor was too thick, too formidable to be penetrated. In his own gun, Quinn had one round left. He watched as Ramos hid behind a car with shattered windows. "Shit. Shit. Shit..."

"Watch out, Quinn!" Hearing Heinreich, Quinn gawked. Thinking it was only him and Heinreich, it wasn't. Ramos Mandilo waved as more of his men approached in a caravan.

How the hell did they find me so quickly?

Quinn stared at this new battalion and was irked by the arrival of these so-called *reinforcements*. There were too many to beat alone. Most were down and dead, but Quinn was faced with the difficult decision of standing his ground while also risking Heinreich's life. To run from a fight was not Quinn's bag. He also didn't know what he was going to do or what the outcome would be.

All the Custodian could do was sit back and wait for the bad guys to come to him.

"Jesus Christ, Quinn," Heinreich muttered, so panic-stricken his lip was quivering. "This plan of yours...really *sucked*."

Sweat perspired around Heinreich's large forehead. In the distance, Quinn heard the sound of a rough, gas-guzzling engine.

It was close now. *Fine*, Quinn thought. *Go, and I'll finish what's left.*

Quinn looked at the squad of armed cartel operators. It was then he felt instant relief. More of Ramos's men began to close in. Quinn could feel Heinreich standing next to him. Apparently, he wanted to be in the fight too.

"This way!" Quinn and Heinreich shuffled together.

Proceeding back into the house, Ramos followed while wielding a gold-plated AK. He stampeded and two other bandits lagged closely behind. Though not as fast or as ferocious, Ramos chased.

But then, Quinn wasn't running, not really.

He was following Heinreich back into the house and toward another door, but he was set to continue the assault. Along the way, Quinn pulled his Glock.

"Go inside," Quinn said to Heinreich. "Hold down and I'll take care of him."

"But there's...there's too many," Heinreich alerted.

"I know," Quinn said. "Just go."

Quinn watched as the head of the most dangerous criminal organizations and his entourage marched along the street. And yet, what Quinn heard loudest of all was the sound of a Ducati soaring in his direction.

Quinn's head shook, utterly baffled by the arrival. He thought he was done with Cane. He was wrong. So far, Heinreich hadn't fled or covered. Instead, he stayed with Quinn.

"Did you hear something? Something's coming."

Quinn watched Heinreich's complexion turn red.

"No," Quinn said. "Not something."

Ramos glided after the sound of the roaring motorcycle. Quinn turned to look back at Heinreich. "*Someone.*" The sound persisted and became louder and louder with each passing second. Quinn looked back at Heinreich. "Get to the house...now."

———

Quinn stood with Heinreich and gazed like a hawk perched precariously on a ledge.

"Ramos is still alive," Heinreich said. "But who the hell is with him?"

Quinn looked down and then away. He didn't know what to say to Heinreich and didn't how to fully explain what was happening.

"Someone I know," Quinn said. "Someone I let go."

"Let go?" Heinreich said. "Who? What do you mean?"

Quinn felt compelled to look away.

If Cane hadn't killed Alessandra when he did, then Ramos wouldn't have run. If he didn't run, then these men wouldn't have come back. In the end, Quinn had to ask: was Cane helping them, or was he helping himself?

Was he settling his own score with the Mandilos or was he settling a score with Quinn?

Uncertain and unwavering, Quinn reloaded. "Can't talk about it now," Quinn said to Heinreich. "Have to finish this."

"*We*," Heinreich clarified. "We have to finish this."

Quinn glanced at the ballsy DEA agent and reached for his sidearm. Quinn wanted his 34 as he looked at Ramos and his brother, both coming in.

"Just keep your eyes open," advised Quinn.

Heinreich joined Quinn in the exchange and did as he was told. Quinn was never one for simply ordering around a subordinate. Most of the time, Quinn couldn't care less what other people did when on a mission. So long as they stayed out of his way, that was all he cared about.

Quinn slipped out from his hiding place. He was unmasked and out in the open.

Still with rounds left in his Glock, Quinn counted down from five. He stared at Ramos Mandilo and his brigade of wannabe badasses. This was essentially all that was left of the legendary and deadly organization feared by so many.

Quinn gawked at Ramos and waited.

"He's here," Heinreich said.

"He's *dead*," Quinn said.

Ramos didn't know how to quit. Quinn should have known this and he did now. Ramos, however, abandoned his wife. Although this was hardly unpredictable, it was still Quinn's mission. He had to eviscerate!

Facing down only one of them, Mandilo should have known he would see its end. He looked dead ahead and spotted a man coming too close to his position. Quinn smoked this fool straight through his chest. Before the other one could reach for his sidearm, Quinn popped him too. Shooting his head, Quinn opened the back of his skull. A quick shot, Quinn sidestepped later because Heinreich gave the best cover. Quinn spread out his shots and worked his way toward the back of the grouping.

Quinn fired again.

"Go!" Ramos shouted as he blew out one of the house's windows. There were more men approaching and Quinn could hear Heinreich screaming before he jumped.

"A phone!" Ramos yelled in Spanish at one of his men.

"What?!" The Narcos's shouts could be heard over the gunfire.

"I need a phone! I have to make a fucking call!"

"A...*what?*" Soon as Ramos's man said this to him, the fool's head exploded as Quinn took down another henchman.

Seeing the brutal sight, Ramos flinched and Quinn reloaded.

"Kyle!" Quinn rarely heard his first name. Always, he was *Quinn*.

But when Quinn heard Heinreich refer to him by name, he felt oddly gratified. He was now awake in ways he never had been before. Quinn rolled, gripped his gun, and capped the group like he was knocking down pins at a bowling alley. Ramos was so enraged, he squealed. Yelling at Quinn, Ramos fired again, and blasted another window. He tried shooting the bloodied mercenary, but it was Quinn who shot first.

"Gotta make a call! Gotta make a call!" Ramos frantically pounded his phone and repeated to himself in his own language. Why he insisted on making this call now provoked Quinn to look at the situation through a more suspicious lens.

Whoever Ramos was calling, familiar or unfamiliar, Quinn saw him lined up perfectly.

Quinn's hand twitched and his fingers eased off his sidearm.

He was never one for killing someone when they weren't looking. Sometimes Quinn did, but sometimes Quinn didn't. Though Ramos did fit into this category, he was one of the most savage, most ruthless men on the planet. He lit his enemies on fire and doused them in acid. He was not just a cartel leader. He was the creator of all things terrible, and it was time for his reign to finally come to an end.

With a clean shot to the chest, the bullet hit Ramos's torso and left him all bloodied-up and gushing. Yet, the phone in his hand was still on and still, flashing.

"*Gah!*" Ramos, crestfallen as he examined his body, the shot left a hole big enough to fit a coffee mug inside. When Quinn saw Ramos's life dwindling, he lowered his weapon.

"You...you mother—" Ramos's finger stayed on the trigger. He was close to pulling it, but before he could, another shot rang out from two meters away.

"Ah!" Another bullet struck Ramos in the shoulder.

Hardly a kill shot, but still solid, Quinn recognized the shooter.

Who else could it be if not Cane?

Sneaking up on people and killing them was Cane's signature. He nailed Ramos before he could nail Quinn. Now joined in killing this drug lord, Quinn watched his brother standing by his bike. After shooting Ramos, Cane drove off.

What was his game? Quinn asked himself.

Why was he always so close?

What did Cane really want?

Quinn asked all of this but was disrupted by the muttering of a belligerent and hysterical Ramos Mandilo.

"Goddamn it," Ramos said. He examined his wound and tried to lift his weapon. It was Ramos's last attempt to go out in a blaze of glory. Quinn didn't rely on a single shot. Instead, he opted for multiple ones. He fired every round at Ramos and motioned closer to the fallen kingpin.

With Ramos's corpse blasted by a storm of merciless gunfire, all that remained after was smoke.

Quinn pulled a grenade from his belt and turned.

Finally, he was done with all this cartel nonsense.

Quinn had been slaughtering them for two whole days, and now they were all dead. Now, it was the end of Ramos and it was the end of Alessandra. While Quinn's initial intention was to wipe out the entire organization, he could not enjoy the bitter-and-sweet demise the way he wanted. No longer was this where his mission ended. No, there was something else happening Quinn could not explain. He was now facing down a greater enemy. He was fighting his brother as well as a new shadow organization known only as KEYS. All of this was piling up and Quinn could see just how full his hands were getting.

The abrasive shifts in his body suddenly stopped. Quinn wiped the blood off his cheeks.

"Kyle." When Heinreich called Quinn by his first name, the Custodian ejected the empty mag and tossed it aside. "Are you okay?" Heinreich was composed. Like Quinn, he was also holding an unloaded weapon.

"Fine," Quinn said. "And you? Are you okay?"

"Yeah," Heinreich said. "It's been a while since I shot someone, but yeah, I'm good."

Quinn's mouth began to twitch. He was almost smiling, though not quite. So far as Quinn was concerned, this was not exactly the best time to celebrate. There was still lots to do, *lots to unpack.* "Right," Quinn said.

"We should go," Heinreich said. "We need to report back to DOD. We have to let them know what happened here, how Sinaloa Cartel was terminated, and how this whole thing is now over."

"No."

Quinn proceeded to the SUV formerly driven by Ramos. Its doors were opened and Quinn held the phone recovered from the scene. He pressed the middle button and examined its many applications.

"Kyle, I said we need to go. Why are you staying here?"

"Because..." Quinn said to Heinreich, "Ramos had this phone in his hand right before he was killed." Quinn didn't mention how his brother Cane was the one who aided in killing him. Quinn was protecting him from Heinreich. So far as Heinreich knew, the only bullets that penetrated Ramos came from Quinn's gun and no one else's.

"Yeah," Heinreich said, "it's a phone, so what? I said we have to go."

"No," Quinn snapped. "It's not just a phone. Never is."

"Well, what is it then?" asked Heinreich.

"Something else," Quinn said, phone still in hand. "He was calling someone when he knew he was about to die. Who was it? I want to know."

Quinn skimmed the names as the sirens wailed. The police patrol cars belonged to local PD. With no idea about what actually happened, the only indication of what had occurred were the slain who were left behind. "Something worse."

Quinn gripped the phone. Still, he was in a place he shouldn't be. Heinreich assured Quinn that they absolutely had to go. Heinreich's hand was on Quinn's arm and he was gradually pulling him away. With the sirens growing louder, Quinn glanced up and placed the phone back into his pocket. He shuffled.

"We have to go."

What Quinn wanted to do now was recover what was in his possession. He clamped the phone to his belt so it was safe.

"We're going," Quinn replied to Heinreich. "We're going."

He and Heinreich hurried to one of the SUVs. From out of nowhere, a new car came in. Inside, Quinn saw a face, a kind one.

"You two!" Ally shouted. The window rolled down in the black Mercedes Benz. "Come on! Let's move!" As the getaway, she was right where she needed to be, as she almost always was.

Quinn did as he was told and slipped inside Ally's Benz. Ally was in the driver's seat and so, Quinn sat next to her. She started the car and headed back the way she came. Quinn gripped the handle above the window.

The entire time, he thought about Cane.

Should he worry about him or the contents in Ramos's phone?

For now, Quinn chose to stay on the phone. This, in his opinion, was more important.

"So...you want to tell me what's so important about that thing in your hand?" Ally said to Quinn.

"Ramos had it when he was executed," Quinn said.

"I thought you said he was using it to call for backup," Heinreich said.

Quinn's head shook. He was adamant about the reasons why he was holding this phone. No, this was *not* why Ramos had this on his person.

"No," Quinn firmly denied Heinreich's claim.

Now that they were gone from this bad location, the SUV was gunning down the road and moving toward a swift sunrise. The fight lasted all night. Quinn was wrecked. He could only assume Ally hadn't slept either, or Heinreich, or anyone.

"He was calling someone, but not back up," Quinn said.

"You think he was calling *them*?" Ally replied.

"Exactly," Quinn said.

"But who and what is *them*?" Ally said. She emphasized the pronoun. *Them* was a title given to anyone who operated behind the scenes.

Asking *who's them* is a lot like asking *who killed Kennedy* or *where's Waldo*?

Everyone asks because everyone wants to know, yet there are very few who actually know the answer.

"What is KEYS?" Quinn asked. "Who's involved with it, who's linked to it, and why..."

"They're clandestine," Heinreich said, sitting behind Quinn. "*Shadow*, they're the ones who we suspect manufactured this Hyper-X."

"We already know that," Quinn said. "But why? What was its purpose? We've heard what it can do, but why? Why make it? What's the directive? What's the endgame?"

"Since when are you a detective?" Ally asked Quinn.

A solid question. Investigations and pursuing truths were not part of Kyle Quinn's job. Yet, the Custodian felt compelled to look deeper. This reason had only occurred to Quinn after asking this question.

"Since I discovered...*this.*" Quinn lifted the phone so he could show Ally and Heinreich what was on the screen. It was encrypted, which said a lot. "Since when does a cartel leader have a military encrypted cell phone?" Mouth gaping and eyes wide, Ally considered Quinn's question. The light from the horizon cast a serene glow on the gentle woman's face. While contemplative, Quinn knew the answer and now Ally did too. "Son of a bitch." Ally's reply squeaked past her lips.

"Maybe KEYS isn't so clandestine," Quinn said. "Maybe it comes from the same world we do."

The life Quinn was referring to was a life filled with secrets, lies, and deception. It was composed of an evil so corrosive it burned everything and everyone it touched. It was a life filled with men who wore suits and sold classified intel to traitors and villains. It included the people who shook hands and made deals. It was a world of those who valued supremacy and victory over ethics, fairness, and truth. It was Quinn's world and yet, something that sprouted in the one place he dared not go.

"I was called back," Ally continued, "because someone told me I needed to be."

"And that's the same person who called me," Quinn said.

Ally looked ahead and Quinn studied her appearance. She was pensive. Touching her chin, she was thinking the same thought.

"No one else is higher than him, and few know what he does," described Quinn.

"But...he...how?" Ally, who was speechless, and when Quinn heard the word *he*, he replaced the pronoun with an actual name.

Priest.

"I don't know," Quinn said, "but now, I keep rethinking the same thing over and over again."

"What thought is that?" asked Ally.

Quinn's hand jammed between the door handle and his bicep bulged so much his shirt nearly ripped. "How well do I know *him*. How well do I know...*Priest*."

CHAPTER 12
THE WORST

THE MERCEDES ESCAPED FROM THE HOUSE WHILE Cane Quinn rode his Ducati all the way back to whatever counted as his home now.

Cane knew Quinn wouldn't execute a member of his own family, even if it was a member who despised him. Cane was aware of his brother's code; his honor. The man Cane was working with had mentioned it. He said it was proof of loyalty and efficiency, but that it was also flawed and broken. In the end, the truth surrounding a Custodian's abilities comes down to a twisted conundrum of hypocrisy and fealty. Still, Quinn's morality was sound.

You don't kill family.

It was the Quinns' father who uttered these words, which didn't make sense. He would turn his own children against one another, and sometimes, Broder Quinn would bring his sons to the very brink of their own deaths. Although so often did Kyle and Cane come close, they still stayed alive and lost so much. Both boys experienced pain and brutality, and both endured their fair share.

And what Cane wanted was more.

So much more.

Not knowing where his brother was headed to, Cane rolled the Ducati down the bright city street. By now, the Mercedes was at least five miles gone, but this didn't matter. It wouldn't be long before the two brothers met again.

Cane, who never let anyone go, slipped on his helmet and placed his feet onto the Ducati's slick pedals.

Cane chased his brother as well as anyone else who might be in the same car. Cane counted the seconds and then felt the assaulting wind as well as the impending light that came from the rising sun. Cane wouldn't stop until he got to his brother, and he wouldn't stop until the deed was done.

All of this was part of Cane's test.

And his test was the same as his brother's.

In the end, both were baptized by the same man, the same...Priest.

———

"How well do we really know Priest?"

In the car, Quinn wanted to tell Ally he didn't trust Priest and never had. He was, however, the only one with the ability to orchestrate this kind of conspiracy. Even still, Quinn didn't care to make it into a thing. Right now, he needed to focus, and...he needed a target.

"Can't think about Priest now," Quinn said. "Can't unravel the truth surrounding this organization until we get someone who was involved in it to actually talk."

"Well that won't help very much," Heinreich said. He was so stiff he had barely turned. "Everyone who's involved is dead. Alessandra Demerez and now Ramos, you made them all go away."

"No," Quinn answered. He was staring out the window and at the rearview mirror. Following a dwindling light, the glint was drawing closer and closer to Quinn and to the car. "Not everyone."

"Who?" Ally asked. Her curiosity forced her voice to get high.

"Who else?" Quinn asked. Quinn didn't tell Ally who.

This person was the same person who Quinn had kept alive throughout the entire Eviscerate mission. Now he was admitting to himself, for the first time, that his very purpose for being alive was to use Quinn himself. Quinn called it mercy at the time. It was honor that forced him to let his own family live. But, as it turned out, Cane was the person they needed to find.

"Blackstone."

"Who?" Ally was captivated with Quinn's response.

"The assassin," Quinn clarified, "the one who has been working with the cartel and, as we've learned now, with KEYS."

"You mean, the one you encountered back on that freighter. Your—" Heinreich said.

"Yes," Quinn said. He already knew what Ally and Heinreich were going to say. "*My brother.*"

"Shit. He's...he's alive?" Ally asked.

"He is," Quinn said.

"Okay," Ally said, "and what makes you think he will even talk to you?"

"I'm not saying he will," Quinn said, "but if there's anyone who can get to him, it's me."

"Right," Heinreich said, "and how exactly are you going to get to him?"

"I'm *not* going to."

"You're not?" asked Ally.

"I don't need to," Quinn said. "He's going to find us."

"And how do you know he will?"

"Because," Quinn said to Ally, "he's been following us for the last few miles."

"What?" Heinreich said, looking over his shoulder.

"Take a look at your rearview," Quinn said. He glanced at Ally, who checked to see if she was being followed.

"Is that—"

"Yep," Quinn said, not letting Ally finish.

"How long?" This query pertained to just how long Quinn's brother, Cane, had been following their Benz. Despite Quinn not knowing exactly how long, he imagined it was long enough.

"So, what, we just grab him and pin him down and demand he tell us everything?" Heinreich asked. At the moment, Heinreich was flabbergasted.

The game was still going and none of the players had quit.

"I doubt that will work," Ally said. "If he is your brother, then I can only assume he's exactly like you."

"Like *me*?" Now Quinn was being cheeky, which contrasted Ally's flirtatious ways. Still, Quinn wasn't sure if Ally meant that Cane was similar to the Custodian, if he was as ruthless and capable.

"You know," she said. "*Crazy.*"

"Right." Quinn glimpsed at the rearview. Cane, on a motorcycle, was now racing to Quinn. The Custodian checked the clock on the dashboard.

It was nine thirty a.m. and so long since he rested. Quinn's eyes felt appallingly heavy. The morning horizon gave Quinn a shot of adrenaline that made him sharper, but only slightly.

"Gotta try," Quinn said. "Gotta try and get him to talk."

"And I take it from your tone that...you actually have something smart in mind?" Heinreich said. In all honesty, Quinn didn't have a clue.

He was thinking it through, however, about whether a plan was in fact a dubious task.

"Some place public," Quinn said. "Some place where Cane won't be inclined to make a spectacle or a goddamn mess."

"I see. Well, do you know of any places?" asked Ally.

"Yeah, I do," answered Quinn. Although he didn't know exactly, he still considered a few places.

"Turn left." Quinn pointed to the freeway exit.

Turning out to be a glorious morning, thick rays of sunlight overwhelmed the sky and brightened everything touched. Highlighting the setting, Quinn could see a park less than a mile ahead. Equipped with a fountain and cobbled walkways, three flagpoles waved giant American flags within the populated area that was ideal for Quinn and his brother's possible meeting place.

"Paisley Park," Quinn said.

"Right."

Ally saw it and cut into the nearest exit. While on their way, Quinn checked the rearview. Precisely as he expected, Cane was there and he was now approaching.

"Ever been there before?"

"No," Quinn replied to Ally. "I don't know. Guess we'll see if it's what we want."

"Don't worry," Ally said. "It will be." Naturally an optimist, Ally was also far nobler than Quinn.

Soon Quinn would come face-to-face with his brother. The outcome would be as unpredictable as everything else that occurred so far. And yet, Quinn was going to go despite the risk. He was going to go because he wanted to, because he needed to.

He *needed* to see his brother.

———

Before heading into this magnificent park, Quinn stripped off his gear, removed all his weapons, and loaded everything into the trunk of his vehicle. With Ally and Heinreich on the lookout, Quinn didn't want to be noticed by any civilians, who were just plain people enjoying what was a beautiful weekend. Quinn observed all the families —the children and the frolicking teens—and he counted at least one hundred in the park as of now.

Quinn submitted his MPX and his tonfa. He surrendered some of his weapons, but not all. What Quinn kept on his person was his Glock 27 and his 34. He had both pistols holstered under his shirt and kept his Ka-Bar there too.

Quinn performed a quick scan of the park.

Cane could easily be hiding in one of the bushes and lining up a potential shot. However, Quinn doubted this. Such was not Cane's style. No, Quinn was never really a fan of long-range elimination. They labeled it as cowardice. And, after Quinn checked the bushes and the outposts, he looked back at Ally and Heinreich.

"Watch my six. If you notice anything, tell me right away."

"Of course," Ally said.

"Also, don't follow too closely, yeah?" Quinn said this to Heinreich. "Keep your distance and stay frosty. You know the drill."

"Yes, but wait." Ally's lip quivered. "You really think

he's going to shoot you from far away? I mean, would you do that shit?"

Quinn continued to survey the region. So far, he hadn't noticed anything out of the ordinary. No one fit Cane's description.

"I wouldn't," Quinn said, "but then again...I'm not him, and he's not me."

"Well, we definitely agree on that," Ally said.

Quinn closed the trunk and he, Ally, and Heinreich motioned across the walkway. Everyone did their best to look casual. Quinn and Ally were nothing more than a married couple here to enjoy the outdoors.

Together, they passed a group of joggers and a mother pushing her baby in a stroller.

Quinn wore his black Oakley sunglasses and checked everyone's hands. He admired people so content with their lives. Quinn questioned whether this was the best to have a meeting. Cane was a disturbed and broken man. Like Quinn himself, he too had chosen to kill for a living. Although he did it for someone else, and although he wasn't quite as skilled as his brother, Cane could be just as unpredictable. Possibly, he could also be more dangerous.

Quinn was glad he was with Ally. He looked again at all the innocuous faces.

No one knew who Quinn was or what he did for a living. Some greeted him and Ally with a nod or a wave. Heinreich chose to stay farther behind them. Technically, he was the lookout. Walking on, Quinn showed zero emotion. The people there were all vulnerable. They were out in the open and in danger.

But that's also why Quinn was here.

He walked with Ally toward the fountain in the middle of the park. They stayed close to the civilians when in public. Quinn trusted his brother to keep things civil. Quinn didn't know this for sure. He gave Cane the benefit of the doubt, something Quinn rarely did but something Ally did quite often.

On more than one occasion, Quinn considered the idea that he might one day come to find a greater truth. Some called this greater truth faith. Yet, this was only something Quinn was starting to consider. He thought it was more real than previously realized.

"Do you ever think about them, Quinn?"

"Hmm?" Quinn thought. It would seem he didn't hear Ally the first time.

"Do you ever think about *them?*"

"Them, who?" Quinn asked.

"You know," Ally said. "People. *Regular people.*"

"What about 'em?" Quinn replied.

"Just..." Quinn could see that Ally's attention shifted.

She was now looking at all the people walking along the path. It would seem Ally was more concerned with them, and so, she was not doing as instructed. Yet, Quinn didn't blame her. At Ally's core, she wasn't the same as Quinn. She was not a natural-born killer. Just because she had pulled the trigger once or twice didn't make her the same as Quinn.

But then, that was the reason why Quinn liked her so much.

She reminded Quinn about how some people didn't need death.

Some were beyond it. In fact, they were far from it.

"How they live, how they can just be...you know... *normal.*"

"Normal?" Quinn said. He repeated the word so it would sound less strange, less uncomfortable. Regardless of whether this was how Ally interpreted it, Quinn didn't believe he was normal. He never was.

"What, you don't want it?" Right now, this was how both Quinn and Ally appeared.

They looked like a perfectly normal couple sitting hand-in-hand, two people in complete harmony and utter bliss.

"Want what?" Quinn said.

"You know," Ally said. She was being direct but also sympathetic.

Quinn had always assumed Ally accepted his way of life.

For Quinn, a normal life was an incomprehensible thing. This was another thing taken from Quinn at an early age. He abandoned his normal life in favor of one whereby he was free to kill and destroy. And so, this was all Quinn knew. For so long, he believed it was all he would ever know.

"A normal life," Ally said.

"I think that option went away for people like me a long time ago," Quinn said.

"Maybe it's not as gone as you think," Ally said. "Maybe there's a way to get it back, you know? You don't honestly believe that someone like you can't be happy, do you?"

Hearing this hurt Quinn.

The very thought might be gratifying to some, but to others, to people like Quinn, it was painful. He couldn't see the world as anything more than a series of Xs and Os. Everything and everyone were just pieces on a board, free to be removed and taken off at any time. A normal life for Quinn was one whereby he could stop killing. It was one where he wasn't serving anyone other than himself.

Quinn liked to think he was on this path now. Quinn wanted to make the world better by killing the very people who infected it. In reality, he felt like he was on a path to finding justice and balance. All of this was part of Quinn's new moral compass. Yet, he couldn't see anything beyond it. He couldn't accept the possibility of killing his own brother because civilized people don't kill their family. Civilized people don't even conceive the idea of killing family.

What Quinn did was not normal, and it never would be.

"Just be where you need to be, okay?"

"Yeah," Ally said. Quinn didn't look at her. He could see from Ally's eyes she was hurting. When Quinn slapped away this idea of normalcy, he was also slapping away Ally's feelings as well. What Ally wanted was a normal life. She wanted a happy and normal life, and she wanted to one day share it with Quinn.

———

Quinn was sitting by the fountain. He rested on a stone poised between two angel statues. Streams of water dispersed from the statues' orifices in the ornate setting as kids tossed in coins and cavorted about with their mothers and fathers.

"Anything yet?" Ally asked while sitting elsewhere. She was speaking to Quinn through a communicator. Her post was approximately eighty feet from where Quinn was now and where Heinreich was too. Ally was next to a tree and as Quinn's Oakleys covered his hazel eyes, he looked up and scanned the region yet again.

"No, but he should be here soon, so stay sharp."

"Right."

Quinn checked his watch. His attempts to figure out his brother's strategy was a measly endeavor. Five minutes had already passed and there was still no sign of him, and then suddenly, he appeared from out of nowhere.

With no visible gear, Cane was dressed the same as Quinn.

And, when the Custodian looked up, he saw his brother's hair disheveled and his flesh all cut up and scarred. Cane's eyes were sunken like he had not slept in days and Quinn imagined this was true. He also hadn't slept in days.

"Kyle." Cane sounded groggy. His tone was fricative and he licked his teeth. In Quinn's eyes, his brother seemed somewhat pleased to be in new company.

"Cane," Quinn said.

Cane nodded. So far, he hadn't moved. And, because he hadn't, Quinn hadn't either.

"Fleeing to a public place so you won't be killed, are you?" asked Cane. Quinn didn't bother to nod or acknowledge the question. "Easiest trick in the book," Cane said. "Some might say it's the most gutless one too. You're still springing tricks and playing dirty, just like Pops taught you to do?"

Again, Quinn didn't care to comment. He was *not* his father.

"Staying in the open has done me good so far," Quinn said. "So, you know it won't do me wrong now, or do you wanna play this thing smart and find out why I asked you to come here today?"

"You asked *me*?" asked Cane.

"Coulda killed you back at that house," Quinn said, "back when you offed Mandilo,"

Quinn watched his brother's eyes go up and then down. Cane was thinking about the moment referenced, when he killed Ramos Mandilo and his wife. Cane didn't seem bothered. A subtle smirk began to appear on Quinn's face and he spoke again.

"I didn't," Quinn said, "because I felt it'd be better if we talked, like two professionals, if you still consider yourself to be one."

Quinn played his hand. The draw was clear.

Was Cane a professional or just another hitman hired by an organization whose leadership was decimated?

So far as Quinn was concerned, this made Cane unemployed. If he was without a boss, then naturally, Cane should return to being a sophisticated and useful hand for himself and no one else. This was Quinn's definition of someone who was a professional.

He hoped it was Cane's too.

"Let's just say I ain't interested in catching easy fish," Cane said.

Quinn's head began to turn. Head turned and tilted; Quinn invited Cane to have a seat. Seconds later, Cane decided to do precisely that.

"So, someone hired you to take out the cartels," Cane stated. "Standard DOD protocol, I imagine. Is that who you're working for?"

"Not exactly," Quinn said. "Kinda work for myself these days."

"I'm sure you do." Cane's skepticism was noted and justified.

Quinn observed his brother's slack-jawed gape. Cane clearly did not buy into the idea of his older brother working solely for himself.

No one did in this profession.

"Was mostly interested in the product that Sinaloa was involved with," Quinn said. "I have to assume you know about that."

"Of course, I know about it," Cane answered. "I worked for Ramos for almost three months. I knew everything he was involved with. The real question is...how much do *you* know about it?"

"From what I understand," answered Quinn, "and it's not my job to understand..." Quinn eyed his brother and, for a moment, he felt like he was back in their basement, about to embark on yet another one of his father's tests.

"It's a *performance enhancer*," Quinn said, "a synthetically engineered compound using chemicals from other narcotics that makes the user numb to all forms of pain. It's an emotion suppressant, I guess you could say. Now, Sinaloa was going to move it into the United States but they were going to do this with the assistance of another organization. They are the ones who allegedly oversaw its manufacturing, an organization called KEYS. They selected the test subjects and were going to supply them. The ideal specimen being kids. Small, helpless...kids."

Cane jeered. Quinn's response sounded absolutely ludicrous. Truthfully, Quinn didn't quite believe he was correct in everything he said. As he stated before, it was not his job to understand. Quinn's goal was to relinquish evil. His purpose was not to comprehend or elaborate on its existence. Oddly, this was precisely what Quinn was doing now.

"Kids, huh?" Cane considered. "Is that what makes you so emotionally invested in all this?"

"Emotionally invested?" replied Quinn. "Is that what you think I am?"

"We're brothers, Kyle," Cane said. "I know you better than most. I know that you would have walked away from all this shit a long time ago if you didn't have some kind of personal stake in all of it. Something's driving you to keep going, something inside of you."

Quinn said nothing, but what Cane said was true.

"Still, now that the cartel is out of the picture," Quinn said, "someone else is going to take their place and finish what they started."

"In all likelihood, yes," Cane said. "But then, that won't matter. Drug war is coming to an end. In exchange for their cooperation in stopping the trade, Ramos and his wife would be given immunity for all their crimes, or that's what he was told by the people in charge."

"They were told they'd be immune to persecution?" inquired Quinn. "By who?"

"According to whoever got them involved, I guess," Cane replied. "Ramos told me they said that so long as he went along with their plan, then he would get out of the drug trade."

"So he's working out a deal, is that it?"

"Possibly," Cane said to Quinn. "Coulda been anyone at the top, behind the scenes, CIA, NSA, DEA, FBI, or any other acronym you can think of? Maybe it's your KEYS, if they are real or just some shit a bad guy made up."

"And he believed it?" Quinn asked his brother with a hard, no-nonsense tone. "Ramos really thought they were going to let him walk away?"

"Fuck no, he didn't," Cane said. "Why the hell do you think he hired me? Why do you think he wanted me watching his fucking back, an outsider and another government reject?"

Quinn said nothing. He had some ideas as to why his brother was recruited by the cartel but chose not to get into any of that now.

"I was part of Ramos's insurance plan," Cane said. "He was always distrusting of everyone and so was his wife. So, he let me come in as someone there to make sure that, should anyone show up unexpectedly, they would have me take care of it."

Quinn looked at Cane. He could see the despondency in his brother's gaze. Cane's lashes fluttered in the presence of the burning sun.

"Little did they know," continued Cane, "I had an insurance plan of my own too, which you know how that turned out. Once he got rid of me, I got rid of him." Cane grinned and Quinn reflected on his brother's recent statement.

Ramos did hire Cane as security to prevent outside threats, either from KEYS or from other government agencies. And, Quinn was the one selected to lay waste to the operation. However, the idea of trusting no one made sense for a man in Quinn's position. It was the only part of Quinn's op that did. In fact, Quinn was here for precisely that reason. He wasn't supposed to trust anyone, and he didn't.

He only trusted one person, and that person was himself.

"So," Quinn said, "the intention was to manufacture a new synthetic, test it, use it, and then what, *cover it up*?"

"It was never about the cartels, only about transportation and using the cartels as canaries, at least that's what Ramos told me," Cane replied. "Whatever is going on, big picture or small, I don't really care. I'm just an employee, same as you. But ask yourself: does any of that really matter? We don't have any moral allegiance to this cause. We do only what we're told to do," added Cane. "We go where the job is, where the money is, or maybe you found a way to grow a conscience in this game of life and death... but me? Nah. I just follow the blood."

The word conscience had a different meaning for Quinn now. Conscience is a tool acquired by so-called good people. It's held by those who listened to their hearts and followed the pillars of their faith—the very laws that govern all humanity. People refused to do bad things because they feared the consequences, either here or somewhere else.

Quinn did vow to change. He swore one day he would.

Now, Quinn's reason for eviscerating the cartels was to make child abusers suffer. The cartels fit into this category and so, they also fit into Quinn's profile for justice and retribution. What Quinn wanted was to live for something greater. It was the only reason he was questioning his brother. Quinn hoped Cane knew more. He hoped he knew why KEYS was manufacturing this Hyper-X as well as why they were testing it on children. Now with a conscience, Quinn chose to believe he had one. Better, worse, good, bad, all were words that meant something to Quinn. And it was meaning he could no longer deny. No, Quinn now weighed all his vast and compelling ideas while gazing at his brother.

Quinn then spoke the truth for the first time since he sat down with his brother.

"KEYS, whatever it is, they're who's behind everything. The Sinaloa Cartel is just a smoke screen. They're patsies summoned by a heavier hand to take the fall."

"Your words, not mine," Cane said to Quinn. "And like I said, I couldn't care either way."

"Do you know anything else?" Quinn asked. "Anything you feel is worth mentioning?"

Cane's lips tightened and he shrugged. "I've told you everything I wanted to, but I could give a shit either way."

"So, you don't have a problem with what's been happening? Experimenting on kids, a possible conspiracy. We could do something about it. We could make it right."

"*Make it right?*" Cane asked.

"Yeah," Quinn replied. "Make it right."

Cane broke into a sarcastic laughter. He looked at Quinn with drooling lips and let out more obnoxious chuckles. It was then Quinn saw his brother not as a man. Instead, Cane was a lost child. For Quinn, the comparison was suitable, all things considered. "The whole operation and all the people involved? The shit they're making, the ones they're hurting, and the impact they may or may not have had on this world? You think we can stop all that? Just who the hell do you think you are? What do you think you've become? Neither one of us were raised to show sympathy or lend a fucking hand. We were taught to survive, to face our fears, and to do whatever it takes to be the last man standing."

Again, Quinn was silent.

Flashbacks of his childhood emerged and Quinn could see all those terrible days and horrible nights, back when he and his brother were torn to shreds for his father's bitter amusement. He recalled the days whereby they were forced to do unspeakable things in order to grow so they could become bigger and stronger.

Quinn remembered and then his hands began to shake.

Trauma is a darkness that carries its own shade. Quinn's previous way of dealing with it was to use his skills to eliminate people. He did this always to prove he was better than his father, that Quinn was the Apex predator. The more he killed, the more he could control the pain growing inside of him. Quinn could see this pain whenever he looked into his brother's eyes. And yet, Quinn was trying. He didn't tell his brother that he was, but he was. He was trying to do this now as he stared at the only person who understood him. Brothers know brothers, and Quinn knew Cane.

He knew everything because he *was* Cane. He was Cane and Cane was Kyle.

"You know this, and yet you pretend like you don't."

When Cane addressed his brother, the Custodian looked at the sun. With his hands on his lap, Quinn's guard was lowered.

"Things aren't the way they used to be," Quinn said to Cane. "I can promise you that."

"Aw yeah?" Cane replied. "Hard to believe after everything that's happened, isn't it? But then, those are the lies you tell yourself," Cane continued. "They're the lies that help you sleep at night, but that's all they are. They're fucking lies. We both know that the only reason you're saying you're better," Cane said, "is so you don't have to live with the shit you've done or the people you've hurt. But just because you want to forget your past, doesn't mean you can, brother."

"I need to know who's behind all of this," Quinn said, ignoring Cane's statement.

He was done insisting on the development of his morality or how he wasn't the man he used to be. Quinn insisted on his ability to change. Quinn was pushing this belief over and over again. And yet, Quinn couldn't convince his brother that this was true. Quinn wanted to get to the bottom of a greater conspiracy and return to the task at hand.

Quinn still had his mission to complete.

"I need to find out so I can burn the whole fucking thing to the ground," Quinn expressed this while Cane hissed to show disdain for his brother's boyish, amateur remarks.

"You're right," Cane said, "I guess you *have* changed.

Your skills have made you arrogant and naïve. You really think you can stop what lies ahead? You think you've grown, have you? But here, now, I see that you're more like Pop than you're willing to admit. He also thought he was strong enough and smart enough to alter the fate of the world through force and brutality."

"I'm not like Pops."

"Sure, you aren't," Cane said, his skepticism noted. "Sure, you aren't."

With the conversation now approaching its end, Quinn accepted how he could not change his brother's mind. Then again, this was never what Quinn wanted. No, what Quinn really wanted was to speak to his brother and acquire more information. This was his only purpose. And yet, at the same time, Quinn also embraced this was the longest he'd been with Cane.

Did he enjoy it? Was it...valuable?

Although what Cane gave wasn't much to go off of, it was still enough for Quinn to plan his next move. When Quinn stood, static crackled in his ear from the comms still there. He said nothing to Ally and he hoped he could simply stand up and go. Whether he could or could not didn't matter.

This was what Quinn was going to do.

"You want to end this thing and tie up loose ends," Cane said, "do it now...while you still can." Peripherally, Quinn kept his eyes on his brother. So far, Cane had not moved an inch.

"I got mine to take care of. You should take care of yours, while you still can."

When Quinn said this to Cane, he stood up slowly.

"Well, that's the thing..." Cane followed Quinn, who was standing too. The tremors in Quinn's hand returned.

"Loose ends...there's only one left for me," Cane said.

"And, you know the main lesson Pop taught us, when you have the chance to take out an enemy, he always said you take it. If you don't, then that enemy *will* come back, and when they do, it'll be too late."

Quinn understood what Cane wanted to do. Although he thought Cane changed, in the end, this turned out to be a naïve assumption. Quinn watched his brother's hand as it started to shift. Now, Quinn could read all of Cane's movements. He could also see into his brother's soul and determine his next course of action.

He remembered how Ally was close by, and so was Heinreich. Quinn remembered how they were both watching him and Cane. Yet, Quinn was still unwilling to drag both of them into what was about to happen here, at this park.

"I'm *not* your enemy." Quinn spoke with his head still twisted. A snort of derision and contempt squeaked from Cane's flared nostrils and his hand slid to his waist.

"And isn't that something enemies all say, right before—"

"Don't do this, brother," Quinn pleaded.

"Oh, I didn't," Cane said. "*You* did. You let me go when you shouldn't have, and you came here to this place, when you shouldn't have." Cane's hand inched toward his weapon. Quinn's did the same.

A fight was now set to unfold between the two brothers.

Quinn couldn't help but feel like a fight like this one belonged in their basement. It belonged in a place Quinn swore he would never return to, but then here he had. He was back, back to where it all began.

"Remember those contests we used to have," Cane said, "how you would always win?"

"I won nothing," Quinn said. "Trust me."

"Once again, saying what all enemies do," Cane echoed, "when they know..." Cane turned and his hand stayed on his weapon. When his arm shot up, he was inches from drawing it out. Quinn knew what he had to do. "They're about to go out!"

What Quinn expected was a pistol. He thought maybe a smaller caliber fitted with less recoil. This was Quinn's prediction but it was far from the outcome. His brother held a Cold Steel Counter Tac 1 knife five inches long and with a satin finish. Quinn recognized the weapon. It was the same tool Cane selected when they graduated from their father's regime.

"Choose your weapon." As it was then, Quinn chose the OTF while Cane chose the Counter Tac.

Here, the first move Quinn's brother made was not predictable or smooth. With the Tac held upside down, Cane drew fast. He swiped up and tried to cut Quinn's chest. Quinn, without body armor, could not afford to jeopardize his mobility or his speed. He watched Cane's slash move up and across. Then, with a quick knife-handed block, Quinn connected with Cane's forearm and stopped the weapon. Quinn pressed the dorsal muscle in Cane's arm and stared at the shimmering blade nearing his twitching eyes. Quinn then used his opposite hand to snag his brother's elbow. From here, Quinn enveloped Cane's wrist and, holding Cane by the arm, torqued his hips. Violently, Quinn turned. Then, in one fell swoop, Quinn whipped Cane into the fountain. Cane crashed into the water. Onlookers gasped as Quinn blitzed before his brother could recover.

"Ally?" Quinn said, hand to his ear. Another crackle of static came before he heard her acknowledge him.

"Yes?"

"Get the car ready. Do it now!" Quinn roared.

"Right," Ally replied.

Quinn sprinted around the corner, turned, and saw Ally twelve paces ahead.

Standing beside a lamp post, she was among a crowd of conversing adults. Quinn raced and thought about how far he was from the fountain. From behind, Quinn's ear filled with the irritating sound of hard exhales. Quinn peered over his shoulder, and as his eyes slipped past his neck, he spotted his brother.

Cane leaped and delivered a high-flying headbutt straight into Quinn. The Custodian took the hit like a champ.

Not even he expected this.

"Ah!" The force of Cane's thrust was painful, even for Quinn.

His brother was evidently more relentless than even Quinn had assumed. And then, as Quinn felt the full force of his brother's brutal hit, his legs collided. With one knee bumping the other, Quinn tripped. He fell to one side and popped his hands out to absorb the hit. His palms pancaked the concrete and he looked back. He could see Cane, still wet and still standing up. Quinn gazed at his brother and bit down on his lips. Silently, he urged his brother to come forward and finish the fight.

Quinn looked at Ally. She was armed. One shot from her gun and she'd put Cane down for good. Even if the shot wasn't fatal, a hit to Cane's arm or the leg would be enough to hold him. And in spite of this heavy-handed outcome, which would benefit Quinn, the Custodian waved Ally away.

No, this was his fight. It was his *mess* to clean up.

And, like all the others to which he had either stumbled upon or created, Quinn was the one who had to fix it.

Go. Quinn mouthed the word to Ally and he began to rise.

A few harmless pedestrians noticed Quinn's hit. All were watching as these two fighters stood opposite each other. Both were locked in a fierce and unrelenting glower. The standoff couldn't be more real, as was what was going to follow.

"How do you want it?" teased Cane.

"I don't," added Quinn, "but I know you're going to give it anyway."

"Of course," Cane replied. "Don't pretend like you wouldn't do the same."

In that moment, Quinn remembered his old self. If he were Cane two years ago, his answer would be disturbingly true. Convincing Cane Quinn had changed was exactly what propelled the Custodian into this mess. Shaking his head, Quinn dabbed the blood glazing his lip. There was no escaping the wrath of Cane. If Quinn ran, as he had, then Cane would chase him, as he had. Unless Quinn chose to fight back, he would never make it back to Ally. He would not complete his mission or know the truth.

Fighting was the only way for him to finish this.

"Then go on," Quinn invited. His hands were up and his fingers were spread. Gradually, Quinn eased into *kamae.* "Make your move, brother. Make your move."

———

A public park was hardly the ideal location for an altercation of this magnitude.

This was why Quinn selected it in the first place. Among so many witnesses, Quinn stood toe to toe with his brother. Quinn knew Cane's fighting style was something

Quinn had only grasped from their last encounter. Although trained by the same man, Quinn could see some of Cane's skills aligned very well with his own. They weren't quite as honed or as perfected. Still, Quinn's brother was a powder keg ready to explode any minute.

"Let's go!" Cane shouted while bouncing with a McGregor-level pizzazz. Both his hands were opened like Quinn's were. Yet, the Custodian's stance stayed strong. His feet were firmly planted and he was *focused*.

Quinn assumed Cane's role as the striker.

His father trained both boys in Shotokan karate, which had evolved into a sick combination of Muay Thai, Jeet Kune Do, and Krav Maga. But, due to Quinn's lack of aggression, he declined to draw the card his brother was currently playing. When Cane stormed at Quinn, the fight commenced with three side-kicks that snapped out in perfect unison.

"*Huh!*" Quinn sighed as he pivoted and shuffled back to avoid the strike. Quinn chose to move in a complete circle while Cane's kicks stayed close and hard. Even dodging them didn't absolve Quinn completely of the pain. They connected with Quinn's hand. His fingers throbbed.

Quinn struggled to decide his next strategy.

"Quinn!" Ally shouted Quinn's name. He didn't have time to see where she was. Perhaps she was close, maybe even closer than Quinn realized.

Right now, it didn't matter.

Cane returned with more strikes and was now inches from Quinn's face. It was then that Quinn emphatically called out to Ally. He told her what to do.

"Go!" When Quinn yelled, Cane's fist shot out and missed Quinn's nose by centimeters. Quinn stepped aside and evaded the punch.

Quinn could see it coming and so, raising his hand, guided the blow away from his face but kept his body turned. Quinn stayed on his brother. He could feel Cane gaining momentum. Quinn rotated his hand and then slid his fingers along his brother's forearm. He moved it one way and then another. Quinn went for the knuckles. He pressed his fingertips hard into the bone. His hand shot down and curved his brother's wrist. Using two hands, Quinn squeezed Cane's joint and did what in aikido is known as the *nikajo* or *second control pin*.

From here, Quinn could prevent Cane from delivering any further moves. It was a temporary hold, but it could go into a straight pin. With one simple alteration and one extra amount of applied pressure, Quinn could break Cane's arm.

"Ah-ha!" Cane grunted to show his frustration.

What Quinn did was a neat trick but delivered with non-lethal intent. He was not here to break, crack, or terminate. Quinn didn't want to see his brother hurt himself. Quinn wanted to go before the fight escalated into something he dared not be a part of.

Quinn enfolded Cane's wrist and squeezed.

Quinn wanted this fight to end soon. While he could push harder, he could break Cane's wrist but chose not to. In response to such a graceful show of mercy, Cane glared. In that moment, Quinn knew Cane was not going to stop. He would not back down, ever.

"Ah!" Cane screamed and he fell down to one knee. Quinn used his back foot as leverage and summoned more power from his hips. Quinn hoped this was where this fight would end between him and Cane. Quinn thought about this, and it was then Cane beckoned again.

"You can't hold me. Your aikido might be strong, but..." Cane's once-opened hand had turned into a fist.

With his head up and with one rapid ejection, Cane plowed Quinn hard in the gut.

"*Grrr...*" Quinn vented his agony through his gritted teeth. Cane's strike was hard and sharp. Though Quinn did his best to absorb the blow as best he could, ever with his side flexed, it was nowhere near strong enough to gain any kind of immunity.

Quinn felt it deep in his muscles as he winced.

Still holding the *nikajo*, Cane's wrist moved and Quinn straightened his hand and kept his feet planted. Solid as he was, more gallant and deathly painful strikes began to follow. Therefore, the primary issue with Quinn's strategy was Cane was always just too damn close. Close was effective, but too close was compromised.

Cane punched Quinn again.

Delivering a straight and clean jab, Cane pumped Quinn's shoulder until his grip gave. While Quinn's strategy was to rely on aikido, such an ambition was arrogant and counterproductive. Quinn could do nothing to stand against what was transpiring. He was too weak, and so, Quinn had no choice but to release Cane. Once the hold failed, Quinn took a step back. He swiped his legs across and tried to return to his kamae, which was the basic stance in aikido. What Quinn could do well, his brother could do too. He just did it differently. Cane was a far more sparkly fighter than his older brother. Cane answered with a spinning side kick and gained more air than Quinn did before.

Quinn crossed his arms and blocked Cane's flashy kick. The strike was more than strong enough to hit Quinn's chest. Afterward, Quinn fell. By now, everyone in the park was gone. Now that the fight had unfolded in a radical and spectacular fashion, all Quinn could think about was how?

How was he going to get out of this now?

Quinn couldn't stop Cane. What Quinn needed was to get Cane to do something other than strike. This was a strange want, all things considered. Cane was in the territory of professional fighters like Anderson Silva and Mirko Cro Cop.

With heavy hands, Cane's hits were hard, fierce, and unrelenting.

Quinn, however, was also a suitable striker. He could break things and had in the past; people and faces. Most often, that was not Quinn's realm. He preferred holds, throws, and locks. Quinn punched only when suitable. He was a gifted grappler. And so whenever Quinn couldn't strike, he went to the ground and this was exactly where he wanted his brother to be now.

Cane hit back at Quinn.

This time, the Custodian deflected using low, sweeping blocks.

Quinn stopped and turned.

What he sought next was to take his brother back to where Quinn had originally put him—in the fountain. There were an infinite number of strikes being produced by Cane. After all were unleashed, Quinn's arms throbbed like hell as each hit left behind a cloud of agony. Quinn could barely stand because his brother was so amazingly strong. In some ways, he was better than Quinn.

"Quinn!" Ally yelled. Quinn stepped back. Everyone had pulled out their phones and were recording what was happening.

In a space this public, everything was visible and so, Quinn was supposed to keep it short and simple. But now, so out in the open, so exposed, Quinn imagined what Priest would say when he saw his prized Custodian all over social media with a hashtag tied to his ass. Then again, Quinn didn't quite care what Priest had to say about anything, not anymore.

"You're too close! You're going backward! You're—"

Quinn knew why Ally was shouting. None of this mattered to Quinn. He waited for his brother to attack so he could redirect his movements. Quinn then extended his brother's arm and swung it up around his head.

Quinn yanked and tossed Cane forward. Cane rolled.

It was no secret Quinn's sibling knew how to handle such attacks. Cane landed all of them perfectly. Quinn sighed. He just wanted to get Cane back into the fountain. Quinn turned and played with Cane. This was not like when the two were younger.

Cane dolefully jabbed and delivered another hit to Quinn's midsection. The Custodian had Cane close to the fountain. Another throw wouldn't work. Quinn whipped his body around and, from there, delivered his signature move. Quinn pummeled his brother dead center with a solid taekwondo front kick.

Quinn knocked Cane into the water.

He was done.

Cane landed in a splash, and Quinn hoped this was where it ended. Soon, Quinn watched as Cane emerged from the slick liquid and let out an exasperated gasp.

"Ah!" Cane popped his head up from the water and Quinn stood over him. Quinn's goal was not to strike. All he wanted to do was neutralize and submit Cane before things got worse.

In this case, Quinn was considering a much simpler technique.

Hearing the commotion from everyone standing around, Quinn could also hear Ally mumbling as she tried to speak. Quinn ignored both and chose to widen his stance and wait for his brother to come forward. Before he could deliver a formidable strike into his brother's cranium, Quinn stopped and controlled his impulse to hit Cane.

Despite this, Quinn's desires remained the same. He wanted to end the fight and do what he didn't back in the basement. Unlike those experiences, which were imbued with trauma and pain, the Quinns' father encouraged them to finish by spilling blood or breaking bones.

And yet Quinn refused to do this now.

He refused, but Cane didn't, and Quinn could see this. He could read his brother's instincts, sense his energy. All he wanted was blood—Quinn's blood.

And, with Quinn bent over, he was prepared to make a clean dive for Cane's legs. And yet, he wouldn't do this until his brother moved. Cane's face was bloody and dented. Quinn gazed at the red blotches lingering on his brother's bruised mug. Rage continued to build. It was then that Quinn stopped looking.

He stopped and he reacted.

Quinn dove, aimed low. He wrapped Cane's leg and pulled. Doing this, Quinn compromised his brother's balance and brought him to the water.

"Ah!" He did his best to resist and it was futile to do so.

Quinn noted this after bringing Cane down. He imagined Cane expected this tactic. It was a simple takedown done so the two could both grapple. Quinn believed Cane would never see this move. And, once he had Cane's thigh between his folded arms, Quinn pulled up. He shot Cane down and around and pressed. Quinn added all the pressure he could until Cane let go or collapsed.

"Get the fu—" Cane planted his heel hard into the wall. He did everything he could to push his older brother away. This proved to be impossible by the time Quinn was done. Now back around, Quinn locked his legs against Cane's ankles and lined up the rear-naked choke.

Keeping his bicep tucked under Cane's chin, Quinn's brother was secured.

He was going nowhere. Quinn's intention was to put Cane to sleep and then run away. This was all that would ensure the fight would come to an end. With everything now in place, Quinn applied pressure.

He pressed and he waited. "Kyle? Kyle, can you hear me?" It was Ally.

Quinn could hear Ally but only barely. He wanted to yell for her to stop talking because he was choking up, *literally*. Quinn grunted as he pushed down on his brother's neck. He waited for Cane to pass out, which should've happened already but was taking longer than expected.

Cane was tough—tougher than anyone else Quinn faced in the past.

But then, *how could he not be?* He was a fucking Quinn. Still, Quinn persisted.

His brother's face was flexed and getting redder by the second. With Cane's eyes turning white, the blood vessels strained, strings of mucky spit spewed from his misshapen mouth.

It was then Quinn let his hands start to slip.

Shit.

Quinn quickly heard the sound of a blade ejecting. The only way to break a choke from a trained grappler, usually, is to resort to a dirtier yet effective means of attack.

Quinn's father said this once. More than this, he encouraged it.

Cane removed his Boker mini strike knife with a curved blade. If Quinn grabbed Cane's wrist to stop the stabbing, he'd have to release the hold. And, if he didn't try and stop Cane, then Quinn would be stabbed and gutted. The only alternative would be to roll over, push Cane's head into the water, and hold him there until he stopped breathing.

But Quinn's goal was clear. He wanted to incapacitate, not to kill.

Still, amid all the pain and all the violence, Cane was someone Quinn knew. He was also someone Quinn cared for, even if he hadn't told him or shown him otherwise.

In the end, Cane was family. He was Quinn's brother!

Quinn heard Cane mutter the word *bastard*. As Quinn's eyes cringed, he braced himself before the weapon was plunged deep into his flesh. Before any of this happened, Quinn's gaze shifted for a second. He could see Ally standing among the civilians in the park. And, when Quinn saw her, it was the same moment whereby the weapon penetrated Quinn's thigh.

"Ah!" Being stabbed is a pain no one ever gets used to.

Quinn screamed. He could feel the pain booming through his every muscle. Quinn held his breath and fought to maintain the hold. Doing this, Quinn knew well he could not sustain it. He couldn't let go, not when he had come this far.

Quinn screamed and then he did what he thought he could never do.

He kicked his brother aside and broke the RNC. Quinn's advantage over his sibling ended as soon as Cane stood in the fountain. He coughed to recover from the asphyxiation. Steady as he was, Quinn was still down. He watched Cane rub his throat and listened to him breathing in big gulps of air. Quinn heard Ally now from only ten feet away.

"Kyle!"

Quinn glared past his brother and was looking only at

Ally. With Cane still in front of him, and with a weapon still in his hand, Quinn gradually emerged from the water. Exasperated and disappointed, Quinn grunted. *This was not what he wanted.*

Quinn wanted to tell his brother to run.

Cane was not trained to walk away from a fight. Boker blade out, Cane spat. He looked at Quinn, broken and weary. "Nice attempt to try and shut me down," Cane said. "Nice swing to try and cut me off, but then you came to a fight with a living weapon. You decided to bring no weapon of your own. Doing that, you broke one of the cardinal rules of combat there, Kyle..."

Cane waved his knife around and Quinn observed his brother basking in amusement. Even still, Quinn took no pride in what he'd done or what he needed to do. There was absolutely no joy in seeing how the fight between him and Cane was not over.

Now back at it, Quinn stood and waited.

"Never underestimate your opponent." Cane reached out to try and stab Quinn but he stepped back.

Unknown to his sibling, Quinn did bring his own weapon. It was the same one he wielded better than anything else. Quinn steadily removed his tonfa from behind his back. He flipped the batons and held them both with the long side pressed into his forearm.

"Son of a..." Quinn cut with his tonfa, but leg bleeding, his stability was compromised. Still balanced somewhat, Quinn was bleeding more than Cane. And, if Quinn was better than Cane, then he would show him just how much he could endure.

Cane struck Quinn's gushing leg. The Custodian's painful screams echoed through the park. "Ah!" Quinn was then hit with an open palm and Cane's new strike shook him to his core.

Quinn saw his brother only as a blurry caricature and then he leaned back when he felt the same strike again. "Ah-ha!"

Quinn shifted the tonfa but wasn't fast enough, smooth enough, or good enough to deflect what came next. And what did come, Quinn should have seen. In the end, he was immune to just how ruthless and daring his brother really was.

Cane was known for his flying high kick. Quinn *could* kick, but *not* like Cane.

What Cane lacked in power, he made up for in flexibility and in range. He was durable. Even when he and Quinn were kids, no matter how many times Quinn hit Cane, he always came back. When he did, Cane was harder and ready for more. Nothing changed now. With Quinn down, Cane pushed off the fountain and swung his foot back and around. He smoked Quinn and lambasted his jaw with maximum force.

Now Quinn knew how to take a hit.

And because he did, Quinn managed to brace himself, but this didn't stop the unrelenting and brutal agony that followed. Quinn's head slumped to one side. He was now an opponent of Tyson in his prime. Although Quinn was tough, few could withstand such power. Quinn felt like he was out of the game. Yet, he needed to keep himself in. He needed to keep breathing!

The last sound Quinn heard was of sloshing water. After this, Quinn could hear Ally screaming. He heard this right before Ally yelled Quinn's name and right before she opened fire.

"Ha!" Cane shouted.

Quinn saw the outline of his brother's body as he moved. Cane grabbed Quinn's shoulder A clear attempt to use his brother as a shield, Ally hit a non-lethal section of Cane's body and effectively ended the assault.

Quinn counted himself lucky. "Ally!" Quinn screamed.

He saw Ally but also saw Heinreich too. Why he was here now, Quinn didn't understand. But he did hear a gunshot and he did see Ally ducking and covering. Cane fired. Fortunately, no one was hit, not as far as Quinn could see. In a flash of movements, Cane disappeared from the scene while Ally sprinted toward the fallen Quinn. Resting her hand on Quinn's bleeding shoulder, she leaned in and whispered, "Kyle, come on...get up. *We have to...*"

Quinn's hearing was disrupted by the incessant sound of police sirens. Lips tingling and head aching, he felt as though someone had poured a beaker of acid straight into his skull. Every muscle in his face felt as though it was being ripped apart. Quinn reached up and wanted Ally to take him by the hand. When she did help Quinn to his feet, the Custodian looked her dead in the eyes. Quinn's expression was best described as gratitude mixed with pain. It was a look of happiness, regret, fear, and optimism.

Except, Quinn wasn't the only one who was silent.

Heinreich stood near the fountain. His hand was pressed to his chest.

"P-p-paul?" Ally stammered.

Heinreich pulled his hand away and looked at the red mark in the center of his torso.

"Paul!" Ally shrieked. A shot had blasted from Cane's sidearm at some point. It missed Quinn but hit Heinreich. It was then that it was all there, all of it was *clear*.

Cane wanted to kill Quinn. He almost did, but then he failed. And his failure resulted in the death of someone else, someone less deserving than Quinn, someone... better.

"Come on," Quinn said to Ally. Heinreich fell.

Their friend and loyal contact collapsed in the middle of the park and Quinn raced after Heinreich and did his best to assist. As Heinreich's body quaked, Ally gazed at Quinn. Fear exploded from behind Ally's once stolid eyes. "He needs to go to the hospital. We *have* to help him."

"Okay," Quinn said. "Let's help him then."

CHAPTER 13
ROUTINE SURGERY

Q<small>UINN NEVER WENT TO HOSPITALS</small>. P<small>EOPLE THERE</small> always asked too many questions.

Quinn did have a name and he did have an address. While on mission, he was supposed to give his list of alternates, which he always did. In this case, Quinn didn't have a list of aliases. Nothing new was provided once Heinreich was driven to the hospital. He was admitted right away. Ally and Quinn stood there in the waiting room. Quinn would heal on his own. He'd rather suffer the pain and avoid the questions. Heinreich was the one who was really hurt.

Together, they were doing what everyone else was. They were sitting, waiting.

"Kyle? Kyle, can you hear me?" Quinn had dozed off while stuck inside this daunting and boring room. It was a long day, and Quinn was in dire need of some rest.

"Hmm?" Quinn said. "Yes, I...I can hear you. How..."

Quinn scanned the room but focused on the door. At any moment, someone could walk through, and Quinn—despite his injuries—was set for another fight.

"How's Paul?" Quinn asked, eyes opening slowly.

"Well," Ally said as she slid closer to Quinn. "We're at a hospital. Regents Medical Center, so how well do you think he's going to be?"

"Right," Quinn said. He adjusted his position and made sure his body was upright when he looked at Ally.

"He lost a lot of blood," Ally explained, "but that's what I heard from the nurse."

"Shit," Quinn said.

"I also heard he's going to be all right, but that's *all* I heard."

"Good," Quinn said. "I guess that's good."

"Hospitals," Ally said. She sighed. "Can't seem to avoid them all, can we? You know what we're doing here," she said. "It's not that different from the last time, is it?"

"Last time?" Quinn asked.

"Yeah," Ally said. "Last time."

Quinn thought back to this *last time*. It was in Louisiana where Quinn had another tango with death, one which he narrowly escaped. Ally arrived just in time. Quinn recalled stumbling into Ally's home bloodied and broken. There, Ally did her best to assist Quinn. She stitched up his wounds and helped Quinn then. She also helped Quinn to get back to his plane so he could return to his home in Wyoming. It was a time not too long ago and it was Ally who ensured Quinn's survival. Such a process was done discreetly. She did it all without the assistance of any medical personnel and thankfully, spared the Custodian from exposure to enemy forces. And because of this, Quinn could not embrace his current reality. Again, Quinn kept his eyes on the door. He did this while continuing to remind himself of his vulnerability and his weaknesses. Today, Quinn was well into a new mission with an entirely different enemy.

"I have to go," Quinn said as he stood.

"No," Ally said. She reached out to grab his arm. "You need to stay. Kyle, you're still too weak. Plus, Paul might need you to protect him should anything happen again."

"This isn't his fight, not anymore," Quinn declared. "And that's why I have to go."

"What?"

"I'm too exposed here," he said, "in case you haven't noticed."

"You're *not* exposed," Ally insisted. "Do you have any weapons on you?"

"I never go anywhere without a weapon," Quinn said. "Never."

Quinn lifted his hands. These were all the weapons he needed. Ally looked down but Quinn was looking up.

"Hospitals are the safest place we can be in right now," Ally said. "Even the dumbest bad guys wouldn't try anything here. And even if they did, I'm here, and the police are right outside."

"You don't know what we're dealing with."

"The cartels are gone, Kyle," Ally said. "Ramos and Alessandra are dead. For now, Sinaloa is dead too."

"Yeah, well," said Quinn, "they're not *our* enemy. They never were, not really." Quinn held his breath and concentrated. He used whatever energy he still had left inside to steady his many unwanted thoughts and feelings.

"Well...who is?"

"Too much to explain," Quinn said. "Lots to do and lots to tell, but not here, not now. Right now, all you need to know is we got to get the hell out of here...*now*." Quinn emphatically recited these words while standing up in the waiting room. His decision was made and there was no denying what was to come.

"Even if you did go, if *we* did go," Ally specified. She

was including herself in this conversation. She wasn't going to let Quinn go anywhere without her. "Where?" she asked. "Where are we going to go?"

"Back," Quinn said. His response was simple and to the point.

"Back where?" Ally asked.

"Back to where it all started," Quinn said. He pulled his collar tight against his neck. "Or should I say, back to *who* it all started with."

"And who's that?" Ally asked.

Again, Quinn had no time to explain.

He was speaking about the one person who stood above all things. It was the same person who was aware of everything Quinn had encountered and everything the Custodian was capable of. Quinn was actually shocked that Ally didn't know who he was referring to.

It was Ally who asked Quinn this single, most compelling question.

How well do you know Priest?

"Never mind," Quinn said. "For now, we just need to get out of here, while we still can."

Quinn checked the hallway and hid near the door-frame. With squinting eyes, Quinn's lips became so tight they turned white. Attempting to see if the only people in his company were medical workers and patients, Quinn was uncertain. He could have been followed. And yet, scoping the scene, Quinn's potential followers had now all blended in.

Quinn grabbed a towel from the room. He was in no mood for drawing attention to himself in any capacity. Quinn rolled the towel taut against his fist.

He looked back at Ally. "Let's move."

Both exited the room. Quinn shuffled along and moved toward the nearest elevator. Halfway there, Quinn glimpsed back. From the other side of the crowded corridor, a group of four men marched.

They could be doctors, could be hospital administrators, could be a bunch of fucking nobodies. They could be this, or they could be exactly what Quinn thought they were. Quinn pressed the button to the elevator and Ally's eyes were elsewhere. As of now, she didn't see what Quinn was seeing. He was happy she didn't. Soon, however, Ally might have a closer look.

She would know exactly what Quinn warned her about.

It was all real, and all of it was bad fucking news.

————

If there was ever a time whereby Quinn was not prepared to fight, it was now.

Quinn and Ally were standing in the elevator. Two of the men stepped inside, and Quinn pushed the button to the parking garage. The elevator was about to take off, but all Quinn wanted was to connect with Priest.

This should have been his goal from the beginning.

And yet, like all Quinn's plans since executing Ramos and fighting his brother, were disrupted. They were hijacked by other men. In this case, there were two who had now come to join Quinn and Ally.

Quinn inhaled and pushed Ally aside, trying to shield her from the forthcoming attack. The two men who entered the elevator were big, although they were not bigger than what Quinn was used to seeing. They did, however, possess certain characteristics. They had no tattoos and were clean-shaven. Their hair was trimmed. They each acquired a unique smell. Such a scent was different from those Quinn encountered from the Sinaloa Cartel.

Therefore, whoever these men were, they were definitely not working for the cartel.

Quinn exhaled a long and deep breath. He remained in front of Ally as if she was not the capable woman that she was. To be frank, Quinn cared more about Ally's safety. Her life meant more to him than his own.

Even in his current state, Quinn could handle these two men.

Ally was secured in the corner of the elevator. Quinn observed these men's mannerisms. Although they were blending in, Quinn thought they were all doing a very poor job at trying to be inconspicuous. Both of these men stuck out considerably. They were basically two bad versions of the bodyguards seen in films. They showed no emotion and were nothing more than furniture. They were chess pieces primed to attack the king and queen.

Quinn, not sure which one he was, right now, he felt like neither.

"Floor?"

"*Hmm.*" The one standing to Quinn's right responded as soon as he heard the question. Quinn's back was pressed hard against the wall. This was no accident. It was an intentional position taken soon as the two men boarded the elevator.

"What floor do you want?" Quinn asked. He was testing these men to see if they hesitated. If they didn't know what floor they wanted, then they shouldn't be in an elevator. This seemed like an obvious tell in Quinn's stable, deductive mind.

"Uh..." The man was about to answer and then the door chimed and opened.

Now was the clear opportunity for Quinn and Ally to

escape. They could blow right past these assholes and vacate the vicinity in favor of a newer, possibly *safer* location. And yet, while this was their plan, it was not what transpired.

When the doors parted again, two more hulking men stepped inside. Both acquired the same characteristics as the first pair. Quinn gasped as he shook his head. Too obvious. Quinn and Ally were both cornered, and although Quinn was confident he could take on these two assholes, there were four standing near him now.

Head shaking, Quinn sighed.

No, he thought. *Not good.*

Quinn looked back at Ally and opened his hand. He spread his fingers and flapped his digits down and up. Signaling to Ally to stand and wait, this was Quinn's own way of letting her know that something bad was about to go down and she needed to be ready. All Quinn hoped was that Ally was *slightly* prepared for it.

"So..." Quinn said. He opened his stance so he was wider, more open, and gawked at the four men. "Who would like to go first?"

The pause between Quinn's choice of words and the men's reaction time produced a gravitational moment of silence. Everyone was pulled toward it. The four men had yet to make their first move. When none did, Quinn took the lead.

"All right then," he said. He didn't use aikido. It wouldn't work well here, in this environment.

No, what Quinn chose to summon instead was another martial art found in his repertoire. Once he had it, Quinn didn't waste a second. He commenced the altercation with a solid push kick and delivered one straight into the man's backside. After, Quinn immediately moved onto the next.

"Let's go!" Quinn roared. As of now, he was dialed up to eight, not quite a ten, but still...he was steadily approaching this level.

"Gah!" Both men fell and Quinn turned and gripped the bar along the perimeter of the elevator. His next attack happened with more panache and flair. After hoisting himself up, Quinn delivered a scissor kick that hit both the other men square in the chest.

Now with heels hitting faces, the two men were knocked back, but unfortunately, none were out of the fight. Being forced into the wall, Quinn split the men up into pairs.

The men to his right were the *twins,* and those to his left were the *duo.*

These names came only because the twins really did look like twins. The duo, however, did not resemble each other at all. With Quinn's aggression starting to build, he landed on his feet after the kick.

He looked back at the twins, both of whom were likely burdened by fear. Still, the men prepared themselves. Ally was pushed back into the corner and Quinn continued to stand in front of her. Quinn's feet throbbed and his knuckles bled. Now that Quinn was going up against multiple opponents, he mapped out his exit early. When anyone faces too many attackers, they are required to hit, break, or shatter whatever they can before moving on. And they have to do this as quickly as possible. This was precisely what Quinn wanted.

It was exactly what he was going to do.

Standing in southpaw, Quinn's fists were up. Ally was set to fight too. Hands up, her stance was the same as Quinn's. He saw this, appreciated it. A power couple, the parallels between them were uncanny.

Subconsciously, Quinn reviewed through all the

Shotokan techniques he could retrieve from memory. Although karate was not a style Quinn frequently turned to, his anger and his aggression propelled him during this exchange. Quinn was a charging battery. And the more he stood his ground, the more power he assimilated. Quinn responded to the first twin. He got on with a straight punch to the man's jaw. Deadly and accurate, Quinn connected with the first two knuckles and felt his bones clattering into his hand. After this, a clean left-handed cross came next. The first hit was a bone-breaking wallop. *Certain* to knock out, the blow pushed the twin out of the fight.

Once Quinn was out, he pushed into the next.

Now he was hearing the imaginary clock *tick-tick-*ticking away. Every fraction of time was monumentally precious, if not also in complete jeopardy.

Quinn's hand stayed tight while the other twin came forward.

Quinn was as clever as he was quick.

Booting the man in the knee, Quinn disrupted the balance. Then, with his leg bent, Quinn popped the man in the chin with a solid push while in the corner across from him, Ally shouted. "Watch out!"

Quinn kneed this fool's neck and gripped his opponent's head with two hands. When Quinn pushed his opponent in, he plunged the man's skull into the wall. He concussed the fool and then peered back at Ally.

Now that the twins were taken care of, the *duo* was next to go.

Quinn never intended to keep Ally out of the fight. Quinn always assumed the fights were his and only his. But Quinn couldn't be more wrong about this assumption.

Quinn saw Ally ignite the same as he had.

She lunged and drove her elbow viciously into the

next man's stomach. How Ally learned such a move was both mystifying and attractive. Quinn sparkled. He was absolutely enthralled. He watched as Ally pushed the same man back. Then, with another hard elbow, struck the man repeatedly in the face.

Much shorter than the man who stood before her, Ally was relentless. She was unleashed too! She did not ease up for a second, not even as the man grunted and cursed her out. "Bitch!"

With a heavy hand, the man tried to hit Ally down.

In unison, Quinn and Ally both punched and kept punching until the man's skull caved in. It had been some time since Quinn beat a man to death. Quinn was ready to christen this mission with this kind of devastation and carnage.

"Argh!" The man's head was covered in blood. His nose had been reduced to a heap of mushed bone and cartilage. The man lifted his arm and tried to shelter himself from Quinn's nonstop blows. Doing this was pointless. Quinn was not going to stop and neither was Ally.

Both amped enough to shatter hardwood, human bone was easy to break. The man pleaded for Quinn and Ally to relent. He begged and yet, both rained down harder blows until this man was all but a broken heap of rancid goo. Tangentially, Quinn could see Ally. Still in the fight, Ally hit again. She kept herself moving while Quinn stepped back and then forward. Abandoning all civility, the man's jaw was shattered. His face was cratered. After, Quinn went for something deadly and shocking. He inserted his hand into the man's mouth. Quinn pressed his hand all the way to the back of the man's molars and clamped down hard. Quinn's knowledge of aikido had gifted him with a near-unbreakable hold over joints or, in this case, *bones*. Once Quinn had his hand in, he squeezed the man's busted jaw.

Solid and ugly, Quinn stared into the man's fading eyes. He continued to hold tight. Like when one pulls the leg off a fresh turkey, at first, one believes the bones to be unmovable. They are stuck and going nowhere. After having one's fingers there for an extended period, all it takes is the right twisting motion to break it. All it takes is the right strength and the right grip, and while Quinn was aware of how much strength he needed, he pulled. Like a crazed lunatic, Quinn ripped the man's jaw clean off his skull. The bones snapped and the muscle tissue peeled like chicken falling off the bone. Blood sprayed Quinn's face and this highlighted his animus in a sight the Custodian thought would scare Ally to death.

Now, she would see what Quinn was truly capable of. Whenever the Custodian felt threatened, he did what he had to. He didn't hold back. It was why he was one of the best. Quinn wielded the torn bone like a trophy. Overkill was not a term Quinn subscribed to. It also wasn't one he often practiced.

Quinn was a damn Custodian, and Custodians left a scene spotless.

No one lived.

Holding the man's torn jaw, the tip of the bone was sharper than expected. Using it as a knife, Quinn stuck the man's jugular and killed him with his own mouth.

Blood everywhere, Quinn's hands were gloved in the grimy liquid. The face and the floor were too. The last man standing shuddered at the sight of his fallen comrade. His voice had reached such high decibels that Quinn had to pummel him in the face again. Hoping for a knockout, the blood on Quinn's knuckles made his hands wet and gooey. This made the blow a little less effective. Nevertheless, hitting the elevator button, the doors opened, and the last henchmen ran.

Now in a new hallway, Quinn stood there, frozen.

"Shit," Ally said. She saw the man with the jawbone sticking out of his neck. "That was..." Ally stammered. There were no words to describe what Quinn had done. To be honest, Quinn hoped she wouldn't even try. With no time left, Quinn shook his head and Ally looked at the still-opened elevator doors.

"I know," Quinn said. "I know."

"He's getting away," Ally said, referring to the man running from the elevator.

"I know that too." Quinn and Ally entered a hallway occupied with doctors and nurses.

The last man limped off like the defeated coward Quinn knew him to be. Unable to get very far, Quinn saw him speaking to a mic pinned to his wrist. Quinn chased and the soles of his feet smacked the surface. The more speed gained, the more people noticed and pointed.

"Stop!"

"Wait!"

"Who are you?!"

Quinn ignored all the voices coming from the barking civilians. He was now gaining on the man, and even amid other screams, Quinn could hear Ally's clear as day. "Quinn, stop!"

Now only five feet from Quinn, he heard Ally yet also heard the last man's voice too.

"Send back up. Third floor. Send—"

While the man ordered reinforcements, Quinn cared less about whatever force might be on its way. Pushing off the wall, Quinn soared and slammed the man's shoulder. Then he grabbed the fool's head and throttled his fucking neck. Using the momentum from the leap, Quinn spun the man back around for a solid takedown.

And he did it right in the middle of the damn hallway.

"Ya!" Pulling and spinning, Quinn had the man's arm locked up. With Quinn also having him on the ground, there were patients and nurses swarming from all around. Some pointed and yelled and some just got the hell out of the way while they still could.

"Quinn!" Ally called out to Quinn again, but the Custodian didn't care.

Quinn pushed his elbow hard into the man's kidney and listened to his pathetic squeals. The sounds made were all the same: weak and pitiful. Now in pain, this man also had nowhere to go. He was a man absolutely defeated. And, what he could and could not do made little difference to Quinn.

All Quinn wanted was to see this man dead at his feet.

Quinn could put him down, yes. He could do this because he still had the strength and grit to get the job done. Yet, that job wasn't over.

The man was still breathing.

Quinn pulled the henchman's arm and added pressure to the elbow and additional strain to the shoulder. About to break it, Quinn was interrupted and forced to stop.

"Kyle!" Whenever Ally referred to Quinn by his first name, it was an urgent call. This was the reason Ally was screaming now. Quinn thought it was to see if Quinn was okay. But now, Quinn could see it was *not* for this reason at all.

No. No, it was instead...an urgent notification.

Two men wielding MP5s cut in front of Ally. Zero hesitation, when these men saw Ally, they also saw Quinn. Weapons up, the wounded Custodian acknowledged with a glower. Depending on his strength left, Quinn waved his hand and yelled.

"Look out!" Now the one shouting, Quinn demanded Ally to take cover.

Peering back, Quinn watched as Ally looked at the men with guns. Now with a fearful gaze, Quinn lunged, and he and Ally jumped into the next room. Opening fire in the bloody hospital, these guns-for-hire were stoic with no faculties whatsoever. Like machines programmed to kill, Quinn was struck with a new thought.

Hyper-X!

They were fueled with it. They were fueled by Hyper-X!

Their appearances could be the result of the famed narcotic currently being pushed by the cartel, who turned out only to be the patsies in this trade. It was what the organization known as KEYS were producing.

This was it!

Quinn could see it.

The substance was said to numb users. It prevented all feelings and transformed their pain into power. These cronies were obviously under the influence of the synthetic. When they shot, they weren't just aiming for Quinn and Ally. They were lighting up the entire fucking corridor like they wanted to shred it to pieces.

They smoked anyone in their way. They killed random patients and nurses and laid waste to everything in sight. When Quinn retreated to a new room, he saw civilians being blown apart like paper mâché. By hiding, Quinn couldn't help but see himself as a coward. He was a fucking hiding coward.

"Son of a bitch." Quinn peeped out from his location. Luckily, Quinn saw Ally.

She was hiding too. Quinn couldn't simply stand by

and do nothing, yet he didn't plan to. As formidable and dangerous as the Custodian was, Quinn was still only human. Tired, weak, and injured, the energy Quinn possessed now was just enough to perform one last stunt. Now, he was not primed to fight. But once he was done with this *stunt*, Quinn would take Ally and get the hell out before these KEYS men had the chance to reload.

Quinn remembered the elevator. He watched the numbers lighting up one at a time. Now on the second level, it was only one above the lobby. Quinn spotted the window in the room across from his own. He knew well he couldn't go back the way he came.

He would *not* go back.

Quinn exhaled and summoned additional waves of calm. What he planned to do next was reckless, stupid, asinine, and just plain insane. But, at the same time, it was the only method for ensuring a safe departure because soon the police would be here. Once they arrived, they would find Quinn, and they would find Ally too. Being arrested was detrimental to Quinn's mission, and he had no plans to go quietly.

Quinn turned to his left and spotted an axe as well as a fire hose locked in a glass case.

Plunging his elbow, Quinn ran right through and shattered the glass. Having removed the heavy chopping tool, though it was not the best idea, it was all the Custodian had to use.

And Quinn wasn't too bad with an axe.

Then again, Quinn wasn't too bad with a lot of things. He waited for the right moment—when these men reached into their pockets, they were going to reload. It was then Quinn signaled to Ally. He mouthed the word *window* and then raised his hand. Quinn gestured to the room across from where he was standing.

This way.

Ally nodded and instantly read every one of Quinn's signals. When Quinn finished, he shuffled to the side and peeped. Soon, Quinn saw one of the men approaching. Wielding the axe like he was Paul fucking Bunyan, Quinn torqued the bad boy up over his shoulder.

"No," Quinn uttered.

Then, in a gallant swing and a heavy turn, Quinn twisted his hip and struck the man's forearm. He cut him down, severing the man's hand from his body. Blood sprayed from the open wounds and splashed into Quinn. Ally and the walls were draped in fat pockets of carmine.

Dark red drained from the man's detached limb. Soon as the first man went down, Quinn headed over to the next. He slipped the meat of the axe behind the man's neck and rested the curve against the fool's collarbone. Spinning the man back around, Quinn threw the KEYS-man as if he was connected by a string.

The man, shouting the whole way, once he hit the wall, Quinn stopped.

Pulling the axe away, Quinn shot it up again. The Custodian was now chopping wood in the figurative sense. In the literal one? Quinn was Jack Torrance from *The Shining*. Splitting the man's skull, Quinn cracked open his enemy's cranium. He gouged in deeply with the axe and decided to leave it in place before taking Ally by the hand.

"Come on!" Why Quinn insisted on doing this didn't matter.

He was just being impulsive.

Quinn wanted to vacate the scene before anyone noticed. And so, after striking all the men down, Quinn refused to wait for another second. He pulled Ally and brought her from the other side of the hall. Together, they stormed into the next room. Passing bedridden patients and visiting family members, an elderly woman wailed. To go back the way the two came was suicide. Although this was a bold and stupid route to take, Quinn refused to do anything less.

"What are we—" Before Ally could finish, Quinn squeezed her hands and the two approached the radiator. With Quinn's right leg bent, he was set to leap.

"Trust me!" Quinn yelled.

Pushing off the corrugated steel, Quinn blasted through the window and plummeted fifteen feet to the ground below. The whole way down, Quinn understood why expecting Ally to trust him was a silly and irrational command. The act was so stupid and outlandish. The only hopeful outcome was to land on something padded and squishy. And this was only the best-case scenario. The worst was they'd end up pancaked onto the goddamn pavement. Quinn and Ally plopped into a dumpster, thankfully, and landed into a soft heap of stinky trash. Even soft, at this height, Quinn collided with the mound dead center. He slammed in a huff and a grunt.

When Quinn realized he hadn't broken anything, he stopped to look up at the window.

Still broken and still clear, Quinn nudged himself closer to the dumpster rim. "Come on. Have to go. *Now*."

"Where?" asked Ally.

"*Away*," Quinn said. "Just follow me."

All the Custodian had now was a new target. It was Priest. He had questions for his employer to answer.

Why? Who? What was the goal, *the endgame*?

And, since the Sinaloa Cartel was massacred, Quinn had a list of new names and a new enemy to deliver swift and horrifying retribution. Any place was better than here.

For Quinn, that was enough. Even better, Quinn was not alone.

Now that the mission was bigger than him, it required help.

And Quinn was glad he had it.

He was even gladder that someone agreed to join him. In the end, Quinn didn't know where he would be without Ally. Quinn wondered if she felt the same way. Then again, she was still here.

So, to Quinn, that was a good sign.

Maybe it was the best sign.

CHAPTER 14
VERSION 2.0

FALLING FROM A TWO-STORY WINDOW, BEING SPARED of injury was impossible, even for a man like Kyle Quinn. When he and Ally climbed out of the dumpster, they were disheveled and smelling like shit. Still, they did their best to leave the scene without being noticed by anyone. Yet, that hope was also ludicrous.

Of course they would be noticed!

They just fell out a goddamn window!

Limping along, the Custodian battled intermittent surges of discomfort and pain. Regardless of how much he tried to ignore it, it still hurt. Quinn didn't want to make this known to Ally, especially now as he caught a glimpse of her busted leg. "Are you good?"

"What?" asked Ally. Her face was contorted as he pointed at her leg. "It's nothing. Let's just keep moving."

Quinn wanted to take Ally's hand again but refused when he remembered how often he had insisted on doing this. While it was a chivalrous gesture, Quinn didn't believe this applied to Ally. She was strong and didn't need his help. Quinn scoped the area outside the hospital.

Everything he saw was a tentacle spawned from the chaos created by his hand. People all scattered in a panic. Nurses and doctors did what they could to assist the wounded patients, but there was a man and a woman who had literally jumped out of a window and everyone who saw them knew this, and many others were dead.

Ally was wounded, and Quinn was banged up worse than a boxer against Tyson in his prime.

Blood smeared his face and flakes of dirt were ingrained beneath his fingernails. He looked like a coal miner from way back when. Should Quinn go anywhere, everyone would recoil in disgust. Quinn couldn't avoid this, no matter what he did. Later, Quinn turned and spotted a bus stop across the street. So far, Quinn only saw a few people waiting there, but not many. As far as an exit strategy, this might be the best one. Ally took Quinn's hand and looked at his feet. They were sore and covered in gashes. No matter, he looked at the bus stop and stepped.

"This way." Quinn motioned along the walkway.

He penetrated the hysterical crowd as more people everywhere ran in all directions.

He and Ally were utterly lost in the presence of all this mania. Able to stand, Quinn and Ally could both get to where they needed to go. Approaching the road, Quinn stopped after a teal Range Rover swiped in front of him and Ally. Intentionally cutting them off, Quinn knew who was behind the wheel. Anyone who knew of their location had to be someone close to them. And anyone who was *that* close might be the same people who sent the men here. He might be the hitman selected to take out Quinn and Ally.

Quinn kept his hands down; a reflex done whenever he felt threatened.

Indeed, this was how he felt now. He felt threatened. Quinn's hand rapidly shot down to his waist, but it was empty. With nothing there to draw, Quinn gazed at the front seat of the luxury car. The window was rolled down and a tanned face poked out from beyond the tinted glass.

It was an old face, oddly distinguished, and with combed gray hair. Quinn gawked at this man whose sudden arrival provided a vague sense of relief. Still, Quinn thought he should have brought the bloody axe with him.

"Kyle, Alexandra," the man said as he acknowledged the two operatives. "What?" he said, grinning. "Surprised to see me?"

Alexandra was Ally, except when Quinn heard her name said in this way, it left a bad taste in the Custodian's mouth. He hated it. Her name was Ally!

"Heinreich?" Utterly baffled, Quinn gazed at the arrival of their much-needed backup.

"Paul," Ally said. She referred to Heinreich using his first name. "What are you...*how*? I thought you were in the hospital."

"What?" Heinreich gasped. "You think I would stay behind while the shit was hitting the fan? I found a way out, and now, I'm here."

"Fuck," Ally said, sounding impressed. Quinn was too.

One minute he was shot, and then the next, Heinreich was in a car, picking Quinn and Ally up when they needed a ride. Honestly, Heinreich was a fucking reliable son of a bitch and Quinn liked reliable.

"Just need you two to get in this car...*now*."

"Right," Quinn said, not wasting a second. "Let's go."

As of now, the mission had been compromised. All of them needed to get moving!

"I know you're surprised to see me," Heinreich said, "and after everything that's happened, I know it's shocking, but—"

"How did you get a fucking car?" What Ally asked made the most sense. Quinn wanted to know this too.

"As I said," Heinreich replied, "I don't have time to explain, but trust me when I say that right now, I'm going to get you both the hell out of here! And once you're out, you'll be one step closer to the truth!"

It was a solid proposal, and Quinn couldn't deny he needed Heinreich now more than ever. The only way forward, despite the risks and the pain, was to not lose a second of time. It was the most precious commodity that Quinn had now.

"What do you want to do?" Ally asked Quinn.

He looked at her shocked expression and could feel her desperation. With the sirens sounding, Quinn was again presented with a narrow list of options. None were desirable.

Quinn pulled the door handle and said nothing. Ally jumped into the back seat and Quinn followed. After boarding, Heinreich shifted into gear and sped away, even running a red light. Nothing was done to disrupt the sounds of clear, ominous silence.

One step closer to the truth. Quinn hoped this was true.

————

Where they were going, Quinn had no idea. How they were going to get there, Quinn could only guess. But, based on the routes Heinreich selected, they consisted of service roads and other side streets. This kept them under the radar. Quinn didn't know what to say, so the first five minutes were spent tending to Ally's injuries.

"Give me your leg," Quinn said to Ally. The veins in Ally's neck bulged as she fought hard not to grimace. Quinn unclicked his seat belt and, in his hand, he held a bunch of bandages. He swiped them from the hospital. It wasn't much, but it was all he had.

"It's fine," Ally assured. "I'm all right."

"You're *not* all right," Quinn commanded. "Just give me your leg."

Quinn cradled the bandages and dampened a few of them with water. He stared at Ally's now gushing wound. "I know this isn't much, but—"

"Right," Ally said. "I know."

Ally's face compressed into a rictus of pain. The wound she suffered was wide and deep. The outline of the cut was almost entirely black. No matter how many times Quinn attempted to stop it from bleeding, more spilled out. In agony, Ally gasped. Quinn was as gentle as his rough hands could be, but still, he was an ape trying to knit a sweater.

"Ah!" Ally exclaimed.

It was just so hard for him to be gentle. Quinn's knowledge of First Aid was extensive, but his ability to take everything slow and easy was not. "Sorry," Quinn said.

"It's okay," Ally said.

"My hands," Quinn said, "they're not the best for these kinds of things, I'm sure you know."

"And yet *your* hands," Ally said, "are what I want."

Quinn enjoyed the warming compliment. Oddly, it didn't get very far. Quinn didn't spend much time saving people.

"I could say the same thing about you. You saved my

ass more times than I care to count," Quinn said, dabbing Ally's wound. "And then I put you in danger shortly after. I would hardly call that returning the favor."

"Just part of the job," Ally said. "Knew the risks when I agreed to come with you, remember? And I still know them now."

"So it would seem," added Quinn. He absorbed more of Ally's blood with a cloth. There was an indentation beneath her left knee. Blood continued to seep out of it. Although it was clean as Quinn could get it, he prepared the next bandage.

"And so, it would also seem," Ally said, "that *this* is what we get for trying to be heroes."

"Is that what we are now?" Quinn asked. He peeled the bandage and was about to lay it over Ally's cut. "Are we heroes?"

"Well, maybe you are more than me," Ally said.

"And how do you figure that?" Quinn asked.

"Well, you got more bad guys than I did, and you're not afraid to die. A hero puts himself in harm's way so he can save those who can't do it themselves, or did you forget that was a thing?" Ally sarcastically recited her cliche lines like she was a child trying to impress an adult. Quinn shook his head. Everything he was told from Ally seemed out of place.

In some ways, it made sense. In others, not so much.

"Didn't," Quinn said. "Didn't because I'm not one. Even if I was, I don't want to be."

"Thought you were trying to turn over a new leaf, you know," Ally said. "Find better people to kill or worse, worse people to kill."

"And yet, there's no such thing," commented Quinn.

"As what?" asked Ally.

"As better people to kill. I think I know that now," Quinn said. "I should have before."

Quinn laid the bandage over Ally's wet wound. What Quinn was doing, he hadn't done in a while. He was talking about things precious and reserved. He was opening up. And for once, Quinn followed this broken trail of honesty.

He did not abandon and he did not deny. He just accepted everything like it was his duty.

It was.

"You're still better than the ones you've taken out these last few days, Kyle," Ally said. "I thought you knew that."

Ally breathed softly, so soft the air massaged Quinn's face.

"By now." Gritting her teeth, Ally gazed at Quinn. Now was the opportune moment for Quinn to truly connect with Ally. And yet, switching back to being a regular operator, Quinn could only speak about the things that pertained to his mission. Nothing else. It was in the time between speaking to Ally and helping her that Quinn asked himself: *was he really a better man?*

He considered this and then he heard Heinreich calling him from the front seat. He was still driving the car.

"We're going to need to get to a better location. We can talk things out there. I know a place."

"Right," Quinn said. He agreed to the suggestion. Quinn could see Heinreich checking on them in the rearview mirror. Quinn always watched out for Ally. He cared for her and the feeling was both appreciated as well as reciprocated.

Never in Quinn's life did he acquire something as valuable as this. Having presented Quinn with this difference, his outlook had become vastly improved. His former fury had been chipped away to form a new kind of empathy. It fashioned him a compass that only good people possessed. Some would call this a conscience. And, when Quinn wasn't watching Ally, he was watching the road. And, with Quinn now watching the road, he was also watching Heinreich. There were so many questions to ask this man who was both mysterious and capable. Quinn wanted to ask Heinreich all he could before it was too late.

Then, he was going to find Priest.

He was going to do all of this and all he could hope was it worked.

He was alive, and so was Ally, and that was enough for now.

———

Heinreich drove Quinn and Ally to a Super 8 motel just off the freeway. It was not at all different from the dozens of others Quinn had stayed in over the years. This one was packed with families for the Fourth of July.

July already?

So often Quinn struggled to remember the seasons.

In Wyoming, the winters were brutal and the summers were nice.

As a result of Quinn's regimented lifestyle, there were no holidays. His days consisted of work and lots and lots of training. Therefore, it's easy to become absorbed by one's routine as well as a lack of spontaneity. When they drove through the motel parking lot, Quinn looked at the kids as they walked with their parents, who carried luggage and fat coolers. A Super 8 wasn't exactly a four-star accommodation spot, this one seemed decent enough.

"This way," Heinreich said, and he walked along while both Quinn and Ally stayed by the car.

"Leg feeling better?" Quinn asked Ally.

They had driven for almost an hour and there was some time for her wound to heal, though not much.

"It's okay. I'm...I'm good," Ally replied.

"You know you should eat something," Quinn suggested. "When was the last time you did?"

Ally's cheeks were sunken. Her lips were so dry they were starting to peel. Quinn assumed it was long.

"At the hospital," Ally said. "But I'm fine. Believe me when I say I'm not that hungry."

Quinn thought about what their recent encounters might do to another person's appetite. Still, Quinn struggled to believe her.

"I do believe you," he said, though not sincerely.

"Good."

"Guys?" Heinreich addressed Quinn and Ally. Standing in front of the door to the first floor of the motel, Heinreich was holding the key card as if he had checked in already. Quinn stepped in, though he was not worried about Heinreich. How long would Heinreich stay with Quinn and Ally? This gray-haired, brittle man was tough as shit so far as Quinn could tell. Although it was never wise to assume someone's skills based on age or appearance, Heinreich was not only about narcotics. He was working with Priest because of this knowledge and *not* because of his combat abilities.

Yet, this was only what Quinn was told. It was not what he had learned.

Nevertheless, Quinn played along and waited for Ally to come with him. She did, seconds later. Heinreich held the door and Quinn and Ally walked in. The setting looked completely untouched. The bed was made and the lights were off. The room was imbued with the chemical smell most rooms exude after they've been cleaned. It seemed to be that way, which was nice.

"Come on in," Heinreich said. "Sit down, please." Heinreich brushed past Quinn and stepped to a desk in the corner. He pulled two plastic water bottles out of the mini fridge and looked back. "You're probably both thirsty, huh? Here..." Heinreich tossed a bottle at Quinn. The Custodian caught it without looking. "Have a drink."

Ally caught a bottle too and Quinn unscrewed the cap and listened to the plastic crunch.

Did he trust Heinreich? Could he...

As Quinn reminded himself again...*he trusted no one. Ever.*

Quinn swallowed his water in big, almost boorish gulps. Once he was done, he crushed the plastic bottle and tossed it aside. He could go for another, but right now, he wanted two things from Heinreich:

1) What did he know? And 2) Who was next on Quinn's kill list?

None had to be answered in that order.

"You want anything to eat?" asked Heinreich. "I can get some stuff from the vending machines outside."

Quinn didn't wish to speak for Ally, but some snacks would hit the spot right about now.

But there was no time.

"It's fine," Quinn said. "You know what we want, and we want it now."

Heinreich's jaw dropped and his lashes fluttered. Quinn's sternness was duly noted. Yes, Quinn was tired of waiting. So, as Quinn stood at attention, both he and Ally gawked at Heinreich and awaited their much-needed answers.

"Yes," Heinreich said. "Very well." Heinreich turned

to the bed, rubbed his hands across his face, and sighed. "Well, there's some things we should have told you from the beginning."

"No shit," Quinn said.

"Yeah," Ally said, "and who's *we?*"

"Well," Heinreich said, "that's where things get complicated, see?"

"No, I don't, actually," snapped Quinn. "Maybe start at the beginning, where things get *less* complicated." Quinn had agreed to the mission because he wanted to punish the cartels for what they were doing to kids. Priest had told Quinn all about KEYS, but what Quinn didn't know was if this organization was working in-house and if they were an enemy that was conceived within Quinn's own country.

Quinn didn't fight his country or his own kind.

He fought corruption, evil...*dishonor.* But now everything had merged into one single problem. The world had become a great big gray thing, and Quinn didn't want to see it expand into something else. And the only one who could clear up the mystery surrounding it seemed to be Heinreich.

For now, he was Quinn's only lifeline.

"Right." Quinn didn't take his eyes off Heinreich.

He was going to tell him more. By god, Quinn was going to make sure he fucking said as much as he could say.

"You were initially hired to remove the cartels, yes? You were supposed to stop them from manufacturing a new narcotic and bringing that narcotic into America, like you said. And by replacing everything with only one substance, or at least introducing a new narcotic, it might effectively end our drug war, correct? Yes, it's a war I've hated and one I've been fighting nearly all my life."

When Heinreich said this, he was pointing his gun at Quinn.

"I was hired to do nothing," Quinn said. "I came to end something that shouldn't exist. I did all of that on my own accord, and that was all."

"Yes," Heinreich said. "But as it would turn out this, this *compound*...it was not obtained by the Sinaloa Cartel. It was actually...*handed* to them."

Paul Heinreich gestured the *handed* part of his delivery. He moved them as to "offer" his hands to Quinn just as he had explained. Some of this, Quinn was already aware of. Cane alluded to it back at the park. But now, Heinreich had confirmed it. He confirmed all of it. The Sinaloa Cartel was officially working with Quinn's own government?

Why? What was its purpose?

Quinn knew what Hyper-X did to its subjects, but believing it was going to end the drug war...*how*?

Quinn required more intel, which, at this time, he did not have. "Handed over?" Quinn asked.

"Yes," Heinreich said.

"By whom? Why?"

"The only people who would be in a *position* to give something so valuable away," Heinreich said. "They're the same people capable of manufacturing it. People who asked you to come here, people who asked you to eviscerate anyone who was ever linked to it. Those people are the people like *me*."

Ally glanced at Quinn. This was something they both had suspected from the very beginning. And now, here it was.

"We already knew that," Quinn said. "But keep talking."

"So...this...this synthetic, right?" Heinreich said. "It

can do many things, but the subjects it was tested on turned out *not* to be quite as programmable as expected."

"Programmable?" asked Ally. "I think I know what you mean."

Quinn's head slanted. He sighed. He didn't understand a goddamn thing so far!

"When it was made," Ally said, "you wanted to make sure it was weaponized, which is why you started testing it on people, *on kids*."

"That's where the project *first* began, yes," confirmed Heinreich.

"And those overseeing this project, this...KEYS...are they the ones behind everything?"

Heinreich nodded humbly. "Yes. I'm sorry."

Quinn ignored Heinreich's apology. It was too late for that.

"I knew the truth," Heinreich said. "I was willing to go along with it because I thought it would finally end what I've been fighting my whole life." The fight Heinreich was referring to was of course the ubiquitous drug war. He kept referencing it like it had taken years off his life, which Quinn was certain it had. "It was going to supplant all the bad shit plaguing our great country and stop it from going any further. See, the goal was to use the bad guys," Heinreich said, now downcast. Quinn didn't care for Heinreich's mood. Still, he listened to the man's long explanation. "Use them and then have them erased. It's why Priest wanted me here, because with me in the picture, and Ally..." Heinreich pointed to Ally as she shrugged. "All of this would be much so much easier to explain," Heinreich continued. "It wasn't until I learned about what was really going on that I chose to come back. I came back to admit the truth."

Quinn was still not persuaded by Heinreich's show of

guilt. When Quinn looked at Ally, she looked sympathetic and also sad.

"So, they manufactured this substance. They're testing it on kids, and the cartels," Quinn said. "They did what? They provided *the subjects?*"

Heinreich nodded. Now Sinaloa's involvement was made impeccably clear.

"Our government would not experiment on its own people, not directly," Heinreich said. "The cartels were going to provide the final piece, so to speak, and then once we had all we needed, we were going to bring in our own teams to bring them down."

"Stop them?" asked Ally. "Who? Who was going to stop them?"

Quinn came forward with an answer. "You know exactly who."

The who Quinn mentioned was himself. He was the one brought in to stop them!

That was his order. Eviscerate!

"We gave them batches of Hyper-X, told them to bring it into the country, stop the regular trade." Heinreich returned to his explaining. "In exchange for this, Mandilo and his wife would be given total immunity. End the drug trade by replacing it with something better."

"Stupid plan," admitted Ally.

"Well, it sounded better on paper I'll admit," Heinreich said.

"So Mandilo *was* working for you?" Quinn asked and put an end to this back and forth.

"He was," confirmed Heinreich. "Yes."

"So then...why was Quinn ordered to kill him?" asked Ally. "And, also, why didn't you say anything about this from the beginning?"

Heinreich bowed his head with shame. He was with

Priest when he explained this to Quinn. The entire time, they neglected to provide the link because KEYS was actually part of the US government! Quinn was not part of the solution. In effect, he was just another piece of the fat and complicated puzzle.

"Because they couldn't risk anyone talking about any of our interactions," Quinn said. He began to put the pieces together. "Mandilo found out though, didn't he? He knew who he was working for, how the walls were closing in around them, and they were going to be given nothing for their cooperation. Mandilo was going to try and kill me and then cash in on his deal," Quinn said. "Little did he and his wife know that there was no deal, not any real one anyway. And so, they hired Cane just in case things didn't work out. They didn't know he was going to betray them, but he did. He was their way out, but he turned against them."

"But why bring Cane into it at all? Did KEYS know the cartel had an assassin of their own?"

Heinreich had no response. Head still bowed, the shame he felt was still very much there. The question of where Cane fit into all of this stayed unsolved.

Did Priest hire Cane to kill Quinn?

Did Priest know about Cane's involvement from the beginning?

Quinn shook his head. Unclear. Unclear. Un-*fucking*-clear!

"As it would turn out," Heinreich continued, "Hyper-X wasn't working on adults or children. The side effects were, you see...too great." Heinreich elaborated, "For a time, it appeared as if the entire thing was about to blow up. Manufactured illegally, the cartels were made to look like *they* had created this new narcotic but that was it."

"Done to finally put an end to the drug trade," Quinn said to himself.

Heinreich heard and he responded. "Like I said. See, what if all the other narcotics would cease to exist, and only one could dominate the market? It was at least a strategy worth considering. And what if the newest drug could be controlled the same as its suppliers could be? What if the entire drug war became about enhancement rather than escape and euphoria? What if we could find a way to satisfy *both* needs simultaneously? That was the plan pitched to me, or, maybe, that's what I thought the plan would be. Then all of this happened, all the bodies, all the people dead, and all the misdirection and uncertainty."

"Sounds a lot like you had a bloody pipe dream there, Paul," Ally said.

Quinn's thoughts were the same. Nevertheless, he was not done asking questions.

"And Hyper-X would have such a level of versatility?" Quinn said.

"We didn't see any limits to its application," Heinreich said. "Except—"

"Except what?" Ally snapped back.

"That's when things get weird," Heinreich said. "*Really weird.*"

"You mean weirder than everything you've mentioned so far?" Quinn asked.

Heinreich nodded. As bad as the story was, apparently, it got worse.

"As the project began to turn," Heinreich said, "we knew it would only be a matter of time before what we were doing was exposed, and KEYS, well, they didn't want their name on any of this as you can imagine. They ordered the testing to be stopped and everyone linked to the project...*gone for good*."

Quinn recalled what Priest told him when he was first briefed on this mission. Suddenly, Quinn's reason for being placed on this path made even more sense. "That's why I was brought here," Quinn said. "Priest wanted me to do it. He wanted me to cover this whole thing up so no one would know the truth. Silence Mandilo, kill the cartel, and kill the truth. I was being used and that's all I ever was. No mission, no retribution, no justice, just...*used*."

"I'm sorry, Quinn," Heinreich said. To Quinn, Heinreich sounded somewhat sincere. "But I hate the cartels, so if someone did have a plan to wipe them all out, of course, I'd be up for it. And I was. *Completely*."

"But then...that would also mean...*he* knows too," Ally said. "Priest knows the truth too. He has the whole time."

"He knew the risks, as well as what KEYS was up to, but..."

"But what?" Quinn said to Heinreich.

"Priest...he...well...he..."

"Speak!" Yelling now, Quinn had reached his limit. There was only so much betrayal he could take. Heinreich danced around all the denial and uncertainty. He distributed too many open-ended responses. He could only hear so much before he began to explore his more creative side.

"KEYS was *his* initiative. It's his project. Always had been."

Another moment of uncomfortable silence surfaced. Quinn heard all he had. After, his heart began to beat faster and harder.

Experimentation on kids?

Was this why Quinn was sent to Louisiana? Was that a cover-up too?

Priest was a user. Always was. And yet, the apparency of Priest using another Custodian to cover his tracks was a reality Quinn could not accept.

How could he be so stupid? How could he *not* see the truth?

He was blinded by his own ambition, his own so-called better code.

If Priest was the one who created the shadow organization, and he was the one who wanted the Sinaloa Cartel destroyed, then he was also aware of so much else. And, because of this, Quinn finally had an answer to the daunting question that followed him wherever he went.

How well do you know Priest?

"Priest has been testing this on kids?" Quinn said. "It was him, him all along?"

"No," Heinreich said. "Not kids."

"Then who?" Ally said. Again, Ally's question was the same as Quinn's.

"If not kids," continued Ally, "and not men, *then who?*"

"Well," Heinreich said. He spoke with his head down. "Women. Lots of *women.*"

After Heinreich finished, Ally turned to face Quinn. When Quinn raided one of the houses earlier in his mission, he remembered what he saw. Quinn did see women, a lot of women. He also saw a boy, age four. Quinn saw everything. Too much.

"Women?" asked Ally. "So, what? Priest is running experimentations on women?" Ally snapped. She was loud because she was frustrated. "How the hell does that work, how would the side effects play out any differently on them?"

Quinn's eyes closed and he was now deep in thought. He was still reliving that moment, whereby he was in that house and then...Quinn recalled the scar. *There was a scar across the woman's stomach.* She looked so lost after being pumped full of painkillers and narcotics.

Quinn should have seen it then, but he didn't. He failed.

"Not just *any* women."

"Who *then?*"

Ally turned toward Heinreich, who was now standing in a corner like a disciplined child. Quinn was right. They *weren't* just any women.

"Mothers," Quinn said. "Pregnant women. It's another commodity owned and operated by Sinaloa. Human trafficking, women, sex workers, the only product more valuable than any narcotic."

With nothing more to say, at this point, Quinn couldn't separate his focus from the two words that now consumed his every thought.

Value and *commodity.*

How people could be referred to as such didn't bother Quinn. It didn't bother him as much as it made him rethink what he'd been doing all his life.

He killed people who were *a threat.*

Now, it was clear. People were being transformed into tradeable assets. And this transaction didn't just apply to those Quinn had removed. It also applied...to himself.

"People," Heinreich said, "and with Hyper-X injected before these *people* can be born. We're talking about the best technology anyone could ever obtain. Trained, capable, programmable *people.* That's the technology. That's Hyper-X, and that's what KEYS wants, and that's why they needed the cartel. It's the next phase, Quinn. *Version* 2.0."

A few heavy breaths huffed out of Quinn's face and his focus increased. Heinreich had finally come to the end of his long exposé. There was a lot to unpack, to dissect. What Quinn needed now was a new objective. Thankfully, he had one.

"I have to get to Priest," Quinn said. "I have to find him and I have to find him now."

Head turned, Quinn looked at his shoes. His Vipers were torn on both sides. Seeing this, Quinn was reminded how long he'd been on his feet and how much running and jumping he'd done these last few days.

It was incredible.

"Where is *he?*" Quinn asked this while biting his lip. Heinreich's head shook and he blinked hard and fast. He was not just anxious as Quinn waited for Heinreich to say more.

Should he not speak, then Quinn truly had no more use for him.

While he had been honest and said everything he knew, Quinn still could not bring himself to trust him.

"Priest...*is*..." Heinreich backed off and Quinn motioned away from the bed. Heinreich was heading back toward the door. It was then his demeanor had changed. He was hunched, and Heinreich moved like all his footsteps needed to be carefully placed. In Quinn's eyes, he seemed like he was dodging a trap. He was moving because, at any moment, something could change, Quinn's nostrils flared.

He sniffed. There was a clear change in his environment.

Quinn's ability to kill was synonymous with his ability to read a fucking room. In this case, a new smell had emerged in the space. Quinn inhaled the putrid scent of ashes and rubber, and he caught a whiff of it soon as Heinreich moved.

It was then Quinn looked at Ally because something was different.

They were *not* alone.

"Ally?" Quinn's fingers curled into his palm. He was reminded again about how he was without any weapons. As of now, he could not be in a worse spot.

"What?" Heinreich stood in the corner. Quinn's heart thrashed in his chest.

When not beating himself up for being stupid, Quinn knew he shouldn't have trusted Heinreich. He ignored his instincts. At the time, he was Quinn's *only* option. Nevertheless, Quinn did it. He did it because he was with Ally. He did it because he desired answers more than he did for watching his own back.

And now, he was about to pay the price.

The shadows shifted. From beyond the windows, vague outlines of armed men appeared. Marching into the room, Quinn approached the door and saw the strike team already in position. Quinn's fists bumped his thighs as he scolded himself.

He should have seen this! He should have predicted the fucking ambush!

"Get away from the door!" Quinn never raised his voice just as he never showed his emotions. Quinn screamed and Ally stopped and looked back. Quinn reacted instantly. Ally jumped while Quinn leaped after her. He reached for Ally's hand, but before he could grasp it, the door to the motel room was kicked in. More men wielding automatic rifles stormed in.

"Down!" Heinreich screamed at Quinn.

Quinn scanned the room. Every man on the premises had itchy trigger fingers and this Quinn knew well before any one of them fired. With all of them ready to pop off any second, it was the same team called in by the same man who called Quinn. Priest knew Quinn, and Quinn knew Priest. Both were made aware of what the other was willing to do. There was zero chance that the team was sent unprepared or undersupplied.

No, they were here and they were fucking ready!

Quinn saw the first man, followed by the second one immediately after. Quinn raced past the window. He pushed off his back foot and soared with his right leg bent. Completing a flying knee, Quinn was aiming for the first man's M16. With much power, Quinn hit the man's gun. He knocked him down the back and the weapon fell. Then Quinn popped the guy with a fierce elbow that cracked the man's helmet visor.

"Ah-ha!"

Quinn struck the man down and then glimpsed back. He swung the first man around and used the fool as a shield. Quinn took over from there and responded with a sharp kick right into the second man's knee. After bringing him down, there was no time in between. Milliseconds passed before one round was fired. Quinn snagged the guy's M16. Lifting the weapon up, he moved it around. Quinn pressed the trigger and sprayed the walls and windows. Delivering some solid cover fire, Quinn's intention was to get the team to back off so he could get away. Quinn grabbed the strap on the man's gun so he could hold the weapon but not pull it.

And, because Quinn couldn't pull it, then technically, he *didn't* have it.

He was *still* without a weapon. Quinn held down the trigger until it emptied. Then, he pushed back the strike team. Fleeing after, Quinn and Ally were still in the motel room. With few places to go, Heinreich stayed huddled by the corner. Cowering there like a child, all Quinn cared for at this point was his escape.

And he needed was to get Ally out, but before he could, Heinreich raised his hand.

"You have to believe me..." Heinreich's face was wet from sweat. Quinn didn't care what he had to say. "I had no choice. I trusted Priest because I thought he knew what he was doing, but I promise...promise you I will fix this! One day, I will find a way to fix it!"

Quinn looked the apologetic man up and down. While somewhat responsible for Quinn's set up, the Custodian's reply didn't require much effort or time.

"We all have a choice," Quinn said. "See you on the other side."

Quinn ended the conversation there with Heinreich and he ran to the door at the back of the room. Exploding through it, Quinn shattered the lock and his highest hope was that the next room was occupied. If there were civilians, the team would still move in, but they wouldn't open fire.

A gunfight in such a public place was not a wise decision.

Quinn was counting on this!

Into the next room, sure to Quinn's assumption, it was full.

There were two people lying in bed. There were no kids, however. Quinn saw that they looked like two young people who were merely in this hotel for a quick bang. He didn't care. Both were startled and gasped when Quinn and Ally sprinted to their room. In the window next to Quinn, the strike team was still visible. Seconds later, the windows shattered and the team began moving in. Quinn looked again at the approaching team and he rammed his shoulder into one of the men's guns. Kicking the next soldier into the wall, and relying solely on his body and his speed, Quinn struck and countered instantly.

He put another man into a headlock and swung him into the table.

Quinn could take one down, yes, but his plan depended on rapid reactions. This was all he could do to keep himself alive. Quinn raced to the door leading into the next room and rinsed and repeated.

This time, however, Quinn was not the one who kicked in the door.

Delivering a hard snap, Ally booted the handle and knocked it in. The fool aimed to put his gun on Quinn. He concentrated his rounds while the Custodian ducked and scurried into the next door. This time, Quinn could not stop to kick. Instead, Quinn drove his shoulder straight in and knocked the door off its hinges. After the door fell, both Quinn and Ally fell too. There was nowhere left to go. The pain in Quinn's body began to spread.

He was getting slower, softer, *weaker*. He was breaking slowly. With each inch gained, part of Quinn died. Part of him did *break*.

Quinn did his best to stand up. His quads hurt so much they were shaking. Quinn also couldn't get up like he was supposed to. He couldn't endure and he couldn't fight. He was losing in the worst way, and that way was slow. Quinn never lost, at least he fought as hard as he could not to lose. So, if he was approaching a place that got in the way of victory, Quinn could either bail out or fight dirty.

Here, he was hardly in a position to do either.

He helped Ally up while the team was closing in and he was then out of options.

"Come on." Quinn slowed. He spoke to Ally and did this because he wanted to offer her something. In this case, it was about detachment. Quinn couldn't bring

Ally with him, not here. Amid these constant attacks, Quinn's plan was to go one way and then let Ally go another.

"You go through the window to the bathroom," Quinn said to Ally, his voice strained from the quick reaction and pressure.

It was a struggle for Ally to hear Quinn. "What?"

Quinn jittered.

The man who was knocked down was starting to get up. And, if he could stand up, then so could the other private operatives. Quinn jerked his elbow in the direction of the room. "Go there and get out through the back. They're not here for you. They're here for—" Before Quinn could finish, he snatched Ally's arm and pulled. Falling back, he dragged Ally into the bathroom and fell near the oval tub in a room that smelled of shit and piss. "They're here for me."

Quinn soon heard the stomping of heavy boots and the sound of a full sweeper team on full approach. There were no plans to make another stand. Quinn didn't know if today was his last day, but if Priest wanted him dead, then he would be already. Ally was a witness now. She was an add-on that was not required. It was not necessary that she stay. She was in the way and, if they had Quinn, then they wouldn't need Ally. And if they didn't need Ally, then she would be perfectly expendable and so, perfectly dead.

And this was something Quinn could not abide by. He wouldn't.

"You go this way. You can escape through there." Quinn jerked his chin to gesture toward the window. "I'll stay."

"No," Ally replied to Quinn sharply. "You *can't* stay. If they get you alive, they'll..."

Kill me. Not saying this out loud, Quinn was aware of what these men would do to him.

"If they wanted me dead," Quinn said. He rethought how he was to phrase this. Initially, Quinn thought the team only wanted him dead. Now he was unsure. "Just go," he said.

Quinn told Ally to escape through the window. He watched her step onto the tub and do as recommended. Quinn didn't see the strike team. In fact, he didn't see anyone.

The team was closing in, but *not* on the location. Quinn was right. They weren't here for Ally. She ran. And then, moving on, Quinn looked at the doorway. They would be here soon. Quinn vowed never to go down without a fight, yet this was not the first time he had tangled with a team like this one.

Quinn grabbed the MP5. This weapon was far from his first choice.

Releasing the clip, Quinn checked the count. It was enough.

Quinn recovered a pistol. It was an HK, not his first choice. There were more rounds in this weapon than the rifle. Quinn holstered the pistol and pulled the Kevlar too. No, he wasn't bulletproof. Time was running out. The team...was getting closer.

Quinn pushed the stock of the MP5 deeper into his shoulder. He counted the rounds.

There were twelve men outside and another six by the vehicles parked in the lot.

Outmanned and outgunned, normally, Quinn was not in this position. His policy when it came to guns was always to have bigger and better. Quinn never went anywhere without double the ammo and three times the arsenal. He never went anywhere without superior firepower, a weapon on his person, or an exit strategy should he need to make a daring escape. None of this were options in this case. And as Quinn held the MP5, he looked back at the window.

It was opened, but Ally was not there.

Again, Quinn reminded himself...that was all he ever wanted. He denied the impulse to consider his own safety. Quinn eyed the door and pressed his back against the frame.

With both eyes closed, Quinn took a deep breath. Then, he continued to count.

Shock and awe and holding back. All out and no mercy.

"All right, fellas," the Custodian muttered. "Let's play."

———

Although not his first choice, the MP5 was still a solid weapon no doubt. It was rapid and easy to reload. It was not outfitted with a scope or a textured grip, which was something Quinn always preferred. Here, Quinn was not exactly selecting rifles at a gun show. Quinn remembered his tonfa. It was the most versatile weapon a fighter could wield and Quinn had them for this exact purpose.

On his back, Quinn lined up his shot.

Unlike previous instances, Quinn was careful with his bullets because now he slipped into new territory. Mad and unhinged, Quinn stampeded toward the first operative. Pressing the trigger to the point where his fingertip burned, Quinn shredded the strike team. He split them up apart like a herd of wild boar. He swarmed one and then another and then another. Aiming primarily for their faces and necks, Quinn found his way around their armor. He shot and reloaded and didn't let up, not for a second. Quinn kicked in knees and punched in heads. He wasn't thinking only about his guns. He didn't care if they were aimed at him or whether they were close enough to even hit. No, Quinn thought only about what *should* happen and what should not. When Quinn emptied the MP5, he flipped it up and held it by its stock. Now holding the gun like a club, Quinn swatted at the other operatives. He struck their joints and Quinn did what he could with this empty rifle. Quinn slipped to the floor. Drawing the stolen HK faster than a magician drawing a card, Quinn fired again. Getting a few headshots, all the men dropped while Quinn's kill count was nearing a solid twelve.

He showered the motel room with bodies and bullets and didn't miss a single target.

Although imperfect, whenever Quinn used any gun, the bullets went exactly where he wanted them to. Even without his most valued and desired weapons, today was no exception.

But the plan was not as exact as Quinn wanted. He was hitting targets, yes, but he was also running low and not just on ammunition. Low on energy, Quinn had to remind himself that he was only human and humans get tired.

They also need things. And when they don't get these things, their bodies and their minds start to shut down. Quinn's vision was blurring. All his muscles felt weak, so much so Quinn couldn't hold the gun without feeling its full weight. No, he was drained and was nearing a place he absolutely did not want to go.

Quinn clutched the HK. He looked at the window.

There, he saw another man. He sprinted with one

hand up while another was firing. Quinn pegged one in the face and then slipped. Aiming from a lower vantage point, the situation proved advantageous. Quinn hit what he needed to and his speed—combined with his rapid ability to deploy quick and accurate rounds—was not just succinct. No, it was also accurate. Quinn was catching fish in a fucking pond. Once Quinn hit the last one with the HK, nothing followed.

But he was out of bullets.

"Fuck." Quinn threw the pistol into another operative and the gun knocked the man's helmet. A clear and effective distraction, the man was left in a daze. Quinn finished him with a straight kick to the chest and watched the man fall. Quinn stepped over him. Then, withdrawing his tonfa, he literally brought a melee weapon to a row of firing guns.

It would be suicide for most, but not for Quinn. For Quinn, it was only *slightly* suicide.

Smacking one man with the long side of the tonfa and, using him as a human shield, Quinn swiped. Every barrel whacked hit by Quinn's spinning tonfa as he kept all the guns away by staying constantly in motion. Quinn was not holding back, not for a second. No, Quinn continued his assault using his most prized possessions.

Going and going and going, Quinn was a battery that would not stop. He hit until his arms were numb. Tiring, Quinn finally did what he never thought he would do.

He let go.

He sunk and he buckled. He did this while the rest of the team closed in.

With no gun and with only one tonfa, Quinn was against five operatives with automatic rifles. He vowed to never go down without a fight, but Quinn knew as soon as he stopped, he was done for.

And so, he couldn't stop.

He screamed as he pushed himself up.

Quinn lifted his tonfa and returned to the assault. He hit another operative in the knees and then rolled. Quinn knocked anyone and anything he could hit. In a state of blissful ignorance, it was a last stand—something Quinn always believed in taking.

He wouldn't go out any other way.

He swore to die a warrior's death, and so, this was how Quinn envisioned his last moments.

Then again, Quinn didn't expect to live past thirty. And here, here he was, as one of the youngest and one of the most prolific Custodians in the order. He knew things he didn't expect to know and felt things he never thought he would feel. One of the most surprising things was knowing someone who *actually* cared about him.

Quinn remembered how it was him who made this person feel safe.

Ally was okay. This was all Quinn needed to know if this was to be his final hour.

He swung again, clubbed another. Another man fell and Quinn hit the legs of one more who was closing in. He continued to keep the guns away. Though moving in a circle worked in some ways, the only question that continued to level Quinn was why?

Why hadn't they shot him? Why were they *not* trying to shoot him?

Their aim was disrupted, yes, but they were still close enough to do better. Something else was happening. Quinn continued to ravage, and eventually, he came across a new figure strolling across the lot.

"Ah!" A clean strike popped Quinn in the chest.

Unlike the others, this hit was delivered with a solid foot. And, because Quinn recognized this kind of strike, he in turn recognized the striker. Landing on his backside, Quinn let his fatigue take over. When Quinn turned his head up now, he was staring at the one who hit him. At the time, Quinn thought it would be Priest, and maybe it was, or maybe it was Kift.

But no. It was exactly who Quinn didn't want to be.

The man who kicked him was his brother.

It was him. It was Cane.

"Don't," Cane ordered a member of the strike team. It was the same operative who had his gun raised so he could shoot Quinn in the face. "Don't do that."

Cane stood in front of Quinn in casual pants and a white shirt clinging to his slim body.

"He told me he wants him alive. He's always wanted him alive," Cane said. "Bring him."

The team member nodded and marched to the now-fallen Quinn. The once weakened grip on Quinn's tonfa began to cease and he could not hold the weapon as he did before.

"Wait," Cane said. He knew entering Quinn's space would only lead to another vicious assault. Therefore, the younger brother did something that the older brother would never do.

Cane removed a new gun—a tranquilizer gun.

When Cane drew this bulky pistol with a long snout, to Quinn, it looked like a kid's toy.

Yet, as Cane pulled the trigger, he fired a dart straight into Quinn's neck. It had been some time since Quinn endured the euphoric sensation. For a second, he felt relieved. For a time, he felt like the shot was necessary. Quinn was unaware of what would happen once he woke up.

He had no idea where he would be or if he would be alive or dead.

At the moment, he cared for neither.

At least Ally wasn't with him.

Ally was safe...for now.

CHAPTER 15
ENDGAME

DYING, NOT DEAD.

This was a phrase Quinn first heard when he was in Delta. He was the youngest to be admitted into the Canadian Special Forces, JTF 2, and was also one of the few to successfully transfer from one special forces division to another, in another country. Quinn had served in two different nations and passed all his training and did so at the age of twenty-five.

Unheard of for most soldiers.

How Quinn managed to pass these tests was for two reasons. First, it was his background, his upbringing, and his mindset.

All of this was sculpted and conceived by Quinn's father's hand.

As it was known, the way Tiger Woods's dad taught his son how to play golf, Quinn's father taught him and his brother...how to kill.

The second was the Quinn family name. Broder Quinn did have a reputation among brutes and operators. He had many kills to his name and he shared all of this with his children. Broder Quinn had many discussions about how many men he slayed, what he learned, and the skills he acquired during his many years of service. Quinn's dad elaborated on how he was going to teach his own everything he knew. At any cost, Quinn's father's advice about dying and not being dead made the most sense. And, now that Quinn was in a new room, he found himself tricked by another member of his family.

In the end, the only people who could trap Quinn were family.

First, it was his dad in Louisiana, and now it was his brother here, wherever he was.

Before, Quinn woke in a cave, but today, he found himself hanging on a chain.

Shoes taken, Quinn's wrists were bound by a metal connected to a rusted hook and he was hanging there like a soon-to-be butchered cow. Quinn had tangled with the torture before and no, he did not fear it. All of this was expected. Slowly Quinn began to lose feeling in his legs and chest and looked down at his body. He wasn't wearing a shirt.

Quinn sniffed.

He thought of all the things that might be used on him now.

There was waterboarding, which was only partially uncomfortable for Quinn.

There was electrocution, which consisted of the zapping of nerve endings with clamps connected to car batteries. There was the usual fingernail, toenail, and testicle-pliers game. Quinn loathed this, but he could take it. His dad did the same thing to him when he was ten. And, though Quinn was prepared for almost anything, what he was unsure about was his location. Still, it wasn't fear he was feeling now. Never fear. No, there is a great secret held among Custodians. When the program was first conceived by Priest, all the candidates met at a warehouse. There, Quinn connected with the other assassins who were part of the same game. Some were ex-military, with tasty and unique backgrounds, and some were civilians, with skills and tactics instilled in enhanced ways. It was then Quinn was made aware of what he was supposed to do if he was ever captured, if a Custodian was ever to be kidnapped or taken prisoner.

There was a solution.

Quinn remembered what it was.

Everyone who was welcomed into the order was given a ring. It was simple: round and so innocuous that, to the regular observer, it appeared only as a black band. Although not an avid reader of comics, the exchange made Quinn think that he was part of the famed Green Lantern Corp. Gifted with a ring from Oa, fueled by a user's will, Quinn was granted something similar. He was impressed by the idea when Priest explained the ring's true purpose.

"This...this will remain with you at all times. Never take it off and never tell anyone what it actually is."

Back then, Quinn didn't know what these rings really did. It was after Priest told him of the sheer power they possessed. It was not only innovative; it was also their greatest weapon.

Built into every ring was a tracking device. This device allowed for Priest to know the location of all the other Custodians at all times. This wasn't surprising. Quinn was aware of this when he agreed to work for the government. Even if it was black ops, there was no way for anyone to disappear off the grid completely.

And so, Quinn abandoned his privacy a long time ago.

But this was *not* the rings' chief design.

Priest said *the rings,* or *beacons* as he called them, were all built with an added feature. The rings were customized to suit every Custodian's fingerprint. If twisted clockwise, they would send a signal directly to Priest.

Only in case of emergencies.

And yet, Quinn didn't know what constituted an *actual* emergency. Right now, he had his own ideas. What Quinn imagined might actually align with what Priest suggested as well.

If any Custodian found themselves compromised, if they were to be tortured or suffer a terrible death, these rings were their way out. The beacons would light up and notify all Custodial colleagues. Then, the compromised Custodian would wait for another's arrival.

How do we know they will respond?

This question was asked by another Custodian back when they were informed of the beacons' true purpose. Quinn thought the same thing.

Because once you join this organization, you have to accept its rules. There are laws to which we are all bound, and breaking these laws will have serious consequences. Incredibly serious consequences.

This was not verbatim. It was all Quinn could remember from years ago.

Priest didn't elaborate on these so-called consequences. There was a classification for those who wanted to leave. It was referred to as an option known as *Extricate*. But Priest's point was clear. Custodians were not just assassins. They were versatile, adaptable, high-functioning professional operators. They were the elite killers numb to the concept of fear and pain. As a result of their level of rarity, they were to be protected and guarded. And, if someone did kill a Custodian—if they even threatened to kill a Custodian—then all the others would be informed. When they were, they were to *unleash hell.*

Ideally, they would do this before the Custodian was killed. If not, whatever happens afterward is a result so brutal it would make Vlad the Impaler look like a kindergarten teacher. Killing a Custodian produced a far worse outcome than offing a guy in the mob, a cop, or a politician.

No, killing a Custodian was like terminating a *sun*.

To do so would bring an end to all existence and creation.

Right now, Quinn wasn't sure what he was dealing with.

Was he about to be tortured? Killed?

Quinn didn't know. He also didn't know who brought him here, if it was KEYS or the Sinaloa Cartel. It could be Priest, but then Quinn couldn't accept how it might be his enigmatic lord. Hanging people on meat hooks wasn't exactly Priest's style, or so Quinn assumed.

Quinn took a whiff of the room. It smelled damp and rank of odorous sweat. Quinn determined where he was based on spatial clues. Quinn glimpsed at the grate, the pipes, the wet concrete floor. Paying close attention to the water dripping sporadically in the background, wherever he was, Quinn imagined, had to be somewhere underground. In the room was a steel door and a dangling light with a pull string. There was also a table with what seemed to be tools for torture. Among these tools, Quinn spotted his tonfa!

Everything about said location suggested CIA black spot.

Only Priest would have access to places like this. He could also be behind everything now. Quinn fidgeted with his ring and tangled with the idea of lighting his beacon. It was a possibility, yet for now, Quinn was still breathing, and that was enough. He could hear the sounds of metal clanking. The door in front of Quinn began to rattle. From the other side, two men in dark clothes proceeded toward him.

"Well, well...look what have here, Fox...another toy for us to play with."

"Yes, and he's one that has a reputation," said the man called Fox. "A Custodian. Lucky us."

How they knew Quinn's title only confirmed the fact that Priest was behind this kidnapping. But, if this was true, he must also know that the beacons could be lit. If Quinn did this, then he would expose him as a traitor.

Also, how well could these men do against someone like Quinn?

All of what Quinn was thinking was possible, it just wasn't likely.

Priest wasn't going to kill Quinn, not here and not now.

"If you knew anything," Quinn said, speaking to Fox. "You'd let me go."

Fox chuckled as he roamed to the table. His cohort stood back and watched Quinn with folded arms. "*Haha.* He said you'd be tough. Even more, he said you were going to do whatever you could to get out of here once you passed your little...*test*. So, if we were smart, we'd just walk away and let you be."

"Torture isn't something you can walk away from," affirmed Quinn. "If you were good at it, which you aren't, you'd know that already."

Quinn looked this Fox asshole up and down. He presumed the reason for Fox's name was because of his orange hair. The shade was similar to the animal's. A mullet running down his neck, he looked like a real piece of trash. Still, Fox was a sadistic fuck but definitely didn't work for the cartel.

Quinn believed he was just a guinea for Priest, maybe. *He did employ a few.*

But Quinn's uncertainty provided no fuel for his predictions. Right now, Quinn was just preparing to kill these two fools so he could walk out the damn door.

"Oh, we know more than you think we do," said Fox. "Like how to add pressure and..."

Fox twirled the blade under the light and his eyes gleamed with sadistic excitement. Like a surgeon about to operate, what Fox was going to do to Quinn was a type of surgery. The only difference was the outcome. It was not to cure or to repair, just to amputate, to cut.

"And how to...make small things," said Fox, "have big consequences."

"That's the torture game," said the other man.

"But..." said Fox. He stepped closer to Quinn. "As we told you...that's *not* what we're here to do."

Quinn's legs were asleep. The tendons in his arms were stretched out. With most of Quinn's strength gone, even thinking about doing a pull-up made his body ache. "Whatever you're here to do," Quinn said, "I suggest you do it fast, because otherwise, you won't be able to appreciate the show that comes after."

"Show?" asked Fox.

Quinn nodded. "The chance to witness a spectacular death."

Fox laughed again. The second man popped a piece of gum into his gaping mouth.

"No one is coming to help you, my friend..." Fox spun his scalpel and let it graze Quinn's lashes. He provided the Custodian with a brief insight of what was to come. "You are trapped down here, trapped in a room that will serve as your crypt, your very own...*tomb.*"

Fox eased the blade in and teased Quinn. Quinn

could only imagine the pain of carving out another person's eyeball. When he was a child, Quinn's father did it once to a wolf. It was some real nasty shit. The wolf had attacked Kyle and his brother and Quinn's father wanted retribution. But, to see an animal endure that much pain and suffering...honestly, Quinn could still hear those horrible screams even to this day.

"So, if I were you...I would make your peace with your God or whatever else you might believe in. I'd say your bloody prayers and hold your breath, because what we're about to do to you...is really going to sting."

"*Hmm*," Quinn said. The scalpel continued to nibble his eyelashes. "And if I were you, I would have spent less time threatening and more time getting the deed done," Quinn said. "As I said, you'll need to make this quick."

"Don't *tempt* me," said Fox.

"I'm not," Quinn said. "I'm *warning* you."

"Warning me? Warning me about what?"

"Of what's about to happen." Although Quinn didn't light his beacon, he did indulge in another feature of the ring.

Along with its tracking, if the ring was rotated counterclockwise, a thin laser could be emitted from within the band itself. And, when ignited at the right time, it could melt chains, ropes, and other binding mechanisms. Burning the steel, Quinn's laser cut right through the coils, which broke well before these men stepped through the door. Quinn watched Fox's head turn. When the chains split, Quinn squeezed the hook.

Hands free, Quinn looked back and smirked.

Time to take these fellas to church!

The ceremony started with Quinn front kicking Fox in the gut.

After generating some serious force, Quinn could

break wood. He could split this man's face completely apart. The idiot henchman fell to the ground and the second man stomped and Quinn pulled his legs up and dropped them onto his opponent's shoulders. Quinn wrapped his knees around this fool's neck and locked him up nice and tight. Quinn flexed his legs and wrestled with the man's neck. The Custodian initiated a traditional triangle hold. The move was done through a person's calf, but unfortunately, Quinn didn't have his arms to assist him.

Fortunately, Quinn did not require them.

Once he had the man in the hold, Quinn shifted. He flicked his torso and snapped the man's neck like a brittle stick. Quinn lifted himself up and slipped off the hooks.

Falling down, Quinn hit the concrete.

By now, the first man had recovered. Quinn saw him right away.

The chain around Quinn's wrist was so long it dragged across the concrete floor. Quinn lifted his hand and spun the metal rings. Spinning and spinning, Quinn was a man who now wielded a whip made of metal. And, with this whip, Quinn smacked the would-be torturer once across the face and then again along his abdomen and thigh. A single hit was enough to cut a person's face in half.

Yet, for someone who was about to torture Quinn, it was going to do more than that.

Quinn struck the man center. He twirled his body like he was doing a gymnastics ribbon routine. Striking again, Quinn shattered the fool in every section of his weak, pathetic body. Once finished, Quinn looped the chain around his hand and wrapped his knuckles up with the steel. Hand sheathed, Quinn glared at the limp piece of shit with a garbage mullet and spat. Quinn never concluded a fight until he heard nothing and saw nothing. Quinn stormed after the man with the chain fastened around his fingers. The fool whose spine was banged up so bad it was almost a plastic straw coughed and quivered. Quinn squeezed his fingers tighter around the coiled steel. It had been some time since Quinn beat a man into oblivion. It's been even less time since Quinn killed someone deserving of such a fate, but then Quinn stared at the man trembling before him and felt absolutely nothing at all.

"Please...please don't. I..." The man quaked. His begs and pleas were so resounding that the Custodian stopped seeing a man but instead saw only a child. This man was following orders, almost the same as Quinn. This didn't justify his actions, but beating a man to death? No, it was not Quinn's way, not anymore.

Quinn let go of the chain and listened to it clank in a sloppy, metallic thump. Soon after he dropped the chain, Quinn's hands felt lighter. He had a request.

"Keys."

The keys Quinn was referring to were the ones that would set him free, not the organization possibly responsible for taking him alive.

"Where?" With not much time left, the shaking man reached into his pocket. Quinn retrieved three small silver cylinders thin as toothpicks. He tossed them at Quinn and the Custodian snatched them with one hand. He dropped his wrists. He had what he wanted.

But this was far from over.

Though Quinn chose not to beat this man to death with a chain, he could still not leave him so capable. His mercy did not align with trust. It was Quinn's choice to let a stupid man live. He unbuckled the chains and finished the man with a quick snap of his leg. Quinn booted the man in the jaw and knocked him unconscious.

Grabbing his tonfa, Quinn now proceeded to the door as a free man, yet freedom was only a relative concept now. First, Quinn needed to discover where he was and how he arrived. Then, he needed to discover just who the fuck had brought him here to this unknown place.

Above all else, it was time to finish what he started.

Eviscerate was still his order!

———

Out the door and without weapons, Quinn wanted to recover anything he could use to defend himself. The hallway, unlike the room Quinn was imprisoned in, was clearer and cleaner.

There were bright lights, the walls were glossy, and the floor was dryer.

Quinn rubbed his wrists. His body was recuperated and his strength was regathered. He was getting faster as he shuffled around the corner. And as his pace quickened, Quinn's fists stayed pressed to his chest.

The next man was behind the corner. He was armed.

What Quinn held was his M4 carbine. Strapped with a Kevlar vest and carried spare rounds, Quinn's feet slapped the ground as he drew closer. He dropped and slipped behind the man and then Quinn pushed his feet into the guard's knees. He snagged his wrist and pulled. Here, Quinn deployed an Open Guard. He chopped the guard's neck and gripped the top of his skull. Quinn yanked the man back and smacked his face hard into the ground, knocking him out cold. With another one down, Quinn stripped this man of his gear and confiscated what he could. Quinn did a quick ammo check of the weapon and also pulled his attacker's pistol. It was a SIG. Quinn slipped it into the back of his pants. No tonfa, for now, this didn't bother Quinn too much. He turned and kept his rifle low. Quinn checked the corners. He had two free mags and watched as another foot soldier stepped in. Quinn shot him in the face while another trailed closely behind. Quinn smoked the fool in the chest and took him down the same as the last.

Two down, Quinn continued to march through the hallway.

What he was searching for was a door. He was also on the lookout for the people in charge. But, as Quinn capped another guard, he spotted a white door in a space brightened by only two fat lights.

Quinn spat onto the floor.

His most recent exploits caused severe saliva build-up. He roamed as two more men snuck up along his right side. Quinn drew his gun before either of them could and fired three shots in their direction. The men dropped and the shots couldn't have been easier if Quinn was playing a fucking carnival shoot 'em up game.

Quinn kept his SIG by his thigh and then carefully opened the door to take a peek.

The room was so bright the light pained his eyes. The first thing to breach the room was Quinn's pistol. Strapped with the Kevlar Quinn took from the guard, he was wide awake as he moved in. So far as Quinn could see, the room was clear of any hostiles. There was nothing from what he could see that posed a threat but this was only just the beginning of what Quinn had witnessed in this underground lair.

Into another room, Quinn pushed open the door. What he saw was an open space absent of any furniture. It was wide and included a set of tables leading all the way to the back of an expansive room. For some reason, it all seemed eerily familiar. Quinn had sworn he'd seen this room before.

Then it dawned on him.

It was the same room featured in the photo Priest showed Quinn earlier in his mission.

This was the *lab* in the photograph.

The same!

Each bed there was equipped with a heart monitor as well as an IV. Screens gave the vitals of all the patients lying there. Confined and tied down, every one of them was identifiably female. All were young. Quinn guessed their ages were between fifteen and thirty.

The women were blindfolded and fast asleep. Quinn's jaw slacked.

Hearing heart monitors, although these women appeared dead, they were alive.

Much to Quinn's satisfaction, the Custodian didn't expect to witness this sight.

It was disturbing and notoriously disgusting to behold. Quinn then remembered the women he encountered back at the house he raided. Then he remembered what Hein-reich said. He was the one who informed Quinn of this greater plan. He was the first to mention *women*. He talked about the smuggling and the trading of people because that's what the cartel was really known for.

What Quinn was looking at now did not fit the mold for human trafficking.

But it did seem pretty fucking close.

There was something else going on here, and Quinn was going to find out what it was.

Quinn approached the first table and looked at one woman. She was young, too young to be an expectant mother, but still, there she was, pregnant and asleep. There was also a chart next to her. Quinn reached with his free hand to grab the clipboard. He brought it to his face and read. Quinn knew jack shit about how to read this information.

But he didn't care.

On his own, he tried to determine the reason as to why these women were put here now.

What was being done to them? What was their purpose?

Quinn reflected on all the possible reasons but was quickly interrupted by a voice he hadn't heard in a long time. Yet, he wasn't surprised when he saw who it belonged to.

"Magnificent, isn't it?" Hand up and gun ready, Quinn pivoted to face the only person he wanted to see.

Now, Priest didn't come dressed in a suit but in a collared shirt made from silk. His pants were khaki and his shoes were loafers. It was not Priest's usual attire. But with his hands inside his pockets, he didn't make eye contact at all with Quinn. In a way of securing his reign of power over this place, Priest didn't look at anything other than the people asleep in their *beds*.

"Not quite as prolific as most will come to realize," Priest said, "but once it's done, everyone everywhere will be wondering how...how was it all made possible? Who did it, and why was it so successful?"

Priest grinned. When he finished speaking, the contractor rotated.

Priest's hands, still pocketed, he kept them there as he displayed his signature maniacal grin. It was the kind of shit-eating smirk that could only belong to a master manipulator—someone who did much and feared little.

"And, when anyone asks, I will only tell them of two names, *mine*..." Priest brought his hand to his chest and gestured to himself. He continued to smile. "And yours."

"It was *you*," Quinn said, chagrined. "You, Priest...you were the one behind all of this?"

Priest circled the room and Quinn watched him like a hawk.

"The mission," Quinn gawked, still aiming his raised SIG. "The cartels," Quinn continued, "KEYS, all of this was *you*. You selected the enemy, you controlled the narrative, and now you found a way to manipulate me into doing the work that needed to be done *for you!* You did all of this just so I could give you whatever it is *you* wanted."

"I suppose..." Priest slowed and bent forward. Again, he refused to look at Quinn. "That's *one* way of seeing it."

"And the other way?" Quinn asked.

Priest shrugged, dismissive of all Quinn's claims. He did all of this in favor of the one that felt more real.

"We *both* get what we wanted," Priest said. "You got to knock out a few bad guys, free some innocents, implement your own form of justice or pain, whichever you prefer, and our country gets to be safe from a threat it was once so afraid of. It's...you know...win-win."

"Except the threat *isn't* won," Quinn said. He looked at one of the sleeping women. "It's still here. It's just... *changed*."

"No, not changed," Priest said. "*Improved*."

"What exactly are you planning here, Priest?" Quinn barked. "What are you up to? What do you want?"

Priest chuckled and Quinn was done with all the pussy-footing. He couldn't stand to hear Priest deny his involvement for another measly second. "What do I want?" Priest repeated, head back and a grin spreading along his jawline. "Is that not the ultimate question to everything we've done together? No, we have a good thing going, Quinn," Priest said. He nodded and appeared pensive with his finger touching his chin. Quinn could see

Priest was remembering everything the two of them had *done* together,

There was so much to remember.

"Some might say," continued Priest, "we have the *best thing* going."

"This isn't about you or me," Quinn said. "It's about *them*." Quinn's gun stayed up, yet he pointed his weapon at the table, to all the women. "It's about the *truth*."

"The truth," Priest said. "And since when do you care about something as small and as insignificant as the truth?"

"Since it began to become so fucking hard to find," Quinn said. "Since it started to conflict with the lines we don't cross. Kids, women, drugs. I wanted to protect this country from being taken over by bad things and bad people. I wanted to clean it up, keep it safe. Wasn't that the reason for creating the Custodians in the first place?"

"It was," Priest said, "but then again, what are Custodians *really*? What makes them who they are, and why are they so necessary to preserving the sanctity and grace of our great nation?"

Quinn didn't know what to say at this point. He especially could not when Priest decided to return to such a lengthy narration. "You asked me earlier what it is I wanted."

Quinn nodded.

"Why am I doing this," continued Priest, "well, the reason is because I want..." Priest turned around to ominously reveal his *other half*. For Quinn, this was true in more ways than one. By doing this, Priest showed the part of himself he had once kept hidden. He was so menacing that, despite the brightness of this room, a few shadows managed to cling to Priest's slender body.

He was a specter standing discreetly in the dark. "I want...*you.*"

"What?"

"As many of *you* as I can get," Priest clarified, "or, in this case..." Priest's hands were out and he set himself next to one of the sleeping women. Casually, Priest placed his hand on her stomach. "As many as I can build."

"*Build?*" Quinn asked. This word made him feel curious and angry at the same time.

"*Breed,* more specifically," added Priest. "How many of the perfect, undeniable, unbreakable warriors can be birthed from each of these...*subjects.* Born and then grown to become fully-fledged, fully capable warriors. They will be the Custodians...*of the future.*"

The future.

Additional surges of bewilderment and fury emerged from deep inside of Quinn. His head was spinning as he tried to piece together the logic behind Priest's very cryptic explanation.

Custodians of the future, synthetic compounds, and, at last, one final act of betrayal?

Why?

"So, you did this?" Quinn asked. "All of it. You set me up. You lied to me. No UBC scientists, and the cartel were just the fucking fall guys. They were just some organization you picked to pin this whole thing on so you and KEYS could get your subjects. It's the next line in our country's defense, at least it will be."

"*Kinetic Enhanced Youth Supplementation,*" Priest explained the acronym. "Yes."

"What?" Quinn said. He thought he didn't hear Priest correctly. Then, his former boss spoke again.

"KEYS," Priest clarified. "That's what it stands for. Kinetic Enhanced Youth Supplementation, and no, you are wrong, Quinn. UBC scientists *did* acquire the formula used in the experiments; it just wasn't a recent discovery. See the photograph I showed you..." Priest said as Quinn reflected back to the time back on the ship, when he was briefed on his mission. He remembered seeing the slaughtered scientists and remembered the story surrounding them. He could see all the men and women in white coats who were supposedly killed at the hands of some assassin.

They were people who once stood here, where Quinn was now.

But, according to Priest, it wasn't now.

"It's old," Priest said. "*Very old*, in fact. Almost thirty years old, to be more precise."

"What?" Quinn said.

"Initially created as a sedative designed to eliminate pain, it was not that different from oxycodone or morphine," Priest said. "Yet, it did have one key factor that set it apart from everything else. The more it numbed the subject, the more strength it gave them in return and the more resilience it granted. However, the pharmaceutical company that acquired it was ordered by our government to shut down. They feared what would happen if it fell into the wrong hands."

"*Weaponization*," Quinn said.

"We *are* the United States of America," Priest said. "If there's any chance something we create can be used as a tool for murder and destruction, then you can be damn sure there's someone out there who's going to want to try it."

Quinn considered this as a plausible reality. As much as he wanted to hurt Priest, nothing he said so far was untrue.

"So it sat in a lab," Priest said. "It stayed hidden until,

one day, I discovered its potential and decided to pursue it."

"By testing it on *kids?*" Quinn glowered. This thought only enhanced his aggression. It fueled Quinn's need to pound Priest until he stopped moving.

He also didn't care.

"Whoa," Priest said. Hands up, he exclaimed. "I'm no child torturer! Come on, Quinn, I would think after all this time, you'd know me better than that."

"Then keep talking," Quinn ordered.

Quinn liked to think he knew Priest, but he could not deny any of the accusations he was considering now. Priest always was a fucking snake. But today, Quinn was going to discover the kind of snake he was. He was a fucking cobra!

"The formula might have been a risk," Priest said, "but how much of a risk...no one knows, not at this point, not until it was tested anyway. So, we struck a deal."

"A deal?" Quinn asked. "A deal with *who?*"

"Who do you think?" Priest replied. "I mean, who was really willing to take an experimental drug and give it to the general public without knowing the consequences?"

"Sinaloa," Quinn said. By now, the answer was obvious. "The world's most dangerous drug cartel."

Priest's cackles were so loud he had to cover his mouth with his hand. "Sinaloa?" Priest's taunting laughter rose to higher, more uncomfortable levels. "No, silly. *Us.* The fucking US of A! We were the ones who were going to send it out there."

Quinn's head shook, baffled for a second time. This bothered him, yet he was not very surprised by it.

"It was given to a number of people already," Priest said, "but all of them...*all of them*, well, let's just say they went a little..." Priest's finger circled around his temple as he whistled and ogled. "*Cuckoo.*"

Quinn was struck again by the sight of the photograph. Yet, only now was he beginning to see the big picture.

"They were the ones who killed the scientists?" Quinn said. "The test subjects. When they were given your compound, they snapped, and what...they...*they all went mad?*"

"Yes," answered Priest. "As it turned out, it wasn't ready to be tested then."

"Hmm."

"See, every time we tested it on people over the age of twenty-five, the synapses in their brain altered and they experienced some kind of chemical overload, apparently. They began to react impulsively, giving into their anger and their rage."

"I see."

"So...what we needed was a different plan," Priest said. "That plan was simple. Test younger."

"On who?"

"Well, we couldn't test on our own, obviously," Priest said to Quinn. "So we decided to turn to an organization that had an unlimited supply of *willing* individuals. What we needed were people who were not technically part of our country, people who could easily take the fall should anything happen."

"It's always been about people," Quinn said, adding another piece to the grand puzzle. "Willing, innocent, *broken people.*"

Priest eyed Quinn with a sultry smirk. It would seem he was actually impressed with the mercenary's detective skills.

"Quite. See, the greatest traded commodity isn't

substances anymore, Quinn. It's *people*," explained Priest. "People who are prepared to do anything for the right price. And so, Mandilo would supply us with these people, and in exchange...we'd bribe him with immunity."

"Which you never planned on giving him in the first place," Quinn said.

"Of course not!" exclaimed Priest, his tongue so sharp Quinn felt like he was being whipped with it. "You think I'm going to let a piece of shit like him and his wife walk away. Fuck that. No way, Jose!"

"And that's where I came in," Quinn said. "That's why you gave me the mission, that's why you asked me to...*Eviscerate*."

"Well, we couldn't have any loose ends, now could we?" said Priest. "See, while working with the world's most dangerous drug cartel might seem like an unsuitable option, the test subjects were once again all failing. As it would turn out, they were just the wrong type. And so, we all began to look deeper. If it wasn't going to work on one demographic, then it was time to look for another..."

"Kids," interceded Quinn.

"Unfortunately, *yes*," Priest said. "Kids were always the answer."

Quinn reflected back to the time when he was first told about this Eviscerate mission.

He thought about when he vowed to stop child abuse because it was synonymous with his own past and his own pain. Quinn refused to let this be traded or explored. And yet, the man who gave him the opportunity to do this was the same man standing in front of him now.

"While the cartel could provide kids, what they didn't know was how I had already begun to research potential new subjects with entirely new ages. And I did that right here, in our very own backyard."

Hearing Priest, Quinn's gaze widened before his pupils twinkled with sadness...remorse.

Our own country. Our own kids...

It was then the next revelation began to dawn on Quinn. It shed light on yet another memory.

"Louisiana," he said. "*The Tenets.*" Quinn thought about his last mission.

The Eradicate mission was done to wipe out a cult that sacrificed young children in the name of a stupid deity. Quinn was always curious how Priest had come across this group.

Now, he knew.

"Yes," Priest said. "Sirius and Alistair, two hillbillies from the bayous who were experts in child trafficking at the time, so I went down there to see what was what."

"You actually planned to take kids, Priest? You were going to kidnap and kill kids from our own country?"

"God no!" The spook snapped at Quinn. Again, he was playing down the idea that he was at all close to the men he described. "I already told you; we didn't supply the people!"

Quinn, however, knew differently. No matter what he said, he was exactly the same as they were. Maybe he was worse.

"I just needed to work within an age bracket. What I needed was a certain...*type*," Priest said. "And I might have needed someone else to take the fall if Sinaloa didn't work out, so I went looking. See, when I considered the possibility, in the end, using orphans and runaways seemed too cliché. I mean, what I wanted to build wasn't some cheap knockoff of the fucking *Halo* or *Hitman* video games." Priest cackled at the reference. "We didn't just want to take children and pump them full of drugs. It's so redundant, so old-fashioned. What I wanted was something much better than that."

"So...why'd you kill them?" Quinn said. "Why'd you kill the Tenets?"

"Well," Priest said, "they knew who I was and I knew who they were. And, they were really fucking evil, and they knew my face, and well, I couldn't have any of that happening, so I sent my best and my brightest to go after them. Thankfully, you succeeded, just as you have now."

"But the cartels," Quinn said, "they know you too?"

"Sure they do, but see, they weren't the only ones connected to this pursuit," Priest said, "but yes...yes, you could say they knew me."

Quinn had said this exactly and he recalled specific instances whereby he killed for Priest, in the name of Priest! Prior to now, Priest convinced Quinn this was for himself, and only for himself. However, clearly, Ramos Mandilo was just a pawn removed because of his poor character and devilish ways.

Yet now, Quinn understood why Priest was not so different. No, he was the same.

"But see," Priest said as he giddily returned to his narration, "that's only where our story begins! Yes, I went to Louisiana searching for children, and yes, the Sinaloa Cartel was willing to provide this to us more than the Tenets were, but it wasn't until later that I discovered a much better way of doing things. I found a more *suitable* way of ensuring our future."

Quinn wanted to ask what this way was, but he declined.

It was only a matter of time before Priest explained it to him.

All Quinn had to do was stay quiet and think. He had a few ideas, but not before he was aware of how involved

Priest was in all this. It was like Priest said back when Quinn asked the ultimate question:

What did Priest want? What did he *really* want?

"Researching the earliest days of Hyper-X, which is a good name, by the way," Priest segued. "We just called it NX-17, but I like Hyper-X a lot better. It's very, *what's the word?* Greek-sounding? Mythological, almost," Priest continued. "Anyway..." Priest waved his hand and returned to making his main point. "The only successful test subject was a woman, from what I heard. Actually, a woman who was, at the time, very pregnant."

"*Pregnant?*" Quinn asked.

"Very early in her first trimester, in fact," explained Priest. "You see, her husband was a soldier, which means she was part of a military family, and so, she agreed to take the synthetic to see if it showed any promise."

"And did it?" Quinn asked. "Did this woman you speak of survive?"

"Oh yes, she did," added Priest. "For some years after, although she was bedridden for most of it and weak...yes, she did manage to survive..." Now, Quinn's memory was hazy. It was compromised by trauma, misguided principles, and the pursuit of absolution. Quinn remembered how his mother was bedridden, how she was sick. Back then, his father told his kids that she had come down with a complicated disease. If not for her family's wealth, the family would have been unable to keep themselves afloat, but they did.

Quinn was aware of how things could be when a person was bedridden.

More than this, Quinn was aware of the madness it created.

"But the compound didn't work on her..." As Priest said this, he was walking between the sections of the beds.

He moved in and out and took frequent glances of all the women as they slept.

"It did, however, work on her child, her *oldest* child."

"Oldest?" Quinn asked. Hands shaking and head throbbing, Quinn had come across yet another piece of the grand puzzle. It was a piece critical to the overall completion—the very one capable of bringing everything together in a great tapestry of hidden, epic truth.

In spite of this, Quinn couldn't stand the thought.

Too real, as the phrase goes. In this case, it was just hit too *damn* close to home.

"Yes," Priest said.

Quinn, battling a myriad of terrible thoughts rattling in his frail mind, they endlessly assaulted him with more memories of his mother. Quinn always wanted to know what happened to her. Always, he wanted to know why his father did what he did.

Now he was starting to see. Now, he was just starting to *realize*.

"Who was it?" Quinn said. "Who was this woman's child?"

Quinn watched Priest's maddening grin continue to spread. Priest leaned over the table and his stare gleamed with infatuation, almost jubilation.

"How do you think I met your father?" Priest asked Quinn.

"What?" Quinn said, flabbergasted by the resoluteness this one question granted.

"Your father," Priest replied. "How do you think I met him?"

"I...I..."

"I was very, *very* young when I did," explained Priest. "Actually, I had just started at the agency as one of their youngest recruits, out of high school you could say. I was working for the CIA. One might even say I was in the earliest stages of building the Custodian program then, but how do you think I met *him*? How do you think I found *you*?"

Quinn didn't answer. Again, he didn't have any power to speak.

"While I did recruit you." Priest now motioned to another table. He sat on its edge and crossed his arms. "I said I had been watching you, but how long do you think I had been, Quinn? Why do you think I came to find you, specifically you? How do you think I came across the great house of Quinn?"

Quinn's head continued to shake. He glimpsed down at his hands. They were shaking uncontrollably. Quinn wasn't sure if it was adrenaline or fear, rage or confusion, but suddenly, all Quinn's trauma surfaced in a giant, daunting wave of bad memories and horrifying thoughts and gripping emotions. He could not end the hold all of this had on him. Priest wielded such power. He had control of it.

"When I heard about an ex-Green Beret living in Canada and training his children to become deadly weapons, I had my suspicions, of course. However, when I heard *how* he was training them and how he was going to use them, well, let's just say I couldn't understand how anyone would survive such a process. So, I began to look closer, to look deeper. Then...then I found my answer."

Eyes closed and head down, Quinn counted down from ten.

"I know your father was a mean son of a bitch," Priest said, "but he was a mean son of a bitch who had a vision, and consequently, it was a vision of who could one day protect this great country of ours! He saw the potential in one specific type of operator, one who could perform at the highest level and achieve all the tasks spread out across our great military. One soldier, one purpose, one type, always...a *Custodian*."

"No," Quinn said, almost rendered speechless. "It's not...it can't be—"

"When I met your dad, sure," Priest cut Quin off from his moment of empathy, "I didn't know much about what he did, but as he educated me on the feats a human being was truly capable of, even if I didn't totally agree with his tactics, in the end, I couldn't argue with his results. I just needed his programming, his methodology. Now, I didn't like the Tenets," Quinn gulped when he heard their name. Priest had coerced Quinn into killing these men because they were pedophile pieces of shit. Apparently, they were just men who knew who Priest was and what he wanted to do. And so, Priest needed them eradicated. Quinn shuddered.

He was used...yet again.

"I just needed to know what they did," Priest continued, "and when I found out your dad was training this family's new security, well, I just weaved my web a little bit bigger." Priest laughed, but Quinn did not. He was being toyed with since the very beginning and he hated himself for not having seen it sooner. Then again, few can see beyond their own trauma and pain, and Quinn was no exception to this. "And if I could get your old man out of the picture," Priest said, "fine, but if he stuck around... well, I left that mission for you to decide."

The Eradicate mission in Louisiana flashed in Quinn's mind like a high-powered searchlight. Was that what it was about? Were Quinn's father and the Tenets ordered to be killed because Priest found someone better to smuggle?

Was he the one demanding test subjects, *children*?

Was that what this was about from the start?

"It's not possible," uttered Quinn. "Not—"

"What?" said Priest. He stood alongside the shivering Custodian. "Not ethical, not moral, not...*right*? All of these ideologies go out the door, Quinn, when you're trying to be the best at something. That's another lesson I learned from your father. He wanted to build a better soldier, and the only way to do that was to start as early as possible. And, by as early as possible, I don't mean as a fucking kid, no. No, I don't even mean when you come out of the bloody womb. No, a soldier moldable from the onset of his or her creation is the way to go. And so, it's by this principle—this idea—that KEYS was born!"

Arms spread; Priest was still joyous as before. At last, he had come to tell Quinn the full and complete story.

Quinn was not bred...he was *chosen*.

He was not trained...he was *made*.

His life and his upbringing had put Quinn on a path that, at the time, appeared only as coincidence. Yet, Quinn's trauma was a tool designed to coerce him into becoming something more. His duty as a Custodian was conceived well before he was ever welcomed into the guild. Priest used Quinn's dad to set him up, to play into his trauma, so he could cover his tracks. It was a ploy done only so he could build more Custodians.

The only problem was Quinn grew a conscience. He grew a soul.

"Sure I was too young to understand, I mean," Priest said, "I'm only what, five years older than you are, maybe? I mean, I met your father when you were still in JTF 2. When I heard about what he had convinced you to do, it all sounded so fucked up to me. But hey, the amount of fucked up shit that we've done, all of that is arbitrary, if you ask me. Does it work?" Priest asked. "Will it work? Those are the questions people in our position should ask and the only ones any of us should care about. And it's all we do. End the drug war, revolutionize our military, win, win, win! *Et voila!* Come on, Quinn, it doesn't get much better than that!"

Priest chuckled like a flippant clown—now relishing in the grand reveal of this masterfully woven narrative. Yes, Quinn was just a pawn and that's all he ever was.

"And where does my brother fit into all of this?" Quinn asked, barely able to say these next few words. "Why bring Cane into this...*web*?"

"Oh, I didn't bring him in," Priest said. "Well, at least, not exactly. Ramos hired him, sure, but once I found out he was another member of your family, I saw...*potential.*"

"Potential?" Quinn asked. "For what?" He never hated Priest more than he did at this moment.

"Completion," Priest finished. "I wanted to see who was stronger, who was worthier of what lied ahead."

"So you *used* me, used *us*?" barked Quinn. He was now also referring to his brother Cane. "You pretended like I was actually trying to do things right," Quinn said. "But, in the end, I was just...what, *equipment*? You were testing to see if I could work your way?"

"Oh, I wouldn't be too self-righteous there, Quinn," Priest replied. "You wanted a new path, so I gave you one. You always need an enemy and there's no greater enemy than the fucking cartels. Besides, fuck Ramos Mandilo," Priest said. "Fuck him and fuck his wife too. The shit they did over the years...they deserved everything they had coming to them. And don't deny how that path made you stronger. So did your mother, she—"

"Don't you dare say her name," warned Quinn.

"But she gave you an incredible gift, Quinn," Priest expressed as if dignity meant something to him now. "She was willing to risk her own life to produce something, *someone...*" When Priest began to rephrase, Quinn squeezed his eyes together so tight he could feel every wrinkle, every taut piece of compressed skin.

Priest speaking about Quinn's mother cut the Custodian deep. Even the slightest mention brought agony and forced Quinn to turn away in disgust.

"Who could protect and serve in ways no one else could. See, your father developed a program so intense that, if properly implemented to fetuses infused with Hyper-X, it would amalgamate all our special forces. Yes, all combined into one devastating unit, Quinn. Imagine it, Quinn, an entire legion of Custodians—true warriors that used your DNA in order to become stronger, to become... *better*."

"My *what*?"

Priest sneered at Quinn and pushed his hands into the table.

"Your DNA," Priest said to Quinn. "It is in *your* DNA."

"What is?" Quinn asked, astonished. Quinn did not simply choose to become a killer.

He was made to become one.

Then, this was not because of a mission or because of his upbringing.

It was because it was Quinn's birthright. *His fate.*

"Hyper-X," Priest said. "It didn't *make* you, no...but what we noticed, based on what your mother said, was it did show greater results in those who experienced some kind of trauma, whether it be early or later in life. See, Quinn, pain produces a specific chemical in the brain," Priest described the process and Quinn gawked. "And so, whenever you experienced pain or trauma, Hyper-X was able to reshape it," said Priest. "And, should the subject acquire the right amount of strength, which you clearly did, it would propel and sustain them in ways nothing else could. Granted, Custodians are known to have many strengths, but given your background as well as your father's regimen, you were the beginning of what would one day be the final piece to this grand puzzle."

"Programmed," Quinn stated.

When he thought about what Priest had said about the nature of trauma and suppression, Quinn instantly thought of his father. Quinn could then see all the days whereby he was fighting his old man but doing so primarily within the confines of his unstable mind. He went toe-to-toe against someone who felt so vivid and so real but was just a figment of his disturbed and twisted imagination.

And now he understood why. It was Hyper-X—the very chemical coursing through his veins and activating all of Quinn's skills, it was reshaping his pain so he could become stronger.

This was why he was made.

"No," Priest said to Quinn. "*Perfected.*"

"So...Sinaloa looked like they were making this synthetic, you effectively end the drug war, and in doing so, you also create an army of new, *better Custodians.* One drug to replace all other drugs and a new soldier to replace all other soldiers."

Now Quinn understood. He could see the whole picture, and it was terrifying.

"Like I said," Priest said. "*It's perfect.* Less pain, more strength, a tool every single person in this country could use."

"Perfect?" Quinn repeated.

Priest said nothing. He said nothing and he just smiled. When Quinn stood next to a sleeping woman, he considered how many were currently with child and how many were soon to be born in his name.

How many would follow in Quinn's footsteps and become part of his legacy of self-destruction and hardship?

How many? *How many?*

"One day, you will come to understand all of this, Quinn," Priest said. "One day, you will see that all your pain and all your anguish wasn't for nothing. No, it was the commencement of a force that will save and protect this country for years to come."

"I was..." When Quinn spoke now, he felt weak because he was fatally wounded by everything he was told.

Betrayed by his past decisions, and the things he could not embrace, Quinn's hand shook against the table. He tried to resist them, but as he was told, this...*this* was part of who he was.

"I tried to be better. I tried to..."

"Turn over a new leaf?" Priest asked Quinn. "Become a *new* man, *better man*?"

Priest hissed. It was clear he enjoyed poking fun at Quinn's supposed revelation and his pursuit of *higher morality*.

"There's no leaf, Quinn. There's no killing people for a greater cause or for preserving life. There's no honor, creed, code, or whatever else helps people sleep better at night. There are just people who know how the world works and those who don't. There are those who are willing to carve out their own path and use whatever they have to use in order to ensure that certain things stay safe and protected. You can call yourself a new Custodian or a bringer of justice or whatever the else you fucking call it, but to be honest, I don't care what you want or are. As long as you keep killing and keep fighting, you'll see, Quinn. You'll see that's how you really make a difference, how you really change the world."

"For *you*," Quinn said, now summoning the strength he needed to stand up and to stand tall. "You had me killing...for *you*."

The clarity of his purpose became jumbled in Quinn's consciousness so much so that it blurred his vision. What Priest had manipulated Quinn into doing, he couldn't stand the thought of. He wanted to gag. Worse...Quinn wanted to kill.

"You forced me to turn against family, my own blood, and you kept turning me because that's what you do. You *turn*."

"And what you do is follow orders," disputed Priest. "That was our agreement from the beginning. I was the one you said you would obey and never deny, no matter what. And don't pretend like you ever cared about your family! All you've ever needed was to put the past behind you, and I am giving you the opportunity to do that now, *finally*. You can finish what you started. Be the last man standing and solidify your place as the greatest among your kin. It's the last step—all that's left for you to achieve."

"No," Quinn said. "I won't."

"What?"

"I won't do it," Quinn said to Priest. "I won't follow you anymore. I will not serve. I will not help you with whatever it is you're trying to build and I will not help you to create more people like me. I will not become him. I will not become my father!"

As Quinn made this epic declaration, his only hope was that it felt true and real.

At least, he wanted it to be.

Yet, Quinn thought maybe he said this because he thought it was the right thing to say.

Quinn recalled the words of a prior enemy, Mr. Sirius Tenet. He was the first who insisted Quinn was not so different than him and his kind. And now, hearing Priest say this exact thing, Quinn repeated the same phrase.

I will not become my father. I will not become my father.

"I know this is difficult for you to accept, Quinn, but as I said..."

"No!" Quinn exploded. He reached a point of vulnerability rarely revealed.

Now was the time to do it. It was time to tell Priest this truth.

"I'm done playing games," Quinn said. "I'm done listening to your lies, Priest, and I'm done pretending like you've ever cared about me. You've never wanted to help or protect. All you've ever wanted was to use, and this..." Quinn looked around the room. Everything he saw made him sick to his stomach. "All of this just proves what lengths you'll go to get what you want!" Quinn's anger was palpable. The veins in his neck looked like weeds growing beneath his skin. "There's no line you won't cross! You'll abandon all your principles just so you can win!"

Eyes shut; Quinn needed a second before opening them again.

"But it's not *who I am,* and it's not who I'm going to be," Quinn continued. "And if that means breaking the cardinal rule to which all Custodians are bound by, then so be it. I'm going to do it because, for once, I'm going to do what needs to be done that doesn't involve murder or suffering. I'm going to walk away, because walking away... *is the only way.*"

"The only way?" Priest beckoned like an impassioned preacher.

Quinn nodded. "Yes."

"You do realize that if you refuse to abide by these new objectives, then you'll be disavowing yourself from our order. If you do that, then you know what you'll be asking for."

"I do," acknowledged Quinn.

"So...what you're saying is...you now wish to be... *Extricated?*"

Quinn nodded.

What Priest said to Quinn was a concept mentioned within the lore of the *Custodial Order*. It was a choice no Custodian ever made but all were warned about.

Should a Custodian abandon the brotherhood, if they were to turn their backs in any capacity, then they would be classified as *Extricated*. Such a path was forbidden. There was no leaving the brethren and there was no denying its code. If a Custodian thought about fleeing from this life, they would be *hunted*.

They would be the *prey* for all other Custodians to feast on.

None survived this classification. Yes, Quinn was skilled and he was strong, but invincible? No. *No one was.*

Quinn learned of a synthetic capable of enhancing performance. It was a compound that used one's pain as a propellent to gain peak level abilities. Even with this inside him, Quinn could not resist the other Custodians. They were the finest assassins and the most gifted killers in the world. If extricated, all of them would be coming for Quinn. And yet, in spite of all the impending danger and in spite of maintaining his honor, Quinn was prepared. He was ready.

"Yes."

As Quinn agreed, Priest snarled. The joy that was a staple of Priest's persona had now vanished. He had returned to the cunning and cold madman without conscience or empathy. Priest gawked at Quinn. "Well then, if that is true, then I am sorry, old friend. I am sorry for what lies ahead."

"I'm not." Quinn's shoulders were pushed back and his chest flexed. He would make no apologies about his decision. It was his and no one else's.

"Not yet, but you will be."

Quinn watched as Priest stood before him. He looked at Quinn with his brows furrowed. With one choice left to make, all Quinn had to do was vacate this secret lab and save these women. He couldn't do this and escape Priest at the same time. Armed with his tonfa, Quinn and Priest both glowered at each other. And yet, not one of them wanted to make the first move.

Never did Quinn see Priest in action.

Quinn couldn't imagine he was capable enough to prevent Priest from getting away.

This was what Quinn assumed, and that was his biggest mistake.

Quinn pulled the SIG and Priest pulled a Colt.

Guns blazing, Quinn fell as Priest took cover behind a pillar. Quinn looked at his body. He assumed he was spared, but he was wrong. A small hole appeared near his ribcage. It was tiny, but wide enough for Quinn to fit his whole finger inside. It was not a killshot, and he was so fucking grateful it wasn't.

The bullet had left Quinn's body but hurt like a motherfucker.

He couldn't believe Priest shot him. He was a decent shot, better than Quinn anticipated.

"Didn't think I'd get ya, did ya?" Priest uttered from

behind the pillar. "You think I'm only good for giving orders? Well, you'd be wrong again there too, brother. I might not have the training, but I do know a thing or two. You'll see."

"Yeah," Quinn said, his hand pressed to his now bleeding side. "I think I'd like to see that."

"Would ya now?" Priest asked. "*Would ya'*?"

"Anyone can shoot someone," Quinn said. "Everyone can get lucky..." Quinn looked at his hand. It was covered in blood. "At least *once.*"

"Is that what you think that was?" Priest asked.

Quinn heard Priest's laughter as more blood spilled from his body.

"You think that was luck, huh?" Priest asked.

"Care to prove me wrong?" Quinn replied.

Priest snorted and Quinn clutched his gun and checked the clip.

There were eight rounds left. More than enough for someone like Quinn. His plan, however, did not align with him using every bullet at one time. He had not once seen Priest fight, but Quinn wanted to see what else Priest, a.k.a. the Lock Smith, could do. And what Quinn hoped to see was a capability best expressed without a fucking pistol.

"Well, you know me," commented Priest. He was now a fucking performer on his way to a stage. "I'm all about proving people wrong."

Quinn glared and Priest glimpsed at the gun.

"What's the saying said before two people get into a fight?"

Quinn shrugged. He didn't know what Priest was talking about.

"Shall we begin?" Quinn asked. He didn't know if that's what the saying was.

"No, not that," added Priest. He blushed excitedly. "Oh, I know, how about...always watch your back?" Priest asked Quinn.

"What?" Quinn was off-guarded.

From out of nowhere, a body dropped from behind Quinn like a ninja. Quinn should have known Priest would never fight by himself. Also, he should have known better to watch his back.

Recently, Quinn had made some fatal mistakes. He was not the killer he once was.

Now Quinn had been whacked with a bamboo Bo staff that shocked him to a whole new level of epic brutality. Fighting back, Quinn raised his hand and tried to block the staff, but his forearm was bruised, almost broken. Afterward, Quinn lost balance and fell. As he hit the ground, the top of the staff connected with Quinn's right temple. He was out before he could grab a new weapon. Cane stood over Quinn.

The gunshot wound and the concussion both compromised Quinn. He could barely see and barely stand.

"Ah-ha." Taking a deep breath, the disappointment began to weigh on the Custodian. He was staring at his brother, now wearing a red shirt, and after Quinn saw him...he also saw Priest. He was now making his way toward Quinn and grinning as he relished in his fall.

"Nicely done," Priest said to Cane. "Very nice, indeed."

Quinn's head was spinning. Once he was down, Priest pulled a vial from his coat. He kneeled and scooped a few drops of Quinn's blood into the glass container. Gathering what he could, Quinn jerked to avoid being touched by his former employer. Quinn moved only an inch and Cane gouged the tip of the Bo deeper into his brother's chest.

Cane kept Quinn from squirming even a millimeter.

DNA, Hyper-X, replication, all were ideas assaulting Quinn like a fearsome storm. After hearing Priest, he provided insight as to why Quinn's blood was being gathered.

"What are you going to do with that?"

When Cane asked Priest this question, he was slipping the vial back into his jacket. "Sustain it, replicate it, and then test it," Priest said. "It's been my plan all along."

"Hmm," Cane said, casual and aloof. "Then you remember our deal then," added Cane. "Once it's ready, you will..."

"Give you the newest dosage," Priest said. "I said I would, and I will."

Priest exhaled. Quinn thought he sounded gratified and exhausted at the same time. Yet, now was the moment for Quinn to make his final stand. Like always, the clock was ticking.

"You spent your whole life trying to be as good as your brother," Priest said to Cane, "and now you will have the one thing that made him better than you."

"I am better," stated Cane as he mounted his defense.

What was said—even Quinn knew—was done out of spite, rage, and torment.

"And now," Priest said, "you will have the opportunity to prove it." Priest turned and placed his hand on Cane's shoulder.

Then, Quinn, struck with déjà vu, he could see that Priest's gesture mirrored all the occasions whereby Cane and Quinn had encountered one another. Quinn regretted every one of them.

"Remember our deal," Priest said to Cane. "I brought you here only as insurance. Should he not wish to follow orders, then you're going to have to make sure he doesn't follow anything ever again. Understand?"

Cane nodded. It was understood.

"Good luck," Priest said to Cane. Then, walking away with his hands in his pockets, he proceeded back toward the door. Quinn glared.

"I only wish you would have seen things the way I did, Quinn," Priest said. "You are good at so much, but the one thing you are not good at, my friend, is...well, you're just not good at keeping an open mind or...accepting the truth."

Quinn gawked.

"You could never see the big picture," Priest continued, "and I always knew that would be your downfall. And now, it will be done at the hands of your very own family. My only hope is that you can do what you could not before..." Quinn scowled as Priest stepped into the elevator. "Finish what you said you would," Priest said before going on his merry way. "End the bonds that have broken you. Will you? Could you? I guess we'll just have to wait and see."

Shrugging now, and with both doors closed, Quinn watched as Priest once again began to flee. Quinn did not see anyone leaving the room.

The Custodian gazed at his brother.

Backing down, Cane gave Quinn some space as he began to remove his coat. He was lighter than Quinn. And, while he was holding on tightly to his Bo, Quinn's tonfa remained secured in his back.

"You don't have to do this," Quinn advised his brother. "Priest is a liar. Don't let him get inside your head. Trust me. Not worth it."

Cane jeered after hearing Quinn's sound advice.

"And now you're going to pretend like you don't know

why I'm here?" asked Cane. "You don't know how I've been waiting for this moment for a very, very long time, do you? You would be so happy to bow out now because you're injured, because the game got the better of you, but you still have to finish it. Then again...maybe you're too afraid to do that too?"

Cane was almost the same age as Quinn was. Even still, Cane was burdened with a pain Quinn understood too well. "I don't want to fight you," Quinn declared. He was clear. This was *not* the way.

"And yet, you have to," Cane replied. Holding his Bo with two hands, Cane pointed its tip at Quinn and extended it as an invitation to their inevitable face-off.

Quinn accepted it now. He could not change his brother's mind.

Still, everything Quinn said was true. He did not want to fight Cane. Blood spilling to Quinn's aching ribs, red drops pattered the floor, and Quinn recalled a time that was now fleeting.

At last, what Priest said and what Cane said, became absolutely true.

Quinn had to finish what he started. He had no other choice.

"Fight," Cane said. "Fight me...*now*."

———

How could anyone kill their own family?

Becoming a monster is determined by a series of tests, each one designed to prove empathy, emotional intelligence, and plain human engagement and self-awareness. Each one is also centered on the universal question that asks how far is one willing to go to get what one wants? What lines is a person willing to cross in the name of victory and power? If you kill, then you have now entered the realm of bad, no doubt. You have lost a part of your humanity and your soul. But, if a person is capable of killing family, then you have lost your soul, or maybe you never had one in the first place.

Quinn knew this.

More than this, he accepted it. This was why Quinn would not kill Cane. He wouldn't even if his own survival depended on it. He couldn't kill, but he also couldn't run. No, Quinn's goal was not to turn away or to deny. It was to do something he never had before. Believing he could still change his brother's mind; Quinn was going to reach out. He was going to tell Cane the truth and he was also going to try and save him.

He actually *wanted* to save his brother.

Now, Quinn was never one for faith. All that was in his heart was the possibility of one day changing and becoming something better. He had faith now. Actually, it was all he had now. Quinn spun his tonfa. He was to initiate no attacks or show aggression of any kind. It was just defense and hope. *A lot* of hope.

"You know I won't attack first," Quinn said to his brother. "So go ahead, make your move."

Cane smirked, cracked his neck, and raised his staff.

Quinn lifted his tonfa. Cane stomped. Quinn held his ground. He refused to do anything less. Having not fought anyone who was armed with a Bo staff, a weapon like that was as versatile as it was unpredictable.

Nevertheless, Quinn remained true to his previous strategy.

Don't end. *Save.*

Quinn's brother twirled his Bo like a propeller, and then he lunged and jabbed. Spinning the baton, Quinn stepped away from Cane and used his tonfa to deflect and spare himself of all blows. The moves summoned by his brother's hand bested Quinn at every turn. And, when Quinn hit the staff, the Bo immediately sprang in a new direction.

Cane clobbered Quinn's chest.

Cane spun the weapon not only in his hands, but around his head, his hips, and back. The Custodian crossed his tonfa and fell down to one knee. While Quinn was down, Cane spun again, delivering a flying tornado kick. The blow smoked Quinn's jaw.

The tonfa did provide some protection, but it was only marginal. Quinn kipped-up without using his arms. It was a badass move but difficult to pull off now. Now back on his feet, still, Quinn was faced with more unrelenting attacks from Cane.

Down and up, left, right, center, all of them came one after the other. Quinn pivoted and continued to sweep his feet. But the effort required was breaking him down, very slowly.

"Ha!" Cane hit Quinn with a straight kick.

Being the superior combatant, Cane was flexing all his abilities simultaneously. In an act of sheer vengeance, Cane was showing off. He was bragging. He was showing Quinn exactly how much better he was than him.

He was the better Quinn!

"Hi-yah!" Cane kicked Quinn to the floor again. The Custodian tumbled over a nearby table. Spinning around, Quinn lost both weapons. He now stood with his hands completely free.

"Pick up your weapon!" Cane yelled. "Go! Do it now!"

Quinn was so stiff he was made of ice. Still, he held his ground and stayed true to his word. No, he would *not* take his new weapon.

"I said pick up your weapon!" Cane jabbed Quinn's chest with the staff and knocked his brother to the floor.

Quinn fell and his bleeding face ricocheted the surface. "No."

The pain that once started in Quinn's cut spread to the rest of his throbbing torso as he stood again.

"Fight!" Cane nailed his brother again with another strike.

Cane wielded the Bo horizontally and pounded Quinn's nose and forced a fracture. Once Cane hit Quinn, he knocked his brother over another table.

"Fight back, you coward!" Cane tucked the Bo behind him and wrapped his hand around Quinn's bruised neck. He pushed Quinn up and thrashed his brother like he was a fucking toy. Quinn took his licks and still refused to retaliate. Whenever he heard Cane yell, Quinn could hear his father too.

"Fight back! Fight back!"

Now in that cold basement where he was bred and made, Quinn wanted to tell Cane to stop but knew damn well he would not.

All of this was Quinn's fault. He was the one who made Cane into what he is. He was the same man his father was. He hurt and he destroyed. And, after enduring whatever Cane produced with his staff, still, it would not be enough.

Quinn would stand and he would stay.

"Ah!" Unleashing a monumental roar of pure aggression, Cane had mustered all his rage. He delivered every blow, and Quinn, now in desperate need of a hospital, when he was hit again, did his best to evade.

When Cane swung the staff back around, Quinn performed the only move he could while so fragile and broken. He lifted his leg, and with the Bo flush against

Cane's chest, Quinn had just enough in him for one final show of action. Quinn severed Cane's Bo in two pieces. The padding on Quinn's shins assisted him when doing this. Being the last strike, it was his concluding demonstration of power and destruction. What came later was Cane holding the broken pieces.

He squeezed the two sticks the way Quinn held his tonfa.

Snapping the Bo, Quinn hit Cane's chest. This forced Cane back as he whipped the pieces aside. Cane jabbed and clocked Quinn in the face. Pounding with the same unapologetic wrath as delivered so far, Quinn let his body go limp. His best bet was to let his brother unload whatever was still left, which Quinn hoped wasn't much. In that moment, Cane dished out a few more blows while Quinn took a step back. Almost falling, somehow, Quinn found a way to still stand somehow. He reviewed all his techniques, but all Quinn delivered was one last aikido pin.

Quinn bent his brother at the wrist and stepped. Executing the pin, Cane returned and kicked Quinn for the last time. Then Cane crawled over Quinn and—grabbing the collar of his brother's body armor—pulled him close.

"Fight!" Cane screamed from so close that Quinn's ears hurt. Compared to the rest of Quinn's body, it was inconsequential.

"Fight!" Cane smacked Quinn again. He struck until every ridge of his brother's mug was bludgeoned and Quinn's face was reduced to a heap of mushed cartilage and torn muscle. Beaten almost to death, Quinn was holding on by a slender thread. He could hold for as long as he could. But, fueled by malice and vengeance, Cane might not continue because the fight was off balance. It was no longer a challenge for either Quinn.

When Cane demanded Quinn fight back, the Custodian had just enough strength to utter one last syllable. "*No.*"

Cane, sweaty from the beatings, he was at the same time so exasperated after feeling his brother's countless shots he could barely breathe. Should Quinn get hit again, then he'd be in the ER for surgery. He accepted it as a fate well deserved for what he'd done.

It was a show of grace—a plea for forgiveness.

Willing to take his fair share of pain, Quinn's lips moved but he couldn't speak. He couldn't speak because his throat was so constricted all he could do was cough and gag.

"You...son of a bitch, Kyle. You son of..." Cane teared and Quinn moaned.

Cane didn't know what else he could do.

More blood dribbled from Quinn's crooked mouth. At this moment, he cared about nothing. He didn't care for his life or his mission. He didn't care that Priest had betrayed him and he didn't care about Ally. Quinn wanted to communicate a message to his brother Cane. By submitting and refusing to fight, Quinn hoped this message was received.

"You won't do it, will you? You won't...*fuck you.*" Head shaking, Cane's voice was fractured and he raised his unsteady hand.

"Who would have thought you...*you* would be the one to get a conscience? You would be the one to follow a fucking *creed*?"

Weakened by agony, even the slightest flinch caused Quinn to feel bursts of intense pain. Still, Quinn generated the perfect response to what Cane had said.

"I'm..." Quinn felt all the muscles in his face starting to stretch. His pain threshold expanded to include so much and now, Quinn could still see his father as a ghost in the room before he willed him away. Quinn made him vanish like he was never there. "I'm *not* our father."

Taking time to finish, Quinn looked at Cane and offered his hand even though he was the one down on the ground. Should Cane take it, then Quinn could still help him. But, should Cane not, then he was truly beyond saving, beyond help. Should any of these outcomes come to pass, then the bond the brothers shared both by name and by trauma would be gone forever.

Yet, Quinn refused to believe this was true. Somewhere, deep inside, there was light.

There was a way back.

On Quinn's hand, Cane was now reaching out of the darkness and easing himself toward the other side. Quinn's offer was a symbol; a symbol of how he was still waiting for Cane to walk away, to follow him out of the shadows and into this new place. So long as Cane was willing to try, then Quinn didn't have to go down the road that most never return from.

Hand steady, Cane inched himself toward it.

Seeing a spark in Cane's dull gaze, for Quinn, this was all the hope he had left. It was a mark of potential and change. And, just before Cane could embrace it, Quinn listened to the hard whistle of a fired high-caliber handgun.

"Ah." Cane's face had suddenly frozen into a pout.

Quinn held his brother. His throat tight, his lashes fluttered...in shock.

A clean shot pierced Cane through his right temple and Quinn caught his brother just as he began to fall. Now the one holding back tears, what Quinn heard seconds after the gunshot was Cane taking his last breath. This was followed by the daunting, conniving sound of Priest's snarling voice.

"Never develop a conscience in this game, Quinn, not when you still have a mission to finish..."

Eyes back, Quinn raised his hand. Burning with his own stream of corrosive rage, Quinn's persona was a potent mix of retribution, anger, and heartache.

"Also..." Holding his Desert Eagle, Priest's choice of weapon was obvious. A weapon like the Eagle shot heavy rounds. Its barrel was still smoking as Priest stared at Quinn with his signature maniacal grin. He gleamed with relish; an almost sexual delight. "Always follow your fucking orders, never go back on your word."

"Priest." Quinn continued to rely on Cane despite knowing there was no way of saving him now. He died instantly in Quinn's arms.

"You break rules," Priest said, "you suffer consequences. This is a reality you should start preparing for. In the end, I am the only one who knows what you're capable of, Quinn."

Quinn's fury had birthed copious amounts of thriving adrenaline and created a whole new brand of hatred for the Custodian to feel.

"You don't know what I'm capable of." Quinn declared. He stepped forward while Priest sauntered toward the elevator. Keeping his gun aimed, Priest began to exit the room. Quinn thought Priest would be gone forever, but he wasn't. "We'll see."

Quinn heard Priest's ominous response. He thought it would alter his current reality. Quinn also thought it would somehow bring his brother back to life. Burdened by so much anguish, Quinn felt one last burst of energy. This was not conjured from passion or desire, will or pride. It did not come from any emotion that could give a man life. And, as Quinn had come so close to death, the only one that served him well was his anger, was his rage.

Quinn's boots pushed into the cracked floor and he was set to sprint.

"Priest!" Quinn stampeded after the man who once owned him. Priest fired several rounds as Quinn veered to an empty table.

Now gripping it by the edge, Quinn brought the table to his chest and flipped it over so he could use it as a shield. Heavy and thick, the table should be resistant to bullets. Now with the table in front of Quinn, he glimpsed at Priest. The first shot clipped the edge and dinged near Quinn's ear. When Quinn felt the second shot, he squatted and, using the table, blocked himself from the incoming rounds.

Feeling another, Quinn's pace quickened.

Now moving fast, Quinn was unrelenting. Priest fired again. He managed to skim Quinn's left arm.

"Ha!" Still channeling rage, Quinn dropped the table and leaped while Priest began to reload. When Quinn landed, he rolled. When he jumped again, he saw the elevator door about to close.

"Too slow, Quinn," Priest taunted. "Too fucking slow."

But Quinn was not done yet. He reached in and jammed his fingers between the doors.

Stretching his shoulders, Quinn gritted his teeth as he pulled. With Priest still in the room he never really left, the madman clutched his Desert Eagle and waited for the next shot.

Quinn knew what Priest was going to do and he didn't care. He was fearless of Priest's plan to retaliate and pushed himself in headfirst. Now inside the elevator,

Quinn turned every which way, looking for Priest. And yet, even in such a close space, he managed to slip away.

But the elevator was empty.

"Priest!" Quinn shouted. Above him, a hatch swayed.

Quinn snaked his way out from the narrow section but screamed his name until he felt satisfied enough to stop. While there was no satisfaction and no end, Quinn persisted until his echo became his only companion.

With little left, Quinn couldn't stand unless he absolutely wanted to.

And he did, because right now, it was *all* he would ever want to do.

———

Quinn was never one for funerals.

He had attended too many throughout his life, but Cane deserved one.

Once Quinn found his way out of the underground lab, he contacted Ally. He sent her what he could, what he knew, like longitudes and latitudes taken from his phone, which was surprisingly still on his person. He didn't care who came to find him. In the state he was, death was not the worst outcome.

He carried Cane's body to a small section of the secluded forest beyond the lab. There, he laid Cane down and gathered as many stones as he could find. Quinn placed them over his brother's body and, being so isolated, imagined none would ever see the makeshift grave.

Quinn stood tall, folded his hands, and did his best to look at the tomb belonging to the only man he ever loved.

"I'm sorry, brother. I'm so sorry."

Regardless of Quinn's intentions or his truth, an apology did not erase the deed or the pain he caused. It didn't provide healing or, for that matter, forgiveness. Quinn's path was one paved with broken memories. It consisted of suffering and much regret, but now it included ways of growing and, maybe one day, recovery and reconciliation.

Where Quinn was going now was a place he didn't think he would ever see again.

In spite of all his attempts to pursue justice and protect those who needed it, the cost of nobility was too great. The man Quinn trusted had revealed himself to be nothing more than a sinister manipulator of epic proportions. So, Quinn was wrong about so much and was possibly wrong about everything else he planned to do too. And now, while staring at his dead brother, helicopter blades chopped above his head and interrupted the moment of solace and silence.

Quinn heard these sounds but he also heard Ally.

Trudging the terrain, Ally called out to Quinn like he was her missing child.

"Kyle! Kyle! My god, are you okay?" Ally sounded off.

Standing there, Quinn had yet to give Ally his full attention. He was not unhappy to see her, only relieved she had found him so quickly.

"I can't believe I found you!"

"Not just me," Quinn replied.

At this moment, he had nothing to say. Even thinking about speaking about what happened left a king-size hole in Quinn's gut. It was so big it practically swallowed his soul.

"Is that Priest?" Ally stared at the grave now while Quinn kept his eyes closed.

Three days ago, Quinn was killing for Priest. Now, he was the one Quinn wanted to bury. "No. Not Priest."

"Who is it then?" Ally asked.

Quinn gulped.

He had just witnessed his brother's head get blown apart by a large caliber bullet. He watched his skull burst into tiny, mutilated pieces just as Quinn was offering to help save his life. Seeing all of this again, Quinn flinched before inhaling. "My brother." Voice cracking, Quinn could barely get the words out.

"Your brother?" continued Ally, surprised to hear what Quinn said.

"He's gone."

"Jesus. And Priest, where's he now?"

"Gone too," Quinn said. "All gone."

"Gone where, though?" Ally said, now standing in front of Quinn. Poised before the assembly of rocks—his brother's grave—Quinn sank deeper into his brokenness and peril. "Where did he go?"

Head shaking, Quinn replied. "I don't know, but he won't be back, and neither will I."

"What do you mean?" Ally asked Quinn.

He wished he had more time to explain, but with so much to unpack and to elaborate on, Quinn needed to bear in mind he was no longer under the employ of someone who could protect him.

He was *extricated* and soon, he would be *hunted.*

"Priest was behind it all," Quinn said. "The cartels, Hyper-X, my brother, he was just using me to get what he wanted. It all started in Louisiana," Quinn explained, "where he tried to recruit the Tenets and use my father to build a new Custodian program. He made me think he wanted my dad killed, knowing I wouldn't be able to do it, and he could use me more and I would just open more doors for him to walk through without considering the consequences. They were working together the whole time, and he was using me to cover up his shit. It was all just a scheme, one big fucking game that I fell for because I thought I could change. It was me. My fault."

"My god. Okay," Ally said, assembling a plan of action. She brought her hand to her forehead and Quinn could see she needed a second to gather her thoughts. "Okay, okay, so...Priest is involved? Okay, well...well that's...look," Ally said again. "First, we have to get you out of here, okay? I can get you to Langley. There, we can talk about your status, maybe find out where to put you until we get this whole thing sorted out."

"No," Quinn said to outrightly deny Ally's proposal. "Wouldn't get half a mile before Priest finds out where I am. He's a beacon of unlimited reach and control. And now that I've told him I'm going to extricate myself. I'm on his list. They're going to come for me."

"Extricate?" asked Ally. "What? Who? Who's coming for you?"

The *who* Quinn was speaking about were them—the other Custodians. Each one was an expert in whatever it is they did, and each one killed without mercy or shame. There were no barriers they would not cross and no world they could not infiltrate or destroy. And so, two, three, or more were enough to bring even the greatest adversary to their knees, including a skilled killer like Kyle Quinn.

But when Quinn heard Ally ask this question, he grunted his response. "*The best.*"

"Okay," Ally replied. "We can still get you out of here. We can help you."

"No one can stop what's coming," Quinn said. "Not you, not the people you work for. No one."

Quinn looked at Ally with a hard stare. Her eyes were closed and she had fallen silent. Quinn assumed she was now imagining the storm now approaching because that's exactly what he was doing. "A war is coming, a storm...*is on the horizon,"* Quinn said. "And when it comes, everyone caught in it will die. The endgame is here—the consequences for trying to be better, and all of it is coming...*for me.*"

Quinn could feel Ally standing by his shoulder, as close now as she'd ever been.

"So much death," Quinn said. "So much pain, and for what, for *who?*"

"You did what you thought was right," Ally said, "and I'm sure you did all you could to save him."

Quinn could not embrace this truth, even if Ally believed it. No, as Quinn's head shook, his lips curled into his parched mouth. "Only after I tried killing him." Quinn said this about his brother. Then, with a deep breath, he kneeled before his grave and extended his hand. "I have broken everything," Quinn said. "And now, I have disavowed myself from the only people who could get me to pay for my sins. I did it even though I knew the consequences."

"This *isn't* your fault, Kyle," Ally said to Quinn. "You were trying to protect people, trying to stop whatever Priest and your dad were doing. That's the only reason why you agreed to his mission, and that's the only reason why I'm here now."

"None of that matters if he's still out there," Quinn said. "It won't matter once he lights the beacons and the others come to answer the call."

Quinn rotated his ring around his finger. The beacon he'd spoken of was *not* the one in his hands. No, he was speaking of another. It was a beacon much larger. It was the light the other Custodians would follow once shown.

"The bell's been rung," Quinn said. "The pieces are moving. It won't be long now..."

"So...you're just going let them, what, come and find you?" Ally's tone was fractured.

She was trying not to cry, but the tears still managed to fill her once affirmed gaze. However, Quinn could see she was considering the idea. She was struggling with the possibility that Quin could—he might—die.

And this hurt Ally. It was painful for her to even think about.

Quinn never doubted Ally cared for him.

Yet now, whatever doubt might've been inside had faded away. Quinn wanted to tell Ally his feelings for her were the same. He wanted to say he had enough time, but he didn't. It never was enough. There was never enough time.

"I made a choice," Quinn said. "I ended the operation but made a new enemy. I started a war against those like me. It's the worst decision, because it's the most dangerous decision, but it's not—"

"The wrong decision." When Ally completed the rest of Quinn's thought, finally, the Custodian stood up and turned. With the will to actually look the love of his life in the eyes, Ally leered and Quinn wanted her to do something other than just stare.

"I have to do this. I have to finish it," Quinn declared. "I have to *end* it."

"I know," Ally said.

"So long as Priest remains, there's no telling what he'll do, not just to me."

"I know," Ally said again.

"And I'm..." Quinn swallowed back his words as they crept up into his throat.

He was neither chivalrous, charming, or romantic. But, with the occasion created, it might be Quinn's last opportunity to tell Ally the truth. As he did this, Quinn took Ally by the hand, and right away, she fell into his arms. Embracing Quinn like it was the last time she ever would, the probability that the two would never see each other again was not only likely, it was an unbearable certainty.

Still, despite his level and reputation, Quinn couldn't kill everyone.

What he possessed was a gift once thought of only as a curse. Born and bred, Quinn would need to summon everything he learned and more if he was to survive. He would need to use all he'd gained if he was to stand even the slightest chance against what lay ahead. And, as Quinn cradled Ally, his chin rested on top of her head. She was his last and only motivation.

"I'm going to make it," Quinn said to Ally. "I'm going to make it, and I promise...*I will see you again.*"

Shedding a tear now would only ruin the moment. Quinn's emotions were connected to his vulnerabilities. None of this could exist if he was not empathetic, and he was. Quinn had now been freed of the unwarranted, mutilated, and abusive chains that once held him prisoner. And, if this was to be the last time he was ever going to see Ally, then Quinn wanted to tell her everything. He wanted her to know that she was his reason for being, she was his heart and his mind, his body and his spirit; *his last and only mission.*

"I will." Quinn pulled back and Ally sniffled to suppress more of her tears. She was awakened by another spirit she also could not deny. Quinn gasped.

"Well, if you're going to go to war, then you're going to need more than what you have. That's for certain. You're going to need weapons, locations, allies," Ally said. "And for that, I can help you. And if Priest is looking for you,"

Ally continued, "and there is nowhere you can go, don't run. You have to take the fight to him."

Such was Quinn's plan from the beginning. Hearing Ally say it offered Quinn affirmation and encouragement. "Yeah," he said. "Yes."

"But for now," Ally said, "you need a way out of here."

"I do."

"Take the Ducati."

"My brother's ride?" Quinn thought back to Cane's motorcycle. He remembered seeing it before.

"The same," Ally replied. "Do you have the keys?"

"No," Quinn said. "But I can get it to go." He provided no details.

"Go now, before anyone sees. Don't know if anyone can be trusted. Best to just assume everyone is against you because, well, when you do the right thing, most people are."

"Yeah," Quinn said. He nodded and darted through the forest like a prowling wolf.

The clock was ticking. At any second, Quinn could be attacked, and so could Ally.

All Quinn could do was run.

He *needed* to run, so he sprinted until he was free of the tree line. He headed back toward the road, but before going on, Quinn heard Ally calling out to him one last time.

"Hey, Quinn!"

The Custodian turned.

"*Spotless,*" Ally said. After saying these words, Quinn's response to Ally was as well placed as the others delivered before.

"Spotless."

Quinn raced.

Out into the vast unknown, Quinn checked every

corner, every tree, every intricacy of the forest that surrounded him. No matter where he went or what he survived, more surprises would await him. Facing a plethora of new opponents, all aching to strip Quinn down to size and sever his head from his body, Custodians did not know the meaning of surrender, nor did they flee or resist.

They do not deny, fall, or lose.

They fought in a game of pain and grit, but still... Quinn had his plan.

And, if Quinn had a plan, then he had a strategy. And, if Quinn had a strategy, then he had a way to attain victory. What he had was a path to absolution, freedom, and choice. Running along, the clouds curdled into a bleak array of gray and the sound of rumbling thunder boomed in the changing sky.

A storm was approaching.

Quinn's next journey would be both deadly and furious, but deadly and furious was all he understood. It was all he knew. Quinn did not fear the storm. No, Quinn belonged to it.

He was molded by it. In the end, Quinn was everything it was and more.

Kyle Quinn was the storm.

ACKNOWLEDGMENTS

I extend my warmest gratitude to everyone else at Rough Edges Press and Wolfpack Publishing for allowing me to share stories about my beloved antihero, Kyle Quinn.

I will always be forever grateful.

Thank you, Jon McManus, Douglas Martin, Jan Clausen, Melodie Campbell, David Bergen, Brian Drake, Mark Allen, and Michael Black. Thank you, Brent Van Staalduinen and Mark Manner, who gave time and encouragement when needed and patience when it was never asked. I would also like to thank a man who is more than a friend but a mentor, Mr. John Corr.

I thank Naben Ruthnum, Lucy S. Snyder, and Andrew F. Sullivan, who have taken time out of their very busy schedules to look at my work, and I offer my gratitude to all my family and friends, including my fellow teachers, good and decent colleagues. Thank you, my buds, Greg Zavitz, Brent Duguid, Andrew Francella, Dave Franciosa, Steve Legge, Christopher Barrett, and my guardian angel, Sharmaine.

I thank my best friend brother, Cody, and my sister, Jenna. I thank my father, a good and decent man, and I thank Bentley, the current love of my life. Above all else, I thank my mother, Sheila. She was the first fan of this series and the first fan of everything, really. Mom, you are an amalgamation of encouragement, power, strength, and truth, which is often inconvenient, but most importantly... of love.

Thank you for being my greatest fan and for following me on my many journeys. I always know where I'm going, and because of you, I am never lost.

A LOOK AT BOOK THREE:

EXTRICATE

The pulse-pounding finale to *The Custodian* trilogy, where justice and survival collide in a high-stakes battle against destiny.

Kyle Quinn, once the elite black-ops mercenary known as "The Custodian," has broken the unbreakable code of his guild. Betraying the manipulative Priest has made him the target of the world's deadliest assassins—his former allies. But survival isn't enough. To free himself from Priest's shadow, Quinn must face his greatest enemy, no matter the cost.

As alliances crumble and friends turn to foes, Quinn is thrust into a relentless war against elite killers. Every move is shadowed by betrayal, every breath a fight for survival.

Even as the onslaught intensifies, Quinn uncovers a sinister conspiracy shaping his life since birth. To destroy Priest and escape the web of deceit, he must confront his darkest fears, heal old wounds, and fight for the family he's vowed to protect.

When justice and vengeance blur, and the line between savior and sinner disappears, how far will Quinn go to end the fight that began long ago?

The final chapter of Kyle Quinn's journey is here. Will he find freedom...or fall to the darkness?

AVAILABLE MARCH 2025

ABOUT THE AUTHOR

Jarrett Mazza is a graduate of Goddard College's MFA in Creative Writing Program in Plainfield, Vermont as well as The Humber School For Writers.

Before completing his terminal degree, he studied writing at the University of Toronto School of Continuing Studies and comic book writing under Ty Templeton and Andy Schmidt. He has had stories published online in the GNU Journal, Bewildering Stories, Trembling With Fear, Aphelion, The Scarlet Leaf Review, and Toronto Prose Mill, The Fictional Cafe. His work is featured in anthologies by Silver Empire Publishing, a best seller, Zimbell House Publishing,NBH Publishing, MuseWrite Press, twice by Dragon Soul Press, Gypsum Sound Tales, Hellbound Books and The Ginosko Literary Journal. All are available on Amazon for purchase. He was also an Honorable Mention for the Freda Waldon Award for Fiction, nominated for an Indie Book award, and was featured as a visiting author for the nationwide We Read Canadian event in 2020. His mystery short story was published in an anthology under the editorial supervision of Michael Bracken and was published by Down and Out Books. He is currently a pulp fiction writer for the companies Airship 27 and Stormgate Press and Rough Edges Press.

He lives in Hamilton, Ontario.

You can follow him on Twitter @JarrettMazza